D0363740

Summer 2021

Dear Friends,

I really loved writing this book. I know an author is expected to say that about every book she writes. If you were to ask me why this one was special, I'm not entirely sure I could explain it, other than to say it comes directly from the lives of several of my friends. We are at an age when our children are grown and starting lives of their own. It's time to coast, travel, and enjoy ourselves with our partners. Except in far too many cases, my friends have found themselves either divorced or widowed. Just when they were set to retire and do the things they had planned for years, all their dreams and hopes went up in smoke. At an age they never expected, they had to start again. I've watched what happened to them and their children, especially if they remarried. The family unit, as it once was, is forever gone. From these experiences was born the idea for *It's Better This Way*.

This book is dedicated to Rick Enloe and Gino Grunberg. If you subscribe to the *Welcome Home* magazine, you will recognize Rick's name, as he writes a regular column. Rick and Gino lead the church where Wayne and I attend. *It's better this way* is something Rick says so often his family has threatened to have it etched on his gravestone. It's a way of saying that life turns out the way it's supposed to, one way or the other.

Thank you for your faith in me as an author to tell a good story and for investing your hard-earned dollars in this book. I hope you'll come away blessed and encouraged, that although life sometimes slings mud at us, in the end, when we can see past the hurts: *It really is better this way.*

Your comments are always appreciated. You, my readers, have been the guiding force of my career. I appreciate everything you have to say. So thank you in advance. You can reach me online on my website, on Facebook, and on every other social media. Or you can write to me at P.O. Box 1458, Port Orchard, WA 98366.

Blessings,

Debbie Macomber

Debbie
MACOMBER

It's Better This Way

sphere

SPHERE

First published in the United States in 2021 by Ballantine Books,
an imprint of Random House, a division of Penguin Random House LLC, New York
First published in Great Britain in 2021 by Sphere

1 3 5 7 9 10 8 6 4 2

Copyright © Debbie Macomber 2021

A CIP catalogue record for this book is available from the British Library.

ISBN 978-0-7515-8115-7

Papers used by Sphere are from well-managed forests
and other responsible sources.

MIX
Paper from
responsible sources
FSC® C104740

Printed and bound in Great Britain by Clays Ltd, Elcograf S.p.A.

To

Rick Enloe and Gino Grunberg

Knowing you makes everything better

It's Better This Way

Prologue

Julia Jones sat at her desk, the divorce papers in front of her, shouting at her to pick up the pen, sign her name, and put an end to this insanity once and for all. Her heart ached, and she held her breath to the point that her lungs felt as if they would explode. Reaching for the pen, her hand trembled with the weight of what she was about to do. Closing her eyes, she set the pen back on the desktop.

She'd fought so hard to save her marriage. She loved Eddie. There'd never been anyone but her husband. When he tearfully admitted he'd fallen out of love with her, she intuitively knew he'd become involved with someone else, although he adamantly denied it. She could understand if another woman had fallen in love with her husband; Julia loved him, too. Even at fifty-three, Eddie was handsome, athletic, and charismatic.

Unwilling to give up on her thirty-one-year marriage, she

pleaded with him to try counseling. To his credit, Eddie agreed, although reluctantly. However, after only five sessions, he said it would do no good. He admitted to the affair with a woman named Laura, someone he'd met on the golf course. He no longer wanted to make his marriage work. He wanted out to start a new life with this other woman.

Still, Julia was unwilling to give up. She was determined. Dedicated to her husband and her marriage. Even after Eddie quit counseling, she continued, seeking ways to build a bridge that would bring her husband back.

Back to their family.

Back to the good life they had created together.

Back to her.

They were a team. Or had been. Julia had shared nearly every important life experience with Eddie. Marriage. Children. The death of her father. Triumphs. Discouragements. He'd been her soul mate.

Julia met Eddie in college. They were young and in love, full of ambition, all set to make their mark in the world. They married, encouraged, and supported each other as they pursued their individual careers. Eddie became a professional golfer, and when his career faded, he became a country club pro and later opened his own shop.

Julia had graduated with a degree in interior design. Her own business had become a success, and she was a sought-after designer, working with contractors from across the state. After marrying and investing their talent and time in building their careers, they'd waited ten years to start their family. Julia was thirty-two before she had Hillary, and Marie a year later. Eddie loved his daughters. They were the pride of his life.

Even now, Julia didn't know how this affair had happened. She'd been completely blindsided. She'd assumed they were happy. They'd been together all these years and were at the point when they were about to enjoy the fruits of their labors. Their nest was empty. Both girls were in college, Hillary was about to graduate, and Marie was a year behind her. The two shared an apartment near the University of Washington, where they attended classes. Hillary was studying to be a physical therapist and played tennis for the college team, just as Julia had while in school. Marie planned to be a respiratory therapist.

Even knowing her husband was involved in an affair, Julia had stubbornly held on to her marriage. Eddie was her best friend. He'd wept with her when her father passed, had been a good father and partner, cheering her successes and comforting her when she faced disappointments. They had been a team, each celebrating the other. They had a good life together, and she wasn't willing to flush it all away.

Julia missed her father terribly. Dad would have been stunned and disappointed in Eddie. Countless times over the years, when life had thrown her an unexpected curve, he'd tell her: *It's better this way*. He'd said it so often that before he died, her mother threatened to have it chiseled on his tombstone.

She remembered the first time he said it was when she was six. She'd been invited to her best friend's birthday party, but had gotten the flu the night before, and couldn't go. Disappointed, she'd wept in her daddy's arms, and he'd comforted her by telling her *it was better this way*. She hadn't believed him until the following Sunday, when she was feeling better and Heather brought her a piece of her special birthday cake. Later, her dad drove her and Heather to the circus, and they'd had a wonderful time. It had been better than sharing her best friend with everyone in her first-grade class.

Again and again over the years, when Julia had suffered disappointments—a prom date who disappeared in the middle of the dance, a missed business flight to New York—she would be naturally frustrated and upset, until she remembered her father's words of wisdom.

Right then, with her marriage at stake, it didn't feel like anything would ever be better again.

Hoping Eddie would come to his senses, Julia begged him to wait six months, praying with all her might that he would change his mind about this divorce. They would find their way through this. Start again. Forgive each other.

All she wanted was those six months, convinced he would come to his senses.

Eddie hesitantly agreed, although he made sure she was fully aware that this was his time limit. After six months, she would willingly sign the divorce papers. With a wounded heart, she promised to abide by his stipulation.

At Eddie's insistence, they spoke with an attorney. Everything would be ready for when the time came. The settlement agreement had been amicably set in place. He kept his business and she kept hers. She promised, at the end of those six months, that they would put the house on the market. Julia would sell her dream home, the very one she had lovingly decorated. They would evenly split the profits. Of the furnishings, there were only a few pieces Eddie wanted.

Four months into the six-month waiting period, things had gotten ugly. It seemed Eddie's lover had grown impatient and wanted matters resolved so they could move on together. She was eager for them to put down roots.

When Julia held firm to their six-month agreement, Laura got involved, forwarding Julia photo upon photo of her and Eddie together, dining out. Selfies on the golf course. Even one of them in bed together. As best she could, Julia ignored the pictures, refusing to take the bait.

When she refused to respond, Laura tried another tactic and sent her ugly text messages, reminding Julia that Eddie no longer loved her and wanted out of the marriage.

You are only delaying the inevitable.

You are being so selfish and mean-spirited.

Why are you beating a dead horse?

You're a jealous witch.

For a couple weeks, Julia resisted, until she couldn't take it any longer. Before she could stop herself, she responded with ugly messages of her own, letting Laura know exactly what she thought of her in words that made her blush now. She hated herself for lowering to Laura's level. She regretted every word of those texts, furious with herself. She wasn't that woman.

At that point, their daughter had gotten involved. Julia had never meant for her daughter to see those texts. When she did, Hillary had gone ballistic. Both their daughters were already furious with their father, and this behavior from Laura didn't help.

Without Julia knowing what she had planned, Hillary confronted Eddie and Laura at Lake Sammamish on a family outing and called her every ugly name in the book. Using the same language Julia had used earlier. Not willing to tolerate Hillary and Marie's outrage, Laura's two sons verbally confronted the girls, and a shouting match ensued. Like a California wildfire, the situation had exploded, as both families attacked each other. Eddie got involved, demanding that his daughters respect his future wife. In the heat of the moment, he said words he would live to regret. If Hillary and Marie couldn't accept Laura, then they could no longer be part of his life.

Unsure what to do, Julia once again consulted the counselor, seeking his advice. She could identify with her daughters' outrage. She'd been angry, too, going through well-documented stages of grief, only in this instance the loss was the demise of her marriage.

Sitting in the counselor's office, wringing a damp tissue in her hands, Julia explained what had happened.

"I'm so sorry, Julia." His expression was full of sympathy. "I know how badly you wanted to make your marriage work."

"I never meant for matters to get so nasty."

"I know."

"Should I sign the divorce papers?" she asked, praying he would give her the direction she needed.

He was silent for several moments and seemed to carefully consider his response. "I can't tell you what to do. I will say this, though: Love that isn't faithful has little value. It really isn't love at all."

With a heavy heart, Julia left the appointment, knowing what needed to be done.

She had put up the good fight. The time had come for her to lay down her sword and accept defeat. Eddie was never coming back. This was the end. It was time to let go.

Let go of her husband.

Let go of her marriage.

Let go of her dreams for their future together.

Tears streamed down her cheeks as she stared at the document in front of her, the words blurred through the moisture that clouded her eyes.

With her heart in her throat, she reached for the pen a second time and signed her name.

As she did, she told herself: *It's better this way.*

Chapter 1

Nearly six years later

Julia woke, glanced at the clock on her nightstand, and wondered how long it would take for her to sleep past six. Old habits die hard, even though she no longer had any need to set her alarm. For more years than she could remember, she had risen at six every morning. Her business, West Coast Interiors, had been sold, and she was easing into retirement, working part-time as a consultant.

The decision to sell had been a weighty one and followed on the heels of her mother's passing. As Julia neared sixty, she felt she had plenty of good years left. Then an offer had come through that was far and above her expectations. Julia didn't feel like she could turn it down. She wasn't ready to give up her work entirely, which was why she'd made continuing as a consultant part of the agreement. The buyers had asked her to stay on, as well. She could work as much or as little as she wanted. After finishing this latest project, she'd decided to take a few days off and test what semiretirement felt like.

This certainly wasn't how she'd once anticipated retirement. There'd been a time when she'd hoped to travel the world with her husband. Julia longed to explore Europe and Asia. As of now, traveling alone held little appeal. Perhaps one day.

As she knew it would, her dream home had sold less than a week after it had been listed. So many changes had come into her life. After her divorce was final, she'd rented an apartment before making a decision on her new home. She knew she wanted to remain living in Seattle, and possibly in the downtown area itself.

The city was her home and there had been enough upheaval in her life without facilitating another major life change. Her girls were close, as was her sister and her family. She waited a year to start looking, and then the search had taken on a life of its own.

For three long years, Julia was on an endless quest to find a place she felt she could call home. The Heritage was an older brick condo building, built in the 1960s, that was filled with warmth and character. So many of the newer high-rise buildings were steel structures, with little to no personality or charm. Set in the heart of the city, it was close enough for her to walk down to Pike Place Market for fresh produce and seafood. The 5th Avenue theater was nearby, as was plenty of shopping. As a bonus, there was a coffee shop next door, as well as several restaurants on the block.

The instant she stepped into The Heritage and viewed the large fountain in the center lobby, Julia sensed this was the place for her. The building, with only twelve floors, rarely had a vacancy. Julia was patient, and in time a unit became available. She'd lived here a little over two years now and loved the community of friends she'd made. Because it was an older building, The Heritage didn't have many of the amenities of the newer condos that attracted the techies from Amazon and Microsoft. This move was a new beginning for her. A fresh start, and she had settled in comfortably.

Tying the sash on her silk robe, she wandered into the kitchen and brewed a cup of coffee. Lazy mornings generally happened only on Sundays, when she attended the late service at church. She needed to create a new schedule for herself—or, on second thought, no schedule at all.

She'd just taken her first sip of coffee when her phone rang. It was her sister, Amanda.

"Hey, you're up early," Julia said by way of greeting.

"I didn't wake you, did I?"

"No, I was up. I can't seem to sleep past six. What's going on?"

"It's Carrie," her sister said.

Julia's niece, an only child, was especially close to her parents. She suspected what was coming. Carrie still lived at home, and the failure to break out on her own was a thorn between Amanda and her husband, Robert.

"Robert and I had another heated discussion about Carrie last night," her sister said with a groan. "He wants Carrie to move out. I mean, she's twenty-eight. It's time. Past time," she added in defeat. "The problem is: How do we tell her?"

"Glad it's not up to me." As Carrie's godmother, Julia dearly loved her niece. She understood her sister's concern. Carrie had graduated from college with a degree in French literature. A degree that didn't offer much in the way of career opportunities.

Never one to be idle, Carrie had applied for several jobs, many of which had lasted only a few months.

Since her graduation from college, Carrie had steadily drifted from one position to another. She'd been a receptionist for a real estate company, worked for an accountant, had done a stint at an employment agency, sold cosmetics at a department store as a beauty specialist. And those were only the jobs Julia could remember. Except for that brief time when Carrie had sold high-end knives, of which Julia had a set. Her niece wasn't lazy, she just wasn't particularly employable. Six years after graduating from college, she still hadn't found a job that suited her unique set of skills.

Carrie was great with people, caring and conscientious, and a good employee while she lasted. The problem was that wherever Carrie worked, she didn't earn enough to support herself, and then she quit when she grew bored. Consequently, she lived at home.

"I was hoping you had some pearls of wisdom to give me." Amanda sounded utterly defeated.

"Sorry, you're on your own with this one, little sister."

"*Grrr.*"

Julia smiled. "Failure to launch."

"I remember the movie." Amanda continued, "The parents plotted to convince their son to move out of the house. I don't know that Robert and I could do that. I know he's right; we aren't helping Carrie move forward in life. Only I don't know what else to do. She's such a wonderful daughter and always has been. It's not like we can kick her out. She's our daughter."

Julia didn't know, either. She felt bad for her sister and wished she knew how to advise her. "Just be honest with her."

Amanda sighed. "You make it sound simple and it isn't."

"I know." Julia sympathized and wished she had a solution to offer. She knew Robert had offered to pay for an apartment for Carrie. She'd refused. Carrie insisted she would make it on her own or not at all.

"There's another reason I called," Amanda said, her voice brightening.

Simply by her sister's tone, Julia again knew what was coming.

"I have someone I want you to meet."

"No," Julia said and moaned inwardly.

"Julia. I haven't even told you who it is."

"Not interested."

"Come on. Don't be so stubborn. Okay, so you've had a few dating disappointments . . ."

"A few, yes. More than enough to know that whoever it is, I'm not interested."

"Really?"

"Yes, really." This was an unwelcome subject.

"Do you seriously want to live the rest of your life alone?"

"Amanda, please, you know how I feel about this." Following her divorce, Julia's sister and other friends had made continual efforts to introduce Julia to a variety of single men her age. Most were divorced and carried more baggage than an international airline. She'd suffered through these attempts until she decided to give up dating entirely, even if it meant living the rest of her life single. She was content, happy, and had moved on, for the most part, without bitterness or resentment. The first couple years following her divorce had been a struggle until she wrote Eddie a long good-bye letter. Although she'd never mailed it, the process had given her a sense of closure. Even more, it helped her accept her life as it was; she didn't need a man to feel complete. The letter and the aftermath had freed her, changed her outlook, which allowed her to move forward.

Eddie appeared to be happy. She spoke to him only about matters that involved their daughters, which were rare, now that both Hillary and Marie were in their twenties and on their own.

"Are you sure?" Amanda asked again. "Frank is perfect for you. Please reconsider."

"Amanda, please. I'm not interested."

"Okay, then, but you're missing out."

"Maybe I am. Maybe I'm not. It doesn't matter. I'm happy as I am."

"If you say so," Amanda said, her words heavy with doubt.

They spoke for a few minutes longer before Amanda ended the call.

Once she finished her coffee, Julia dressed and headed down to work out. The Heritage had an exercise room that, although small, was state-of-the-art. There were a couple treadmills and exercise bikes. Plus some weight-lifting equipment.

As a matter of habit, she exercised every afternoon, when she returned from work, walking off tension on the treadmill while listening to an audiobook or music. It was a good way to keep herself in shape. Before she knew it, she'd be sixty. She certainly didn't feel that age. Not anywhere close. Her daughter had recently commented that sixty was the new forty. That was a stretch, but Julia would take it.

Most afternoons, the exercise room was empty. She wasn't

sure what she'd find when she altered her schedule to morning workouts. She preferred to have the room to herself.

To her disappointment when she arrived, she found a man, busily walking on the treadmill. He was big, easily over six feet, with broad shoulders. He wore a sleeveless shirt that was damp with sweat, as if he'd been going at top speed for some time, and shorts. She noticed how well defined his legs were. He had a full head of salt-and-pepper hair. Julia had seen him around though she didn't know his name. As best she could remember, he'd moved into The Heritage about a year ago but hadn't partici-pated in more than a few of the social gatherings. The other times she'd seen him, he'd been dressed in a suit and tie and made for a fine figure of a man. As she recalled, there'd been some speculation floating around about him and the condo con-cierge. Julia didn't generally listen to gossip and couldn't re-member what the story was, since it was none of her concern. What she did know was that the management was taking appli-cations for a new concierge.

Seeing him, Julia hesitated before stepping into the room. "Morning," she said casually.

He nodded in return.

She got on the treadmill next to him and put her earbuds in and started her routine. He finished and moved to the exercise bike. Julia walked three miles, and he was still going at the bike, leaning his well-defined upper body forward and pumping his legs at a furious pace.

The next morning and for the following three, they exercised side by side, never exchanging more than a simple greeting. She felt him glance her way on occasion, as if he wanted to start a conversation. Julia discouraged it, as she was there to exercise. Nevertheless, she noticed him, probably far more than she should. When he didn't show on Friday, she was surprised to realize she was disappointed. Without exchanging a word, he inspired her to work harder and longer, and she missed the challenge.

When she arrived Monday morning of the following week, he seemed to be waiting for her. He stood next to the treadmill, a towel around his neck, looking more appealing than ever.

"Heath Wilson," he said.

"I beg your pardon?"

"I'm Heath Wilson. I thought it was time I introduce myself."

"Julia Jones."

"I figured if we were going to exercise at the same time each morning, we should introduce ourselves."

She smiled. "It's nice to meet you, Heath."

"Have you lived at The Heritage long?" he asked.

"A couple years. You arrived last year, right?"

"Right. A friend of my son's lives here. Eric Hudson. Do you know him?"

Julia shook her head.

"Not surprising. Eric has a home office and works odd hours since he has several overseas clients. I don't think he's attended any of the condo functions. I've only attended a couple myself."

"I love living here. It's a fresh start for me."

"Me, too. I hung on to the house following my divorce thinking I wanted to keep it. That was a mistake. So many memories and more room than one person would ever need. I decided it was time to move on."

"I hear you. I'm divorced as well, over five years now."

"About that long for me. Did you hold on to your house?"

"No. I needed to sell, as it was part of the settlement." Putting her home on the market had been one of the hardest aspects of the divorce for Julia. "It was probably for the best." Like Heath, the house held a lot of memories, and would have been a constant reminder of all that she'd lost.

Plugging in her earbuds, she set about her routine. When she'd finished, she gave a wave to Heath and headed back to her condo to shower. She intended to stop by the shop to advise the new owner at some point that day, and thought she'd head out early before it was too hot to walk the seven blocks to West Coast Interiors. Since Julia hadn't taken time to eat breakfast, she decided to stop on her way for a latte at the Busy Bean, a tea and coffee shop next door to The Heritage.

Three people were in line in front of her. Her phone beeped, letting her know she had a text message. Taking it from the outside pocket of her purse, she saw it was from her niece, Carrie.

Can u talk?

Julia called and Carrie answered right away.

"You okay?" Julia asked.

"Not really." She sounded as down as Julia could remember. Carrie was generally upbeat and happy.

"You want to tell me what this is about?"

It wasn't uncommon for Carrie to seek Julia's advice. Her niece was like a third daughter. Carrie was the same age as Marie, and the three girls were tight, having grown up together. Carrie often claimed she had two mothers.

"I'd rather do it in person."

"Great. How about lunch tomorrow?" Her niece had been on her mind ever since last Monday's conversation with her sister. And when Heath had introduced himself, she'd gotten an idea. The condo was looking to hire another concierge, and Carrie would be a perfect fit. Plus, a small apartment was offered with the position.

"Sure, I can do lunch."

"How about the Thai place," she suggested, knowing it was Carrie's favorite. "Noon?"

"That would be perfect. Thanks so much, Aunt Julia."

If this panned out, it would solve a big problem for Carrie, and her sister and Robert.

Chapter 2

"What's got you so down?" Marie asked Carrie.

Carrie sat with her knees bunched up beneath her chin in the middle of her cousin's apartment. "It's Mom and Dad," she said, releasing a slow, frustrated breath. Rarely had she been more depressed.

"Your mom and dad," Marie repeated, her eyes widening with alarm. "They aren't splitting up, are they?"

Carrie supposed this was a natural assumption after what had happened with Marie's parents. Even now, after nearly six years, Carrie found it hard to believe that her uncle Eddie would leave a woman as wonderful as her aunt Julia.

"Not yet," she said, "though I have a feeling if I don't find a job that pays me enough to move out, they might consider it." That would be the extreme, but after hearing their argument, she couldn't discount the possibility. Her parents rarely raised their voices at each other. The shock of hearing them argue had hung over her head for a week now. They were miserable, and so was Carrie.

"They were fighting about you?"

Carrie nodded. "They didn't know I was home. They hardly ever argue; it shook me to hear them yelling at each other." They must not have heard her come in, and she didn't think it was a good time to interrupt. Sneaking up the stairs, she silently went to her room without letting them know she was home from work. "Their raised voices were amplified from the foyer like it was being broadcast throughout the house. Dad insisted that it was time I move into my own place. He was adamant they weren't helping me by letting me live at home."

Marie lowered herself from the sofa and sat on the floor next to Carrie. "What are you going to do?"

"I don't know. Dad's right. It's time I accepted responsibility for myself and had my own life."

"You could always move in with Hillary and me," Marie suggested.

Adding a third person in a two-bedroom apartment wouldn't work. Carrie had a good relationship with her cousins. Becoming their roommate had catastrophe written all over it.

"Where would I sleep or put my things?" she asked, hoping the question was answer enough. Carrie's cousins were close, both in their late twenties. Living together wasn't ideal for them, either. But the cost of housing in the Seattle area made it nearly impossible for each to rent their own place.

"It wouldn't surprise me if Blake and Hillary announced their engagement soon," Marie offered. "I'll be looking for a roommate once they get married. Do you think you could wait a few more months?"

"No way. I need to find a solution as soon as possible. Besides, even if they do get engaged, it could be months before the wedding."

It did cheer Carrie to hear her cousin was ready to make the leap with Blake. They'd been dating for more than three years. Marie had once mentioned that Blake had hinted at marriage a year earlier. Only Hillary claimed she wasn't ready.

"Yeah, I know." Marie drew her knee up and rested her chin there, mirroring Carrie's position.

"I'm happy for Hillary. Blake's a good guy."

"He is. She's lucky," Marie agreed. "I think Hilly would have accepted his proposal last year if it wasn't for what happened to Mom and Dad. They were married thirty-one years. Even now it's a jolt, you know?"

"I do." Carrie had been stunned when her mother told her the news that her wonderful uncle Eddie was leaving her aunt for another woman. While that was bad enough, it had deeply affected both Hillary and Marie. After the shouting match at Lake Sammamish, neither cousin had anything to do with their father or his new wife. From what Carrie had heard, Uncle Eddie had made several attempts to reconcile, only her cousins weren't interested. The problem was, he insisted they meet and accept their stepmother, which Hillary and Marie refused to do. They considered the other woman to have ruined all their lives. That their dad had put this woman above them wasn't something they were willing to forgive.

"Hillary's convinced Dad never wanted girls."

"That's not true," Carrie said, surprised her cousin would say such a thing. Her uncle Eddie had been a good father. He doted on his daughters, teaching them to play golf and taking them on skiing vacations. She'd often joined them on their outings. Carrie knew it must be hard on her uncle to be separated from them entirely. And especially hard on Hillary and Marie. But they were as stubborn as their dad was.

"I told her that, only Hillary doesn't believe me. He has stepsons now and is constantly doing things with them. When she heard Dad took Laura's sons to a Seahawks game, she blew a gasket. That was all the evidence she needed to prove he'd always wanted sons. According to my sister, we were poor replacements."

"You don't believe that, do you?"

Marie lifted her shoulder in a halfhearted shrug. "I don't know what to think any longer. I miss Dad and then I don't. This is what he wanted; he should be happy, only I know he isn't."

Carrie didn't know what to think. She'd hoped that after all this time her cousins would be willing to move on and accept their father's choices even if they didn't agree with them. Then again, she wondered how she'd react if her father had left her mother for a woman far less deserving of his love.

"I don't want to talk about my dad," Marie said. "It depresses me. Besides, you're the one with the problem."

It was easier to get sidetracked than to deal with her own seemingly impossible situation.

"Didn't your dad offer to pay for an apartment for you a while back?"

Carrie wondered now if she should have accepted. "I told him no. Dad has no idea how much a studio apartment costs these days." She refused to drain her parents' savings account because she couldn't find a job that would support her on her own.

"Do you have any other ideas?"

Carrie wished she did. "Justin suggested we move in together." As if that was going to happen! He lived with his mom, and with them both working jobs that paid slightly above minimum wage, they would never make it financially.

Marie's head came up and she looked aghast. "You aren't going to do it, are you?"

"I'm not that dumb. Justin is . . ." She paused, not knowing how best to describe her sometimes boyfriend.

"Not the one?" Marie offered.

"Not even close." They got along fine, shared expenses whenever they went out, and could laugh together. Carrie could never see the relationship going beyond what it was—on her end, at any rate. Even though Justin was thirty, he acted more like someone in his late teens. Life was a party. Responsibility was for someone else. Carrie knew if they were to get an apartment together, she'd be left worrying about paying their rent and utility bills because Justin couldn't be bothered.

"I'm meeting your mom for lunch tomorrow," Carrie said. "I'm hoping she might have an idea of what I should do. I feel like such a disappointment to my parents."

Her frustration was overwhelming. Carrie didn't know what she'd been thinking to major in a subject that didn't lead to a career. Her love of all things French had led her down a dead-end path when it came to finding employment. The only viable option was to teach, which would mean returning to school for an additional degree. She refused to put that financial burden on her parents, after they'd already paid for one degree. Besides, knowing herself as well as she did, Carrie accepted she didn't have the temperament to be in a classroom all day.

"Mom will think of something," Marie said confidently. "She's good like that."

Carrie sincerely hoped so, as she was at her wit's end.

At 11:50 the following day, Carrie arrived at her favorite Thai restaurant ten minutes before their scheduled meeting time. She'd been eager to get out of the house and spend as much time as was comfortable away, hoping to give her parents breathing space.

The restaurant was only a block from The Heritage, where her aunt lived. She loved that building. Her aunt claimed it felt like home the instant she walked inside. Carrie understood; she'd experienced that same warmth and welcome. Very few buildings built of brick remained in the Seattle area. Not with the constant threat of earthquakes. The Heritage was set in the middle of a thriving neighborhood, filled with restaurants and small businesses. The location was ideal for her aunt, as she could walk almost anywhere in the downtown area.

The server handed her a menu and Carrie ordered a pot of jasmine tea. Even though she never ventured beyond her favorite avocado-and-shrimp green-curry dish, she scanned the front and back of the single page while she waited for Julia to arrive.

"Carrie," her aunt called as she approached the table.

Carrie set aside her empty teacup and slid out of the booth. "Aunt Julia," she said, cheered by the warmth of the greeting. Carrie enthusiastically hugged her aunt.

Julia sat opposite her, and Carrie poured them both a fresh cup of tea. Her aunt quickly scanned the menu and made her choice before setting the menu aside. She had her own favorite dish and they often shared.

"It's good to see you," Julia said.

"You, too." Despite her joy at seeing her aunt, her shoulders slumped.

"I think I know what you wanted to see me about." Julia reached across the table and gently squeezed Carrie's hand.

Carrie looked up. "Did Mom call you?"

Julia nodded.

"I heard them arguing. They think it's time I got my own place, and I agree. Only how can I ever afford one on what I make? As it is, I'm hardly able to make my car and insurance payment. Mom has me on their phone plan, and I give her money for that, and I contribute what I can toward groceries." That was all she could afford. She had a measly hundred dollars in savings, and that wouldn't last a millisecond in a real emergency.

"Your mom is in a tough spot."

Carrie was aware of her mother's feelings on the matter. "I feel awful about this, I really do. It's just been so hard for me to find a job that pays me enough to afford to move out."

The server stepped forward, cutting in to their conversation, and they placed their order.

Carrie waited until he left before continuing. "Hillary and Marie were smart in their career choices." As a physical therapist, Hillary could work as many hours as she wanted. And Marie, a respiratory therapist, had skills that were in high demand. She could have her choice of work in any one of the area's hospitals.

"Don't say that," Julia said. "You graduated magna cum laude."

"It doesn't feel like it," Carrie whispered.

Their food was delivered, and as eager for Thai as Carrie had been earlier, she no longer had an appetite. Reaching for her fork, she rested her elbows on the table. "What did Mom say?" she asked.

"She loves you, Carrie, and wants what's best for you."

That was a given, seeing how long Carrie had been living off her folks.

"I have an idea for you, though."

Carrie looked up from her plate as a fleeting sense of hope filled her chest. "You do?"

"Have you ever considered being a concierge?"

"A concierge?" She frowned and shook her head. "You mean like in a hotel, booking reservations at restaurants and such?"

"Sort of. The Heritage is looking to hire one."

Her interest was piqued. She loved the idea of working at The Heritage. "What would I be doing?"

"I don't have a full job description; the only thing I can tell you is what my experience with the concierge has been."

Leaning slightly forward, Carrie was eager to listen.

"When I first learned a condo was up for sale it was the concierge who showed me around. My real estate agent was with me, but the concierge is the one who answered my questions. She collects packages and handles all the details for scheduling repairs. I'm sure there's much more."

Carrie listened intently. "Do you think I could do all that?"

"Of course I do. In fact, I think you'd be perfect. You're a natural with people and have a way of smoothing ruffled feathers."

Carrie was willing to admit she enjoyed her role of peacemaker. "It sounds good; I just wonder if I'm qualified."

"With your broad experience, I think you'd be fine. The board is gathering résumés this week. I would encourage you to apply."

"Can I do it online?"

Julia hesitated and appeared to give it some thought. "You could, of course, as I'm sure that's what the vast majority will do. If it were me, I'd stop in personally. You're only a block from The Heritage now. It wouldn't take much effort to walk in and fill out an application. If you like, I can print out your résumé at my place."

"I'll give it a go," Carrie decided.

Her aunt gave her hope when she badly needed to see the light at the end of the proverbial tunnel.

"One more question. Do you know what the position pays?"

Julia shook her head. "I don't, sorry."

She'd find that out soon enough, although she desperately hoped the salary would allow her to find a place of her own. "Can I use you as a reference?"

"Of course. I'd want you to, and I'll be happy to put in a good word for you, although I don't know if it will be of much help."

"It can't hurt."

Carrie sampled a bite of her lunch, feeling a tad better. Working at The Heritage was bound to offer more than her position at the drugstore, and would certainly be more enjoyable. It was a beautiful building and the residents seemed friendly.

"Like I said, Carrie, I can't be sure what the pay is; however, there's one major benefit that comes with this position that I didn't mention."

"You mean other than I'll be able to see you on a daily basis?"

"Yes, more than that. Much more. The concierge position includes a studio apartment."

Chapter 3

Julia was happily taking a day for herself. She planned to meet Hillary for lunch, and had scheduled a massage and hair appointment for the afternoon. The new owner of West Coast Interiors was starting to rely on Julia a bit more than she liked, especially when it came to dealing with contractors. It would be far too easy to fall back into the pattern of working full-time, and that was something she wanted to avoid.

Following Julia's advice, her niece had applied with The Heritage for the concierge position. Carrie had apparently made a good enough impression for the condo board to check with Julia as a reference. From what she knew, the decision was going to be made either today or tomorrow, once the board had completed the interviews. Julia felt Carrie had a more than fair chance of getting the job. For everyone's sake, she hoped so.

After her workout, Julia returned to her condo to shower and change clothes. As he had for the last two weeks, Heath had arrived at the same time as she did. Other than exchanging their usual morning greeting, they basically ignored each other. She plugged in her earbuds and went about her routine as if she had the room to herself.

When Julia first switched her exercising to the mornings, she'd been disappointed not to be able to work out in private, and even briefly considered altering her schedule. She wasn't sure what changed her mind. Since they rarely spoke other than a brief acknowledgment, it seemed a little silly to change her schedule.

Seeing that she would be eating lunch out, Julia opted for a light breakfast by stopping off at the Busy Bean. The line was short, with only two people in front of her. She was considering ordering the daily drink when she heard someone come to stand behind her.

"Hey," Heath said, sounding surprised to see her.

"Hello," she said, smiling over her shoulder. As she looked his way, she noticed her sister walking into The Heritage, and she wasn't alone. Twice now Amanda had mentioned Frank, the man she was hot for Julia to meet. Julia had refused both times. It seemed her sister had decided that if Julia wouldn't meet Frank on her own, then she would bring the man to her. Noticing the two of them walking side by side, her face fell. "Oh no."

She was willing to admit Frank looked decent enough; looks, however, were deceiving, as she had painfully learned in her brief sojourn into the dating world.

"Something wrong?" Heath asked at her whispered protest.

Julia's shoulders slumped as she turned her gaze away from Amanda, whose intentions were good, though misguided. "My sister is heading to my place and she's bringing this man she insists is my soul mate, despite the fact I have repeatedly told her I'm not interested."

Heath looked toward The Heritage. "Hide out here with me," he suggested. "If she happens to see you sitting alone, she'll bring him over. But if you're with me, most likely she'll leave."

She wasn't about to refuse this small gift. "Thanks. I'd appreciate that."

"Get us a table, and I'll order the drinks."

"Perfect." She opened her purse to get out cash when Heath stopped her. "My treat."

This was an even better offer. She told him what she wanted and quickly secured one of the few tables available. Within a matter of minutes, Heath handed her the latte and then sat down across from her.

"Does this sort of thing happen often?" he asked.

"You mean my sister and/or friends pushing me to meet a man who will be perfect for me?" she asked in an exaggerated voice, and then answered her own question. "All the time. You?"

"Some. Not so much lately, as my friends have gotten the message I'm not interested. Shortly after the divorce I thought it would be a good idea to move on, give dating a try. That was a mistake."

Julia understood all too well. "It was a while before I was ready to meet anyone. I was lonely, and thought *Why not?* All I wanted was someone to share experiences with, someone to laugh with and enjoy life. I'd been married over thirty years, and I wasn't accustomed to life alone."

"I hear you. That was my thought, but after a few pretty hairy experiences I was done."

"I met my share of duds as well," Julia said, and she had. It didn't take her long to discover the men who were single were that way for a reason.

Heath relaxed against the back of his chair and tossed out a challenge. "Bet my dating experiences will be worse than yours."

"Oh yeah?" Julia said with a smile. "First time out was with a guy who was the friend of a friend. Sheryl thought we would be perfect together. Have you noticed how that is what they all say? 'I know someone perfect for you'?"

"Heard it enough to realize my friends don't know me near well enough."

"At any rate, Sheryl said this about Harry, that was his name, claiming we had a lot in common. Like me, he had been recently divorced. We met for dinner and everything was going along fine until after half a bottle of wine, when Harry started talking about his ex-wife and his children. Then, out of the blue, he started to cry. And when I say 'cry,' I mean howling sobs and tears. There I sat in the middle of a crowded restaurant, with a man weeping into his napkin so loudly that the waiter asked if there was something he could do to help. I assured him there was and asked if he could call for a cab. I thanked Harry for dinner and left."

Heath grinned. "My first time out was equally bad. An old college roommate set me up with a woman he knew, convinced we would hit it off. Callie worked in social media and was seriously into her job. Like you, we met for dinner, and she—I am not exaggerating—snapped at least forty selfies, which she posted on Facebook. I don't think she swallowed more than two bites of her lobster, and yes, she ordered the most expensive item on the menu. Then she asked me to take her photo for Instagram. Not one photo, mind you, several, none of which pleased her. Later she let me know I didn't make her look as good as I could have. With that, she informed me it would be better if we didn't see each other again."

Julia shook her head in sympathy. "Apparently taking a good photo for Instagram is a prerequisite for a relationship these days."

"It seems so," Heath agreed.

Julia was enjoying this and wasn't about to let him win this challenge. "Okay, okay. See if you can top this. Another friend-of-a-friend situation. I trusted Susan. She's smart and assured me I was simply meeting the wrong kind of men, and I should put all my past failures behind me. Typically, she claimed she had the perfect man for me. In fairness, she did mention he was a bit older. She described him as mature, established, and financially secure. He sounded too good to be true."

"Don't they always?" he asked.

"Right. Anyway, once again we met at a restaurant and Lloyd had to have been in his late seventies, if he was a day. This guy was on his last legs. If that wasn't enough, when we went to order dinner, it took him ten minutes as he listed off all his physical ailments that prevented him from eating almost every item on the menu. He asked the server so many questions, needing to know every detail of the preparation, that I nearly dozed off. That server had the patience of a saint. The worst was when he went into detail, as to the reason he couldn't eat red meat, which he claimed gave him diarrhea."

"Good one," Heath said with a chuckle. "I had a stalker."

"A stalker?" she repeated, not sure she could beat that.

"We had a total of two dates. I should have followed my instincts after the first one. Nothing terrible happened. She was pleasant enough, and by this time, I was getting discouraged. Of all the women I'd met, she showed the most potential. I liked that she was enthusiastic and could carry a conversation, so I decided to ask her out again to see how it went.

"We attended a concert, and afterward she was all over me. It felt like an octopus who had all eight of its arms wrapped around me. I had to pull over on the side of the road and explain I couldn't drive with her trying to undress me.

"That was enough to tell me it wasn't going to work. When I dropped her off, she asked when I wanted to see her again. I said I'd call her, to which she responded July worked best for us to schedule the wedding date. Foolishly, I thought this was a joke. If so, it was on me."

"She was talking marriage after two dates?"

"Oh yes, and that was only the start of my troubles with Candace. It took me nearly three months, a lawyer, and a restraining order to get her out of my life."

"Okay, you win," Julia said, lifting her hand in defeat. "I have nothing to compare to that disaster."

"I'm sure you heard what happened with the concierge," he said, slowly shaking his head, as if the memory continued to traumatize him.

"Not really. There was some talk around the building, only I didn't pay much attention."

"I had to report Melanie to the condo board. She had this business opportunity she wanted me to finance. I explained I wasn't interested, and left it at that, hoping that would be the end of it. But she refused to give up. It came to the point that I couldn't even walk into the lobby to collect my mail without her pestering me. If that wasn't bad enough, she suggested she would be willing to do 'anything' if I would back her in a venture even an amateur entrepreneur knew would fail."

"Oh dear, she was that desperate?"

"It's unfortunate the building had to let her go. I felt bad about it, only I wasn't about to invest in an idea that was doomed to fail. After what happened with Candace, I was leery, and felt I had no option but to report her to the association. As far as I'm concerned, I'm finished with dating. I sincerely doubt I'll ever remarry."

"Exactly. It isn't worth the hassle. The men I've met came with a lot of baggage. I'm carrying enough of my own."

They continued talking long past the time they'd finished their drinks. Julia learned Heath worked as a hedge-fund manager and, like her, was semiretired. She told him about her daughters—he had two sons—and that she had recently sold her interior design business and worked as a consultant, hoping to ease into retirement.

When she happened to catch the time, she was surprised to see that if she didn't rush, she'd be late for her lunch date with her daughter. They had talked, nearly nonstop, for the better part of two hours.

Scooting back her chair, she stood and reached for her purse. "Thanks for the latte and for saving me from my sister. If not for you, I would have been forced to meet yet another man who is absolutely perfect for me. Not."

Heath rose with her. "My pleasure."

She hesitated, and then added, "I enjoyed this."

He grinned. "Me, too. See you tomorrow."

"Tomorrow," she said, and even to her own ears it sounded like a promise.

Hillary glanced across the table at Julia. "Mom?"

Julia looked up from her salad. "I'm sorry, honey, were you saying something?"

"Where's your head? You look like you're a million miles away."

"Sorry, I was thinking about this morning." She'd thought of little else since leaving Heath.

"Did something happen?"

"Not really . . . I shouldn't say anything. I had coffee with a friend and rather enjoyed myself."

"That's nice." Her daughter raised her finely shaped eyebrows in speculation. "Is this friend male or female?"

"Male, but don't make more of it than there is." Julia could almost see Hillary's head spinning. Like Amanda and most of Julia's friends, they assumed she needed a man to be happy. Nearly six years alone—the anniversary date of her divorce was only a month away—had proved otherwise. Yes, life as a single woman had been an adjustment, and yes, she was lonely at times. However, that wasn't reason enough to compromise herself.

"Tell me about your friend. Divorced? How'd you meet?"

Julia answered her daughter's questions, downplaying it as best she could. "We both agree we're finished with dating."

"What if he asks you out? Would you go?"

Her immediate response was that she would, but she didn't

admit it. "I might, I don't know. I barely know him. I will say that we seem to be comfortable with each other; like me, he would want to keep this on a friends-only basis."

"This is encouraging, Mom. Go for it."

Her daughter's words lingered in her mind as Julia left for her appointment with the masseuse. It'd only been since the divorce that she'd indulged in this luxury. Amanda had suggested a massage would help relieve her body of the tension of dealing with Eddie, following their separation. It helped, and she'd been hooked ever since, scheduling one every two weeks. As the masseuse worked on her, Julia closed her eyes and reviewed once again her conversation with Heath, and how good it had made her feel.

Her next stop was the hair salon, where she had a standing appointment every five weeks for a haircut.

"You're in a good mood," Terri, her hairdresser, said as she clipped away.

She was. Her step was lighter, and she had the almost irresistible desire to break into song. She giggled at the absurdity of the thought. She was losing it.

When Terri finished drying Julia's new cut, she twisted the chair around and handed her a mirror for Julia to look and approve.

"Great as always," she said.

As she returned to The Heritage, she found herself eager for the next morning, when she would see Heath again.

Chapter 4

Heath couldn't stop thinking about Julia for the rest of the day. It had been a long time since he'd felt this at ease with a woman. For the last couple weeks, they'd exercised with each other and had barely spoken a word. When she first showed up, he'd resented the fact that his space and time had been invaded in the smallish room. He'd hoped her arrival was a one-off, and that she wouldn't return. She had, and after a week, he felt obliged to introduce himself. After his negative dating experiences, he'd gone out of his way to avoid conversation with her or make any effort to become friends.

When he saw that she was at the Busy Bean, he'd surprised himself by asking her to join him. He realized she genuinely wanted to avoid her sister and he knew he could help. Because she sat with her back to the window, Julia didn't know her sister had come out of The Heritage looking for her. She walked toward the Busy Bean, saw Julia with him, and then, just as he'd predicted, had walked away.

He noticed that Julia hadn't mentioned one word about her divorce, which he found rare. It proved that she truly had moved forward. That was the exception, if his limited experience was anything to go by. Every divorced woman he had met to this point felt it was necessary to enlighten him to the horrors of her marriage and the unfairness of the divorce.

Heath preferred not to discuss his own disillusioned marriage. It stung that his wife had left him for another man. In many ways, he blamed himself. He'd been oblivious and hadn't noticed the subtle changes in their relationship. Over the years, they'd fallen into a pattern, and without him being aware, they had grown apart.

He should have suspected something when Lee said she wanted to sleep in another bedroom, claiming his snoring kept her awake. It'd been months since they'd last made love, and her moving to another bedroom hadn't upset him.

The day she asked for the divorce, he'd been stunned. At the time, he didn't realize there was someone else. He could have fought the divorce harder, insisted they go to counseling and attempt to save what was left of their marriage. Lee wasn't interested. If she didn't want to find a way to save their marriage, then he felt he couldn't do it alone.

His son was the one who enlightened him to the truth. Their mother was involved in an affair. The news that Lee had taken a lover shocked him. Once he learned she'd cheated, he was glad he hadn't tried harder to resuscitate the marriage. As far as he was concerned, it was over. Way over. He was done.

He left the details to the two attorneys to sort out, and other than negotiating a couple points, he was happy to let her go, and twenty-six years of married life circled the drain. Of course, there were regrets and recrimination. He probably hadn't been the best husband. Since Lee had sought out another, it made sense that he hadn't met her emotional needs. He accepted responsibility for his part in the failure. Heath wasn't looking to remarry, but, as Julia had mentioned, he was accustomed to being a couple, and single life challenged him. All he was looking for now was companionship.

Heath spent part of the afternoon at the office, checking the stock market and his accounts. Repeatedly his mind drifted to Julia, and every time it did, he found himself smiling.

His assistant brought in a report he'd asked her to retrieve. She paused when she set it on his desk. "You're in a good mood," she said.

And he was.

A very good mood, better than any he'd had in a long while.

The following morning, he arrived in the exercise room five minutes early, eager to see Julia. He had an idea he wanted to float past her. When she was a few minutes late, he found himself watching the time and growing anxious.

When she entered the room, it was with a smile. "Morning," she greeted him, her eyes bright.

"Morning," he returned, and was surprised by the relief he felt that she had showed.

Julia walked over to the treadmill. Before she could adjust her earbuds, he said, "Do you have time for coffee this morning?"

"Sure. What time do you want to meet?"

"Does ten work?"

"It does."

"Great. See you then."

As he started his regular routine, Heath noticed that he didn't need exercise to get his heart going. All that was necessary was seeing Julia.

When she arrived at the Busy Bean, Heath had already secured a table and ordered their drinks. In the late morning, the coffee spot wasn't as crowded, and getting a place to sit wasn't much of a problem.

He stood when Julia approached and handed her the same drink she'd ordered the day before.

"Thanks, only I was hoping you'd let me buy this time."

"No need."

"I disagree," she said, taking a seat.

The summer sunshine fell over her, lighting up her face. She was lovely. Not beautiful in the classic sense. Her face was heart-shaped, and her dark hair—she'd done something different with it, he noticed—was stylish in a flattering pixie cut. Her eyes were the color of warm topaz.

"Why's that?" he asked, when he realized he'd been staring.

"I should pay, otherwise this might be considered a date, and we have both decided to not date again."

He nodded. "You're right. My mistake. Next time you buy."

"Next two times," she said with a smile.

A smile that made his insides stir. He lifted a finger and pointed to her hair. "You did something with your hair."

"Just a cut."

"It looks nice."

She seemed pleased that he'd noticed. "Careful with the compliments. They could be considered flirting."

"Not flirting, just a comment."

They each sipped their drinks.

"I had something I wanted to ask you," he said, easing into the conversation.

"Fire away," she said, and gestured toward him.

"I've been in my condo for a year now. Lee didn't take much with her, and I sold almost everything and bought new. With no experience in this sort of thing, I walked into a store, picked out a few items that appealed to me, and left it at that. Lee was the decorator. Not me. My place is sterile, without any accessories or personality. I was hoping you would give me a few pointers."

She looked interested.

"Naturally, I'd pay you your normal fee."

"Don't be silly, I'd love to help. I do this sort of thing for friends all the time. It's what I love."

"When would you like to take a look?" he asked, eager to spend more time with her.

"Is now convenient?"

"Now is perfect."

They finished their drinks, and Heath led her to his condo on the top floor. He had the penthouse, and a lovely panorama of the Seattle waterfront. He didn't know how much longer he would have that spectacular view, with office buildings and condos going up every other week, it seemed. Which made him determined to enjoy the scenic wonder of life on Puget Sound while he could.

"Oh," Julia whispered, as she entered his condo.

He noticed how her gaze immediately went to the view.

"It was that sight that sold me on The Heritage."

"Little wonder. It's breathtaking."

"I'd been house-shopping for a while. When I first started my search, I was looking to downsize, perhaps a three-bedroom place in an upscale community. The longer I looked, the more disenchanted I became.

"Growing frustrated with me, the agent suggested condo living, something I hadn't considered at that point. This was the first place she showed me. I'll admit when I saw the older brick building, I wasn't impressed. I almost discounted it without even entering. Once I did, it was such a pleasant surprise—I felt an immediate sense of welcome, of home. Then I learned that Eric, my friend's son, lived here as well, so naturally Michael was keen to have the two of us in the same building."

"It was the same for me," Julia said.

"The only unit available was the penthouse, and I made an offer immediately," he said, although he would have welcomed any of the units, had it suited his needs.

"I found The Heritage early on in my search and loved it immediately. The same as you, I realized right away that this was where I wanted to live, only there weren't any units available. My name was on a list, and when one went up for sale, I made an offer, sight unseen."

"Brave of you."

"In retrospect it was daring, probably the most out-of-character purchase I've ever made. The condo itself didn't matter. I could turn it into whatever I wanted. If it needed updating,

I knew plenty of contractors who would do a brilliant job. If it was too small, I would adjust. All that was important was the feeling I had of finding home."

"Home," he repeated, unaware he'd said the word aloud until she nodded and smiled.

"That's what drew us both here, I suspect," she added. "We'd lost more than our spouses. We'd lost our homes, and that feeling of familiarity, of belonging. My house ended up selling quickly, and I realize now that was a blessing. I should have known I couldn't live in the same space that I'd shared with my husband with all the memories. It would be like facing that loss every time I walked through the door."

"I hear you."

After Julia stepped away from the large windows overlooking the city, Heath gave her the grand tour. He noted how Julia studied and appraised each room.

"Do you mind if I make a few notes?" she asked.

"Not at all." He led the way to his home office and grabbed both paper and a pen.

Julia stood in the doorway, surveying the room. When he gave her the pen and pad, she immediately started writing.

After viewing each room, she made a second journey through the rooms, adding to her notes. "This kitchen is amazing," she said, coming to stand behind the long white marble countertop that faced the view. The stainless-steel appliances and white cabinets were behind her.

"The way the light comes in and floods the living area makes this entire area stunning," she added.

"I was drawn to that myself," he said.

"Other than a few accents and decorative additions, I wouldn't change a thing."

"What do you think?" he asked, once she'd finished, curious to hear her thoughts.

Julia guided him back into each room, giving him a detailed list of what she would suggest in the way of accessorizing the area.

"You did a good job choosing the furnishings," she told him. "They show your personality in every way."

This was news to Heath. "And what's my personality?" he asked, interested in hearing her thoughts.

"You're a man's man. Big. Bold. Intelligent."

He laughed. "You're saying that because my office computer has two monitors."

Smiling, she shook her head. "It's far more than that," she said, and didn't elaborate. "How do you feel about my suggestions?"

Everything she'd recommended suited him fine, and he told her so.

"What's your budget? I shop economically and promise not to spend money needlessly. The reason I ask is that it gives me parameters, so I know how much to spend in each room."

Never having worked with a decorator before, Heath wasn't sure what to tell her. "I don't have a problem with anything you suggested. The one thing I would ask is to preview any paintings you purchase."

"Perfect. There's an art show coming up at Gas Works Park this weekend. If you'd like, we could go together and check it out."

"I'd like that." Although he didn't admit it, he'd enjoy any activity that gave him more time with Julia.

They met midmorning on Saturday. Julia greeted him with two coffees and handed him one.

He grinned as he accepted it. She'd been serious about buying him coffee, and serious about being friends and not dating. Now that he was coming to know her, he was inclined to bend the no-dating rule. He'd wait and see how she felt after she'd had a chance to know him better.

Gas Works Park was located on the north end of Lake Union and south of the Wallingford neighborhood, which meant they would need to drive. After Lee moved out, Heath had foolishly splurged on a red Ferrari convertible. He sold it after a year, kicking himself for the indulgence. These days he drove an electric car, which was far more practical. And, frankly, better for the environment.

It worked well that they arrived at the art fair early enough to find parking, which was never easy in the Seattle area, especially on such a glorious July summer day. The artists had set up displays all around the nineteen-acre park. It would take more than a day to visit every booth.

Julia wore a yellow summer dress with a white short-sleeved sweater and a big straw hat to shade her from the sun. With her round sunglasses and her smile, it was hard to keep his eyes off her. He couldn't remember seeing any woman look more relaxed or lovely.

He soon learned shopping with Julia was an experience. He

was inclined to see something he liked and buy it. Not Julia. She had her notes and her tape measure and collected photos with her phone. It surprised him that she knew several of the artists personally. It was apparent that Julia was well respected and genuinely admired.

They broke for lunch, eating deli sandwiches, which he insisted on buying, seeing that she was giving of herself and her time. As they sat in the air-conditioned deli, sipping their drinks, Julia reviewed the paintings, pulling each one up on her phone for him to appraise again. She'd made meticulous notes about each one, the artist, the asking price, and the location of the booth.

"I'd purchase every one of these," Heath admitted.

"You don't have the space."

"I know."

"I like the old-world navigation painting for your home office," she told him.

That had been one of his favorites. He'd been drawn to it immediately. "How much was the asking price again?"

"Twelve hundred. However, I know the artist and believe I can persuade him to lower it to nine hundred."

"I would be willing to pay full price." And he would, without question.

"This is why you have me. I will get whatever you need, cheaper than what you would normally pay. It's what I do, and I'm good at it."

"That's a twist. A woman who saves me money."

Julia grinned and shook her head. "Now, that was a sexist comment if I ever heard one."

"Forgive me. I'm old-school. Be patient, I'm learning."

"Good." She patted his hand, and he felt an immediate surge of warmth and electricity shoot up his arm.

For the next hour, they made their decisions about which paintings to purchase. When they finished, Heath was pleased, eager to finalize the deals that afternoon.

When they returned to Gas Works Park, Julia went to work. She claimed she was good at negotiations, and she was. With finesse, she was able to get each and every painting he decided on, at a price below what was listed. Heath had the feeling these talented artists recognized having Julia Jones purchase one of their art pieces was a positive career move.

On the way back, Julia got a call. Heath was driving and the traffic was heavy, and although he could hear one end of the conversation, it didn't make much sense. All that came through was Julia's excitement.

"Good news?" he asked when she ended the conversation.

"Terrific news. My niece, Carrie, got the job. She's going to be the new concierge at The Heritage."

"That's great. I look forward to meeting her." Julia's niece was sure to be an improvement over Melanie, the previous concierge.

Chapter 5

Carrie was thrilled to have gotten the job, although no more so than her parents. From their reaction, one would think she'd been awarded a gold medal in the Summer Olympics.

Before the day was up, her mother, along with Carrie, had her bedroom packed and her father had loaded the boxes into her car. Eager much? The relief she felt was overwhelming, and clearly for her parents as well. Once at The Heritage, her mother helped her unpack and set up what she needed for the night. As soon as she finished, she fled, as if she feared Carrie would change her mind.

The studio apartment that was part of her employment package was small. The furnishings were mostly new and modern; it wouldn't take much to make the place her own. She was sure her aunt Julia would advise her what to do to brighten up the space.

She was surprised at how busy she was. This was a job she

could lean in to, as every day offered a learning experience and a challenge. She intended to make the most of this opportunity. Her aunt Julia, whom she deeply loved and admired, had given her a recommendation, and Carrie refused to do anything that would let her aunt down. Carrie made a point of introducing herself to each of the residents and found them all to be friendly. The only one she had yet to meet was Eric Hudson, as he had yet to appear to collect his mail. From what she'd learned, he had a home office and worked odd hours. At some point, she would introduce herself.

The Friday night of her first week on the job, she was making notes for the following morning, when her cousin Hillary strolled up to the counter where Carrie sat.

"Hey," Carrie said, looking up.

"Hey." Hillary beamed back at her, looking unusually happy and cheerful.

Before Carrie could ask the reason, Hillary's sister, Marie, entered the lobby.

"What's up?" Carrie asked. Her two cousins looked as if they were ready to burst with good news.

"We've come to see Mom. Can you join us, or are you on duty?"

"I'm finished for the day, so sure." Obviously the two had some fabulous news to share.

Carrie put aside her notes and followed her two cousins to the elevator. Julia must have been expecting them, because she had several appetizers set out. There were the usual cheese and crackers, and Julia's special vegetable dumplings that were a family favorite. At any family function her aunt Julia was required to bring these, as no one else seemed to make them taste like hers.

"Oh good, Carrie's here," her aunt said, ushering them past the appetizers, which she had set on the counter, and into the living area. Her aunt Julia's condo was one of the nicer ones, and of course it was decorated beautifully in soft shades of gray with teal accents.

The four sat, and Julia looked expectantly toward her daughters. "Well, don't keep me in suspense, what's the good news?"

Marie looked to Hillary and then Hillary raised her left hand, splaying her fingers. A beautiful diamond engagement ring sparkled from her ring finger. "Blake asked me to marry him," she announced, "and this time I said yes."

Carrie knew that Blake had been after Hillary for some time to take the next big step in their relationship. He wanted to start a family and buy a house, and he wanted to do it with Hillary. Carrie never fully understood why her cousin kept putting him off. She kept insisting she wasn't ready, and according to Marie, Hillary's delays had become an issue with Blake. Carrie suspected Blake had given Hillary an ultimatum; either make a commitment or he was moving on.

Carrie had gotten to know Blake a bit over the last few years. He was a catch, and if Hillary didn't want to commit to him, she knew plenty of other women would. He worked at the University of Washington in the IT department.

At her daughter's news, Julia leaped to her feet, and with tears glistening in her eyes cried out, "Hillary, oh Hillary, that's wonderful!"

"I knew it would make you happy."

"I'm more than happy. I'm over-the-moon thrilled." Mother and daughter embraced and swayed back and forth a few times, overcome with joy. Like Carrie's own mother, her aunt Julia looked forward to spoiling grandchildren one day. It would happen, only not anytime soon.

Although she'd never tell her mother, Carrie knew how deeply Hillary's parents' divorce had wounded her cousin. Carrie had been afraid Hillary would never marry, for fear of what would happen in her own marriage. If her parents could divorce after being together for more than thirty years, what was to say any marriage would last? For reasons Carrie never fully understood, her cousins seemed to believe that in divorcing Julia, her uncle Eddie had divorced his daughters at the same time.

"Do you have a date for the wedding yet?" Julia asked, sitting down and pressing her hands between her knees, as if to hold herself back from hugging them all half to death.

"Not yet. Blake and I are looking at different venues, and it all depends on what dates are available. We were hoping for mid-November, sometime before the holidays."

Julia nodded approvingly.

"Pastor Rick has agreed to perform the ceremony and will be counseling us. As soon as we know where we can have the wedding dinner and reception, we'll coordinate the date with the church."

The whole family attended the same church. Pastor Rick had been their pastor for as long as Carrie could remember. They'd all grown up with him. If she remembered correctly, Rick had been a youth pastor to her mom and aunt years earlier, when they'd been teenagers. Their history went a long way back.

"I've asked Marie to be my maid of honor and I'd like Carrie to be a bridesmaid," she said, looking to Carrie.

"I'd love to. Hill, this is such great news."

Her cousin glowed. "Now that I've accepted Blake's proposal, I'm sorry I waited this long."

Julia reached for Hillary's hands and stared at her daughter. "Have you told your father?" she asked, her voice low and serious.

Hillary immediately stiffened. "No."

"Honey, you need to let him know. This is wonderful news, and you should be the one to tell him. He'll be happy for you."

Carrie knew that Hillary'd had little contact with her dad since the divorce. Her uncle had made several attempts to break through, with no success.

"I'm not telling him, Mom."

"It's been six years. It's time to let all this anger go. The only one it's hurting is you. Your dad loves you and he'd—"

"Mom, please, don't bring Dad into this. He made it clear who he loves. When he left you, he walked out on us, too."

"He didn't walk away from you. He never would; you're his children, his precious daughters. You need your dad, and I know you might not think it, but this separation has been just as hard on him as it has been on you."

"Not likely," Hillary insisted, her back as stiff as a broom handle. "I don't believe he cares about us the least bit."

"He misses you."

"Good. I hope he's miserable and that this new wife of his makes him suffer."

"Listen," her mother said, her expression one of regret and

anxiety. "If you believe having a relationship with your father is somehow being disloyal to me, then you're wrong."

"Mom," Marie butted in, coming to Hillary's defense. "It isn't that. Dad is the one who is making any kind of relationship impossible. He refuses to see us unless Laura comes with him. Neither of us wants anything to do with her."

"He's trying to force that parasite he married on us," Hillary added, and shuddered as if she'd bitten into a lemon. "If seeing Dad means I have to deal with Laura, then I refuse."

"Has Laura reached out?" Carrie asked. She knew her uncle had at least tried, and she wondered about his new wife.

Hillary snickered. "The only time I've spoken to her was the day her son and I had it out. She stood between us and shouted at Marie and me to leave, which we were more than happy to do. She was rude and horrible. I have no intention of speaking to her ever."

"Honey," Julia said, as if looking to interject reason into this discussion. "Laura was standing up for her son. Had the situation been reversed, I would have leaped to your defense."

Carrie knew her cousins' actions had been less than civil. It was shortly after the Lake Sammamish incident that her aunt had finalized the divorce. Whatever had happened that day had deeply impacted her cousins. It was from that point forward that Hillary and Marie refused to have anything more to do with their father.

"You should be able to talk to your father without Laura," Julia suggested gently. "He'll want to know you're engaged."

"Not doing it," Hillary said, and shook her head for emphasis.

"You say Dad misses us?" Marie scoffed. "Mom, I think it's

best if we drop the subject. Dad made his choice and so have Hillary and I. As far as we're concerned, he can live with the consequences."

Julia slowly shook her head, as if disappointed by their unwillingness to bend. "Oh girls, you're as stubborn as your father."

"At least we come by it honestly," Hillary said, as if making a joke.

In a blatant effort to change the subject, her cousin walked over to where Julia had arranged the appetizers. "I have always loved these dumplings."

"Okay," Julia said, sighing loudly. "Message received. I won't bring up your father again, although someone needs to let him know the news."

Hillary paused from loading a second dumpling onto her small plate. "You can tell him if you want. You appear to be the only one in this family willing to talk to him."

Marie shrugged. "Yeah, Mom, you tell him."

"And while you're at it," Hillary added, "you can remind him that he isn't invited to the wedding if he plans on bringing Laura."

"Hillary!" Julia protested. "She's his wife!"

"I'm serious, Mom. I have no intention of letting her ruin my special day. As far as I'm concerned, when he walked out that door, he made his choice. I no longer consider him my father."

Perhaps she shouldn't have asked, but Carrie was curious. "Who will walk you down the aisle?"

"I haven't thought that far ahead. Maybe I'll just walk myself. Daddy gave up the privilege a long time ago."

Julia's face fell. "You need to seriously think about this, Hillary. You might regret this decision down the road."

"No, I won't. I'm the bride-to-be, and if Dad wants to be part of my wedding, I'm willing to let him, with one small stipulation. I don't want Laura there. If he can agree to that, then he, and he alone, will receive an invitation."

"I shouldn't have said anything," Carrie murmured, regretting asking the question.

"It's better to get this out now," Hillary said, "so there's no misunderstanding."

"And if your father refuses?" Julia asked.

"Then so be it. What was it that Gramps always said?"

Carrie and the two cousins recited it together: *"It's better this way."*

After her cousins left, Carrie headed back to her desk to complete the list she'd been working on earlier. When a meal delivery came for Eric Hudson, Carrie saw this as the perfect opportunity to meet the elusive resident. Seeing that the meal had already been paid for, she decided to deliver it herself.

Standing in the hallway outside his door, she waited for him to answer.

"Give me a minute," he shouted from the other side.

"No problem," she said. If he didn't care that his dinner was growing cold, then she wouldn't worry about it, either.

The door opened a couple minutes later. He grabbed the sack from her hands and was ready to close the door when she stopped him.

"Eric?" she said, making it more of a question than a statement. She hadn't expected him to be so young. He had to be around her age, perhaps a year or two older. She couldn't help but notice he was easy on the eyes. His hair was badly in need of a cut and it didn't look like he'd taken the time to comb it. He was dressed in sloppy jeans and a T-shirt and had bare feet.

He glanced up as if noticing her for the first time in her pencil skirt and silk blouse. His eyes widened, as if he was as surprised as she was. "Yes. I'm Eric. Is there a problem?"

"No, not at all. I wanted to introduce myself. I'm Carrie, the new concierge. I'm here to do whatever I can to make life easier for you. If you need me to collect packages, or book a reservation, or if anything needs repairs, don't hesitate to ask." She bit her lip to keep from suggesting an appointment with the barber.

His gaze briefly held hers. A beep came from somewhere inside his condo. He glanced over his shoulder, then said, "Nice to meet you. Now, if you'll excuse me, I need to get back to my computer."

"Of course. Have a good evening."

"You, too," he said, as he swiftly closed the door.

Well, that was interesting, Carrie mused. Even though their interaction had been brief, she was intrigued. From what she'd observed and what she'd heard, Eric was something of a recluse. As far as she could tell, he collected his mail in the wee hours of the morning when no one else was about. He ordered take-out meals, and the only visitor who'd signed in to see him appeared to be a businessman. The guy had scribbled his name down and the only part legible enough to read was Michael. One visitor, and that was it. Everything else—groceries, laundry, meals— was all delivered.

When she'd gone to meet him, she'd expected to find a senior citizen with a long white beard, not a man in his late twenties or early thirties. There was more to him than met the eye, and Carrie found herself curious about what had led Eric Hudson to hide away in his condo. She'd do a little digging and find out what she could.

Chapter 6

Julia knew if she had a conversation with Eddie it probably wouldn't go well. Because neither of her stubborn daughters was willing to tell him about Hillary's engagement, it had been left to her.

She debated with herself all weekend, unsure she even should. The last thing she wanted was to stand between Eddie and their children. Before she left, Hillary made sure Julia accepted the fact that she had no intention of enlightening her father as to her wedding plans. If Julia felt he needed to know, then she would need to reach out. Hillary was content to leave her father completely in the dark.

Julia couldn't let that happen. If Eddie were to hear the news of Hillary's engagement from one of their mutual friends, it would devastate him. Eddie might be her ex-husband, but she had no wish to hurt him.

Before making the call, she carefully reviewed how best to tell him without stirring up hard feelings. Which meant not mentioning Hillary's dictate that Eddie attend the wedding without Laura. Excluding his wife would put Eddie in an impossible situation. To Julia's way of thinking, their daughter was being unreasonable. She feared banning Laura was the one thing Hillary could do that would keep Eddie away. This would prove what Hillary had said all along—that her father had never really loved her.

It hurt Julia to see her daughters punishing themselves by keeping their father out of their lives. And if it made her own heart ache, she could well imagine what it did to Eddie. She wondered if he had ever considered the fallout when he'd started his affair with Laura. And if he'd had any inkling of the havoc it would cause, would it have made any difference? Silly thoughts, really, seeing that it was all water under the bridge now.

Sunday evening, when she didn't feel she could delay it any longer, she reached for her phone. It rang three times before Eddie answered.

"Hello." His voice was gruff and unwelcoming.

He didn't greet her, although he knew from caller ID it was her. Perhaps he was with Laura and didn't wish to say her name aloud. Already, her nerves made this harder than it should ever be.

"It's Julia."

"I know who this is."

Oh dear, this wasn't starting out well.

"How are you?" she asked, hoping to ease into the conversation with small talk. Her hand tightened around her phone, trying to remain calm, despite his lack of warmth or welcome. She didn't make a habit of contacting him out of the blue. It'd been months, probably more than a year, since they'd last spoken.

"Did you call to inquire about my health?"

"No. I . . .

"I'm good, Julia. More than good. I'm happy."

She swallowed hard, not wanting to read any more meaning into his words than what he'd said. From the tone of his voice, he seemed to suggest that the only way he'd found such unbound well-being was by separating his life from hers. He seemed to be looking for a way to hurt her. She could either take offense or ignore it.

"Glad to hear it. I feel the same," she said, after an awkward moment, choosing to take the high road by assuming his comment had not been a dig.

"Wonderful. Now that it's settled how happy we both are, is there a reason for this call?"

Julia strongly suspected Laura was sitting next to him or was within hearing distance.

"I have news I thought you'd want to know," she said.

"Is it important?"

She closed her eyes, wishing it could be different between them. "Would I call otherwise?" she asked, keeping her voice even and controlled, unwilling to let him intimidate her. It hurt that their relationship remained strained.

It didn't need to be like this. She had released him without malice, and she hoped that after all the good years they'd shared together, they could part without hard feelings.

Her throat tightened, and she waited a moment, the pause awkward. "Does it need to be like this?" she asked, softening her tone.

"How do you mean?"

She wasn't fooled, he knew. "I only wish you well, Eddie. It used to be we were friends as well as lovers. We have children together. It shouldn't be awkward between us, because we have both moved on. I don't harbor bad feelings toward you, or Laura."

His sigh was heavy. "You're right. I'm sorry, Julia. I saw your name and my mind went back to places it shouldn't have. Now tell me what prompted the call."

"It's Hillary."

"Everything okay with her?" His concern was immediate.

"It's great. She was by on Friday to let me know she and Blake are engaged."

Her announcement was met with silence. "And you're the one telling me? Why is that?"

"Trust me, Eddie, I urged her to reach out herself."

"Did you?" His words were full of skepticism. How quickly he reverted to being suspicious and annoyed.

"Yes," she returned emphatically. "I have repeatedly encouraged both girls to put aside their resentment and reconcile with you. You're their father, and while they might never admit it openly, they miss you."

He huffed as if he found that hard to believe. "The ball is in their court. Heaven knows I've tried to have a relationship with them. The problem is they're both too stubborn to listen to reason. They won't have anything to do with Laura. They won't meet her, won't speak to her. It's as if my wife doesn't exist."

Silently, Julia wondered how much of an effort Laura had made to connect with their daughters. She quickly put an end to that line of unproductive thought. Once Laura's sons and her daughters had gotten into a nasty verbal exchange, Laura had basically ignored Eddie's family.

"I know you've tried, and I'm genuinely sorry, Eddie."

He sighed again with frustration and regret. "Guess I shouldn't complain, I can be just as strong-willed."

Julia grinned in full agreement. She didn't know how long it had been since his last attempt to connect with his daughters. Neither had mentioned their father in several months, which told her he hadn't made any effort for quite some time.

"When's the wedding?" Eddie asked.

This was the point where their conversation was sure to get sticky. "She's hoping sometime in November, before the holidays. As soon as she sets the date, I'll let you know."

"I wish Hillary would tell me herself."

Julia felt the same.

"Will she let me help with the costs? I'd like to do that. That might build a bridge between us."

The offer was generous, in light of the fact Hillary had barely spoken to her father in the last six years. "I don't know. You'll have to ask her. My guess is that she and Blake will want to cover the expenses themselves. I offered to pay for the photographer and the cake."

"Hard to believe Hillary is close to thirty."

The years flew by far too quickly.

"She waited long enough, didn't she? Any particular reason she held off as long as she did?"

No way Julia would admit she feared the divorce had destroyed her daughter's view of love and marriage.

"Again, that's a question for Hillary to answer."

"Would you tell her that I'd like to help with the cost of the wedding?"

"Eddie, I can't. You should tell her that yourself."

He waited a couple seconds, mulling it over, and then said, "She'd probably reject the offer anyway."

"You won't know unless you ask," she gently reminded him.

"She ignores my calls."

"Then text or email." She didn't know why she should be the one advising him. He knew how to connect with his daughters. She shouldn't be the one pushing him. If it was up to her, she'd stay out of this messy situation entirely. Even being put in the position of telling him about Hillary's engagement was more than she was comfortable with.

"Do you remember when she was little, how she loved to play bride?" Eddie asked. "You sewed her a veil, and she moved the chairs around in the dining room to make an aisle. What was she, six or seven at the time? She insisted I needed to walk her down the aisle."

"I remember."

"Marie was her maid of honor." His mind seemed to drift back to the days when their girls were small and filled with imagination and wonder. After attending the wedding of Eddie's cousin, they'd returned home wanting to be brides themselves. Julia had constructed a small veil for Hillary, and she'd worn a pair of Julia's high heels and carried a bouquet of yellow dandelions.

That seemed a lifetime ago now. Her daughters had once dreamed of happily ever after, never suspecting that one day that dream would shatter when reality set in and their parents divorced. At the time of the divorce, both girls were adults. She'd assumed they were mature enough not to be affected by the disillusionment of the marriage. Even after the clash with Laura's sons, Julia had hoped the girls would accept their father's decision to remarry and move on. It stunned her even now how personally they had taken his choice.

"I want to be the one to escort my daughter down the aisle."

Oh dear, Julia had hoped to avoid this. It wasn't up to her to report what Hillary had said.

"It's what I always expected," she agreed, perhaps a bit overly emphatically.

Her voice must have given away some hint of discouragement, because Eddie picked up on it right away.

"What aren't you telling me?" he demanded.

"If you do or don't escort Hillary is between the two of you," she said, as gently as she could. "I have nothing to do with this, and I don't plan to get in the middle, either."

"She knows as well as you that's my right as her father."

Julia agreed. Hillary had made it plain she had no intention of letting her dad know her plans. Hearing the pain in Eddie's voice made her heart ache for him. Even though they were no longer married, and he'd betrayed her, she continued to have feelings for Eddie. She always would.

"This is a matter you need to discuss with Hillary. Please, Eddie, all I ask is that you leave me out of it," Julia said. "Don't use me as a go-between."

"Come on, Julia. Hillary isn't talking to me."

"Then try again," she advised. No way was she stepping into this cesspool of hurt and anger.

"It's Laura, isn't it?"

"Eddie, did you not hear me? I refuse to get in the middle of this. I was uncomfortable even telling you about the engagement. I would have left it, only I knew if you heard the news and didn't know, you'd be hurt."

He paused for a moment to digest this. "I suppose I should be grateful you called. My guess is Hillary is going to use this wedding to—"

Julia cut him off. "Don't go reading more into her actions than warranted. She would never admit it, but I know my daughter. She misses you. If she's using this wedding for anything, it's to bring her father back into her life and save her stubborn pride at the same time."

"I wish that was true." Eddie sounded utterly defeated. "She made it clear how much she dislikes my wife. From the moment I moved out of the house, Hillary and Marie have refused to have anything to do with me if Laura is involved."

If there was anything Julia could personally do to make this better, to get her daughters to be logical, she would gladly have done it.

"I'm sorry, Eddie, I wish . . . I wish the girls would listen to reason about you being with Laura. I've tried talking to them. Laura is your wife, and sooner or later they need to accept that there's no going back for either of us." Julia had moved on, and she wanted her children to do the same.

His voice dropped, weary and sad. "I know."

Julia sincerely wanted to help. She'd tried numerous times pleading with the girls to be reasonable about their father and Laura. They, however, weren't open to their father or his relationship with his new wife.

If ever there was a time for reconciliation, it was Hillary's wedding. "Eddie, listen, this is your life. I don't mean to interfere; that's the last thing I want. What you should recognize is this may well be your last chance to reconcile with your daughters."

"What do you mean?"

"Being indifferent and avoiding reconciliation simply isn't working. This engagement is a gift. An opportunity. Fight for your daughters. Let them see your heart and how important they are to you."

Eddie's sigh came over the line. "You're right. Thanks for the call, Julia."

"You're welcome, Eddie."

What had started out as an uncomfortable conversation had ended on a gentle note. When she disconnected the call, Julia leaned back and closed her eyes, praying that Eddie would take her words to heart and do whatever was necessary to be reunited with his girls.

Chapter 7

Heath spent the weekend thinking about Julia. More than once, he'd been tempted to call to ask if she'd go sailing with him. He'd kept his boat in the divorce and often enjoyed time on Lake Washington. Lee had never taken to the water, so he'd frequently gone out with friends or his sons. Since both Michael and Adam had plans for the weekend, Heath had ventured out with a friend he'd known since his college days.

As it so often did, time spent on the water had relaxed him. As he leaned back, letting the wind carry him across the choppy waters near the University of Washington, his mind had continually drifted to Julia. He would have enjoyed sharing this day with her. The desire to ask her had been strong. He would have given in, if not for fear he was coming on a little strong.

They were together nearly every morning as it was, and recently they'd fallen into the habit of having coffee together following their workout. He enjoyed her company, far more than any other woman he'd met in the years since his divorce. Like him, Julia was gun-shy, and he didn't want to overwhelm her.

But he was interested in Julia. Very interested.

Monday morning, after they'd exercised, parted, and showered, they met at the Busy Bean. It was her turn to buy coffee, and he let her, although he would have preferred to pay himself. Probably a sexist thought, but he couldn't help that. It was how he'd been raised. The man paid. Any woman paying for his half made him slightly uncomfortable.

He was early enough to get a table, and stood when Julia arrived, after collecting their coffees. Standing was likely another faux pas, but again, this was how he'd been taught. Ever the gentleman.

Once seated, he asked, "Did you have a good weekend?" He hoped to feel her out about joining him on his boat the next time he went out on the water.

She seemed to be weighing her answer. "It was a mixture of the wonderful and the not-so-wonderful."

"How do you mean?" With anyone else he might have left it at that and awaited details. He wanted to know, and so he asked. "If I'm prying, stop me. What happened?"

She smiled, letting him know she hadn't taken offense. "The best part was when my daughters stopped by. My oldest, Hillary, just got engaged. She's been dating Blake for three years and I'd been hoping, of course."

"That is good news." His own sons were getting to the age where they should be thinking along those lines themselves. To this point, neither of his boys seemed to be in any hurry to make a commitment. Heath wondered if the divorce might have something to do with their reluctance. It could be what had held Julia's daughter back.

Julia's eyes lit up with happiness, as she relayed what she'd learned about her daughter's plans to this point. "It's wonderful news and I couldn't be more pleased."

"And the not-so-wonderful part?" he prodded.

"Yes," she said, sighing, "Hillary remains on the outs with her father. I was put in the uncomfortable position of being the one to tell him his daughter is engaged."

Heath didn't envy her. "I take it the conversation didn't go well?"

"It actually ended up being fine, after an uncomfortable start. Naturally, Eddie was hurt that I was the one to tell him. I'd rather stay out of this conflict between my ex and our daughters. The last thing I want is to be caught in the middle. The only reason I called was because I was afraid if word got out, and Eddie heard about the engagement from someone else, it would devastate him."

Julia's sensitivity toward her ex-husband's feelings impressed Heath. "It sounds like your girls haven't forgiven their father."

Julia groaned. "That's putting it mildly."

She didn't elaborate, and he didn't press her with more questions.

"What about your sons? Do they have issues with their new stepdad?"

Quite the opposite, from what Heath could make out. He never wanted to put his boys in a position of having to choose; consequently, he didn't ask, and they seldom volunteered information. "Apparently not. They don't mention much about my ex and her husband, and frankly, that's just as well."

"You're fortunate. My girls took the divorce personally. They don't seem to understand that while Eddie no longer wants me in his life, he loves our daughters and wants a relationship with them."

Seeing that Julia was struggling with this situation, Heath sought a way to brighten her day. "Let's concentrate on the positive. Your daughter is engaged, and you're pleased."

"I am," she said, brightening at the reminder.

"I say this news calls for a celebration. Let me cook you dinner," he suggested. Since living alone, Heath had become adept in the kitchen. The first year following the divorce, he'd dined on takeout most nights. Within a few months, he was tired of the same menus and the same restaurants, and decided to teach himself to cook. He signed up for an online cooking class, tried out a few basic recipes, and was pleased with the results. It was possible to teach an old dog new tricks! He was eager to show Julia he was a man of many talents.

"When?" she asked, and then playfully narrowed her eyes. "Heath Wilson, are you asking me out on a date?"

"Ah . . ." He was unsure how to answer. Thinking quickly, he said, "Not a date. A meal between friends." Then, because he was eager to spend time with her after the long weekend, he added, "How about tonight?"

Her shoulders slumped in disappointment. "I can't tonight. I've signed up for a charity pub crawl."

That sounded like fun. "How about tomorrow, then?"

"Sure, anytime," she readily agreed.

He mentally reviewed possible menu choices. He considered

three different recipes that were sure to impress her: two with shrimp and another with sole. He had a couple good chicken recipes, along with a few others.

"Heath?" Julia said, pulling him from his thoughts.

Looking up, Julia had a huge smile. "Come with me," she said, and then, reading his bewilderment, added, "on the pub crawl. I have a ticket I got for my sister. Amanda intended to go and then this morning she called to say she couldn't make it because of some quilting class she wants to take. I'd rather not go alone. The event would be much more fun if you were able to join me."

"You're on," he said, grinning. Then he jokingly added, "Remember, this isn't a date."

She smiled. "Not a date. It's two friends enjoying good draft beer and having fun together."

"Count me in."

He was in, all right. Nearly over his head when it came to this woman.

The thick line of people around the bar awaiting their beer made it nearly impossible for Heath to maneuver back to Julia. Loud voices echoed off the walls, making conversation difficult.

This was their second stop, and Heath held the flight of beer over his head as he waded through the mass of customers to return to Julia. She was at a high-top that was shared with a young woman who lived at The Heritage. They'd been introduced before the event, but the chatter was too loud to clearly hear her name. It sounded like Kennedy. She had a friend with her. They both taught high school—at least that's what he thought he heard. Kennedy didn't look much older than her students would be.

He set the beer down and claimed his seat. They were lucky to have found a table. At the first pub, they'd been forced to stand at the bar. It was something of a surprise to discover these microbrew beers were to his liking. Heath had never been much of a beer man, preferring fine single-barrel scotch or a dark red wine over canned beer.

He'd already learned the difference between IPA, ale, and lager in a short lecture given by the proprietor of the first pub. The woman had been informative and entertaining.

"You first," Julia said, motioning toward the flight. It was suggested they start with the pale beer. The color and texture in the flight grew darker and richer as they continued sampling. Julia liked the paler beers, which he'd learned had a more distinctive flavor of hops and were closely aligned with the British ales. The IPA stood for India pale ale, which, he had been informed, was the most popular of the American craft beers.

Heath swallowed the first sip and nodded approvingly. Julia tried it next and agreed. "This is good. I've never really appreciated beer before."

"A whole new experience for us both," Heath said. He didn't frequent taverns and rarely drank beer, unless he was with friends who did, and then only sparingly.

Julia set the pale ale aside and as best they could exchanged notes with Kennedy and her friend. Next, Heath indicated she should be the first to sample the blond. From the short lecture, he recalled the brewing process included pale malt hops and yeast. He was good at taking mental notes and was impressed with the different varieties. It was enlightening to learn how many different types of beers there were.

"What do you think?" Julia asked after he tasted the blond ale.

He nodded, giving it his limited approval. If their first stop was any indication, the darker the beer, the more he enjoyed the tasting.

He reached for the third sample, which he had learned was a German beer known as Hefeweizen. After his first sip, he frowned and handed it to Julia.

"Tell me what you taste."

She took a tiny sample and then raised her eyes to meet his, full of question.

"Well?" he asked.

"Don't laugh," she said. "Banana?"

He could barely hear her above the rowdy crowd. He nodded. "I thought I was losing it. Banana flavoring in beer?"

They both laughed, the alcohol loosening them up more with each drink.

The last two tastes in the flight were a porter and a stout. They were heavy and not to Julia's liking, so he drank them both. The flavors were strong and distinctive, to the point that he felt he could almost chew them.

By the time they left for the third of the four pubs, they were in good spirits and even a little tipsy, which surprised Heath. He wasn't sure this heady feeling was entirely due to the alcohol. Julia had gone to his head as potently as any fine scotch. He felt at ease with her, comfortable. It had been a long time since he'd experienced anything close to what he did with her.

Had it been like this when he'd first met Lee? He couldn't recall, and decided it was a mistake to look back instead of forward. He didn't know what the future held when it came to him and Julia. What he did feel was encouragement and the eagerness to learn more about her. He'd basically given up on relationships, and to find a woman who seemed perfect, living right under his nose, was a complete surprise.

As they left the pub to walk to the next one on the crawl, Heath reached for Julia's hand, using the excuse that he didn't want to lose her in the crowd. It would have been easy to get separated. Heath was determined to hold on to this woman in more ways than simple hand-holding.

At the end of the evening they were on the Seattle waterfront. Heath felt the need to get some food in his stomach. He hadn't eaten before the crawl. They passed Ivar's, a well-known and beloved fish-and-chips restaurant.

"Are you hungry?" he asked Julia.

"I'm more drunk than hungry," she said, smiling up at him.

It demanded every ounce of his restraint not to lean down and kiss her. Her lips were moist and parted, and her beautiful eyes smiled up at him. He'd never been one for PDAs, but for the life of him, he was tempted.

"How about fish and chips?" he said, purposely looking away.

"Not on a date, right?" she teased, slightly slurring her words.

Yup, they needed some food in their stomachs to counterbalance the beer. "Date or no date, I'm buying. You paid for the crawl tickets, so dinner is on me."

For a moment she looked like she wanted to argue, then seemed to change her mind. "One piece of cod with a side of chowder. Their chowder is the best."

"You got it."

Heath approached the window and placed their food order, along with two cups of coffee. When it arrived, he carried it to a picnic table on the pier and sat across from Julia.

Summer in Seattle didn't officially begin until after the Fourth of July. It continued to get better with every passing day and reached a peak in August and September. Heath loved the Seattle summers. This July evening couldn't have been any more perfect. The sky was clear, and the stars were just starting to come out as dusk settled over the city. Shadows fell from the skyscrapers. A gentle breeze blew off the cool waters of Puget Sound, and Heath sat with the most beautiful woman he'd ever met. How any man could walk away from Julia left him speechless. The woman was the entire package.

They took an Uber back to The Heritage and Heath rode the elevator up with Julia. Being a gentleman, he walked with her to her condo. When she unlocked the door, he stepped inside without waiting for an invitation. She didn't look surprised or agitated, and he was grateful. Either he kissed her or he would go insane. He'd been waiting for this moment all night.

"I had a great time," she said. The light remained off, and moonlight glowed through the window, bathing her in its golden softness. He couldn't take his eyes off her, and she looked up at him.

Neither spoke.

Heath placed his hands on her shoulders and said, "I had a great time, too. Thanks for inviting me."

"I wouldn't have enjoyed it nearly as much alone. Spending the evening with you made this experience a thousand times better."

"I agree." And then, because he couldn't wait a moment longer, he lowered his mouth to hers.

Julia's arms circled his middle, and she stood on her tiptoes as her mouth eagerly met his. Heath wasn't sure what he'd expected, but it wasn't the shot of electricity that zipped through him like a spike of lightning. He deepened the kiss, and Julia opened to him like a rose in summer.

He didn't know how long they remained in the small entry with their arms around each other, kissing like love-starved teenagers. Eager now, their kisses were long enough to steal his breath away.

Julia was the one who broke it off, leaning her forehead against his chest. She didn't say anything, and Heath was afraid if he spoke it would spoil the moment.

"Thank you," she whispered after several seconds.

He grinned. He should be the one thanking her.

"It's been a long time since anyone has kissed me like that. Or made me feel beautiful and wanted."

"Oh Julia, how could anyone not see your beauty?"

She closed her eyes and smiled.

"Remember, I'm cooking dinner tomorrow night."

"A man with culinary skills. Not turning that down."

"Good. I'd be disappointed if you did."

"I can help. We can prepare it together."

Heath would enjoy nothing better. "Sounds good. I better go." He said it more for himself than for Julia. If he stayed any longer, he'd end up kissing her again. Stopping was hard enough as it was.

She opened the door and then remained in the doorway as he backed out, wanting to hold on to the image of her as long as possible.

"Good night, Julia."

"Good night."

Heath returned to his condo and found he couldn't keep still. He walked from his home office to the kitchen and then back again. All he could think about was Julia. Her unique taste remained with him and he wanted more. Needed more.

After ten minutes of mindless arguing with himself, he left his condo and rode the elevator down to Julia's floor. This was crazy. He was acting like a besotted high-schooler. He didn't care.

After ringing the doorbell, he stepped back and waited.

Julia answered and surprise showed in her eyes. Surprise was followed by a smile as she literally fell into his arms with a small cry of welcome.

Heath kissed her again and again, unable to get his fill of her. Unable to stop.

Pulling away from him, Julia's hands framed his face as she smiled up at him.

For the longest moment all they did was stare at each other.

"About dinner," Heath said.

"Yes?"

"It's most definitely a date."

Julia smiled and nodded, and then he kissed her again.

Chapter 8

"Hey, Mom," Carrie shouted as she arrived, bursting through the front door of their home.

"Carrie." Her mother stuck her head out from the kitchen. "This is a surprise."

From her mother's look, it wasn't a pleasant one. "Something wrong?" Carrie asked. It felt like she'd interrupted something. Her mother looked guilty, as though Carrie had walked in on her parents running through the house naked.

Her mother shook her head. "Everything is fine at The Heritage, right? You didn't lose your job, did you?"

"Mom, what would make you think that? I'm enjoying my job." If she lost her position after only two weeks, it would be something of a record. Besides, she had come to love the variety of each day. It'd been fun getting to know the residents and their particular quirks and personalities. Every day was different, with fresh experiences.

She'd gotten to know Kennedy, who was about her age, and had a soft spot for Eric, who rarely showed his face, although she'd taken to delivering his dinner every night. At first he seemed eager to get rid of her, which she found both amusing and challenging. Now, though, she was beginning to make a dent in the wall he'd built around himself, and a few times they'd engaged in brief conversations. From what she'd seen of his condo, she could tell Eric was a tech geek. Computers and monitors took up every bit of available space. She wasn't sure what he did exactly, although she could guess. Even from their short conversations, she was learning more about him every day. He was different from any guy she knew, and the more time she spent with him, the more intrigued she became.

Carrie's dad came out of his den and wore the same anxious look. "Carrie, what are you doing here?" he asked, breaking into her thoughts about Eric.

It hit her then. Her parents were afraid she was going to move back home. It was almost comical. For half a minute, she was tempted to toy with them, and then decided that would be childish.

"Stop fretting, you two. I'm collecting my bike. Justin and I are going to ride around Green Lake."

"Oh thank goodness." Her mother heaved a relieved sigh.

Carrie started up the staircase, taking the steps two at a time. "I need to get my helmet," she said, rushing down the hallway toward her bedroom. She opened the door and was dumbfounded by what she saw.

"Carrie . . ." Her mother shouted from the bottom of the stairwell. "I moved your things."

Carrie could barely believe her eyes. Her entire bedroom had been dismantled. Gone were her bed, dresser, nightstand, and desk. Her room had been transformed.

Where her bookcases had once been was a large rack that contained spools of thread of every conceivable color. A rainbow didn't have this many colors. A cutting table had replaced her bed, and a monster of a sewing machine covered up one entire wall. Out of curiosity she opened her closet doors, and, sure enough, the entire space was stacked with fabric from floor to ceiling.

Where her mother had stored this volume of fabric before Carrie moved out was a mystery. She must have had it tucked in every room in the house, under beds, in boxes and drawers. Hidden. This was unbelievable.

Closing the door, she stepped back, unable even now to believe the evidence staring her in the face. Her room was gone. The one place in the house where she belonged. Seeing it completely converted this way was a jolt.

A few years earlier her mother had joined a quilting guild. Carrie hadn't paid much attention. A smaller version of her current sewing machine had been set up in the laundry room, and her mother had attended classes and seminars. The quilts she made were works of art. She made them for friends and relatives, for homeless shelters, and for nursing homes. Her mother had always been generous with her gifts and talents. No way would Carrie begrudge her this space.

Her mother joined her, looking guilty. "Are you upset?" she asked.

Putting on a brave smile, she shook her head. "I have my own place now, so no worries. I'm grateful you've put my room to good use." How her mother had managed to do all she had from a tiny laundry room before was amazing.

"Has Dad seen your stash?" she asked, gesturing toward the stuffed closet. Her father would have a conniption fit if he was to know how much money her mother had spent on fabric.

"He knows," she said, lowering her voice.

Carrie couldn't imagine her dad not being appalled at the huge investment her mother had made in her passion for quilting. "Did he look inside the closet?"

A smile wiggled at the edges of her mother's mouth. "He did."

"And what did he say?"

The smile grew until it covered her mother's entire face. "He was aghast and claimed all that fabric must be worth over a hundred dollars."

Carrie burst out laughing, and her mother joined in until tears rolled down their cheeks.

"And what did you say?" Carrie prompted, knowing her mother.

"I looked at your father, gasped, and said, 'Do you really think I spent that much?'"

The comment told her how often her father went shopping. He probably believed bread still cost twenty-five cents a loaf.

Her mother grew serious. "You meant it, didn't you? About not being upset I commandeered your room?"

"Not upset as much as surprised. No wonder you wanted me out of the house. You needed the room for all this equipment and for your fabric stash."

The two hugged. "Now, where did you say my biking gear was?"

"In the garage. I've got it tucked away in boxes. Come on, I'll help you find it."

A half hour later, Carrie was at Green Lake straddling her bike, patiently waiting for Justin, who was notoriously late. She should have known he'd be thirty minutes behind schedule. Normally, she'd tell him an earlier time to compensate for his lateness.

When he finally rode up and joined her, she looked pointedly at the time.

"Don't give me grief. You know I'm always late," he said, charming her with his smile. He looked great, another bonus. They'd met in college in a study group and dated off and on through the years. The relationship had never been serious. Not on her end. Justin seemed to enjoy the chase, and the connection had never been strong enough for Carrie to take it seriously.

Carrie set her feet in the clips and glanced his way. "You ready?"

He laughed. "I'm always ready. You're the one holding things up."

That smile of his was far too convenient, and he used it effectively.

"Come on," she said, adjusting the strap on her helmet as she prepared to join others circling the popular lake. The summer day was perfect for biking, the weather in the midseventies. Justin was good company. For all his faults, and they were plentiful, she enjoyed being with him.

The one serious drawback with Justin was his complete lack of ambition. He was content to work for a few weeks, then collect unemployment for as long as it lasted, while living at home.

To the best of her knowledge, he had never lived on his own. His mother was a soft touch and his father was out of the picture. Justin made it sound like he was doing his mother a favor by living at home. From short conversations she'd had with his mother, Carrie knew that wasn't the case.

At the end of their ride, they were both sweaty and in need of a break.

"How about grabbing lunch?" Justin suggested.

"Sure."

"Hot dogs and soda?"

"Perfect." It'd been a month or longer since Carrie had enjoyed her guilty pleasure. Frank and Mustard's was a favorite stand of hers, with their specialty hot dogs. No inside seating, although there were plenty of tables with umbrellas for alfresco dining. Carrie liked her hot dog piled high with jalapeños and coleslaw. Justin preferred chili dogs.

They parked their bikes at the stand provided and located an empty table. Carrie waited for Justin to place their order and reached for the money to pay for her own meal.

"Do you mind covering me?" he asked. "I'm a little short."

Carrie paused. "Seems to me like I covered you the last time we were out."

He shrugged. "Things are tough out there."

This was his way of admitting his reputation had finally caught up with him. Justin seemed unable to hold down any position for longer than a few months.

After they'd graduated, Carrie had sympathized. Like Justin, she'd drifted from job to job herself. The difference was, she'd never left any position with hard feelings. Each one of her employers had been impressed with her work ethic and were sorry to see her go. By contrast, Justin either didn't show up or made it known he'd prefer to get laid off.

Determined this would be the last time, Carrie took out extra money and handed it to Justin.

"Next time," he promised.

She'd heard that before. Rather than stew about it, Carrie was determined to enjoy this special treat. Within a few minutes, Justin was back with two plates heaped high with their orders and large sodas. He pulled out the bench and sat down.

Savoring their food, they were silent for several minutes.

"Been missing you," Justin said after he'd wolfed down his chili dog.

Carrie found it hard to believe and let the comment slide. He hadn't called since her move into The Heritage. Hadn't even sent a text. She was the one who'd asked him about biking this afternoon.

"So, what's it like living in that hoity-toity condo, rubbing elbows with all those rich folks?"

Again, she preferred to ignore the comment. "It's great having my own space. You should try it sometime." It was a small dig that seemed to go over his head.

"Naw," he countered. "Mom needs me."

"I think it might be the other way around. You need your mom."

He shrugged. "I'm not complaining. She does the laundry, cooks the meals, and pays for my health insurance. I've got it good."

Yup, Justin was much too comfortable to make the transition to becoming a full-fledged adult. It wasn't a stretch to realize he wasn't likely to move out on his own anytime soon.

"Did I mention my cousin Hillary is engaged?" Carrie said, changing the subject.

Justin set his drink down, and his eyes rounded. She had the feeling that if he'd still been eating, he would have choked on his chili dog. "Hey, Carrie, this isn't a hint, is it, because you know—"

"Stop." She held up her hand before he stuck his foot in his mouth any farther. "No way am I suggesting anything of the sort. I'm sharing news, not making any implications regarding the two of us."

No way.

She wouldn't say it out loud, for fear it would damage his fragile ego. Justin would be at the bottom of the barrel when it came to her choice for a husband. If lunch was any indication, she would end up supporting him.

"I mean," he said, smiling now that any implied pressure was off, "you're the full meal deal, Carrie. Any guy would be lucky to have you. That said, I wouldn't be opposed to us moving in together."

"Are you kidding me? That's not happening."

This wasn't the first time he'd casually tossed out the idea. One Carrie would never consider. First off, if he assumed once they shared an apartment, she'd sleep with him, then he was delusional. They would be strictly roommates.

As far as any living situation with Justin was concerned, she could read the handwriting on the wall. He'd move in, and before long she'd be forced to pay his share of the rent.

"Hey," he joked, "I was serious."

"So was I."

He laughed in good-natured humor. "This is what I like best about you, Carrie. You're a straight shooter."

Following lunch, Carrie and Justin went their separate ways. Carrie returned to her parents' house to store her bicycle and helmet.

Seeing that she was back, her mother joined her in the garage. "Did you have a good time?"

Justin was fun, and she could count on laughing with him. "I did," she admitted, although reluctantly.

Her mother cocked her head. "Really?" she asked. "You sound hesitant."

Carrie stored her helmet in the container where her mother had packed it. "I don't think I'm going to do much with Justin after today."

"Why's that?" The same look of surprise was back. "You always seem to enjoy time with him."

"I do, that's the thing. Justin's fun and good company. He's easy to be around."

"What changed?"

Carrie followed her mother into the house, and her mother opened the refrigerator and brought out a pitcher of iced tea. She poured them each a tall glass.

"It's more who changed," Carrie admitted, after giving the question some thought. Leaning her hip against the kitchen counter, she paused, gathering her thoughts, finding it difficult to explain her feelings to her mother, let alone herself.

"Don't get me wrong," she said finally. "I like Justin. I always have. Like I said, he's fun. The thing is, he's one of those guys who will probably never grow up."

Her mother smiled. "You mean like Peter Pan?"

Carrie nodded. "Exactly like Peter Pan," she agreed. "It never concerned me before. For whatever reason, it did today." The contrast between Justin and Eric was profound, especially their work ethic. "When I left Green Lake, I realized it was time to move on. He's a friend, and we most likely will see each other now and again through mutual friends." No longer would Carrie seek him out, though.

As her grandfather used to say: *It's better this way.*

With her thoughts full of Justin and her decision, Carrie returned to The Heritage. Her decision really was for the better. She knew without a doubt that after three or four excuses why they couldn't get together, Justin would likely shrug and move on. They'd never been exclusive. She was aware of at least two other women he saw, and they, too, seemed willing to pay for his chili dog or whatever.

Soon after Carrie took the position as concierge, she discovered the roof of The Heritage. It was lovely up there, with potted plants decorating the corners. Someone had put up a few lounge chairs, which invited her to sit and enjoy the evening.

The view was spellbinding, especially at night. A cool breeze blew off the waters of the Sound as the clatter of the street noise echoed far below. Every so often a siren would scream, announcing another emergency, followed by a stillness that reminded her how far removed she was from the chaos.

Being in a thoughtful mood, she decided to head up with a glass of wine, unwind from her day, and let go of the past and look instead to the future. Carrie was happy for Hillary, although she had to wonder if she was ever going to meet "the one."

Nestled in the chair, dusk settled over the waters of Puget Sound and a few stars blinked in the darkening sky. Sipping the wine, she relaxed and felt the tightness ease from between her shoulders. Time on the rooftop had the ability to do that.

The creak came from behind her as the door to the rooftop opened and she realized she was no longer alone.

"Oh."

Whoever had joined her seemed as surprised to find her as she was to have her space invaded. Glancing over her shoulder, she saw it was Eric Hudson.

"Eric," she said, pleased to see him outside of his condo.

He stood next to the lounge chair with his hands stuffed in his pockets, looking as if he wasn't sure what to do. "Sorry, I didn't mean to intrude."

"You didn't." She patted the chair beside her. "Join me."

He hesitated, as if he wasn't sure this was a good idea.

"I don't bite," she assured him, with a welcoming smile.

"You didn't bring me dinner this evening," he mentioned as he took a seat.

He'd noticed, which pleased her. "I was off today and out with a friend." The less said about Justin, the better. "Did you miss seeing me?" she asked, jokingly.

"If I did, I wouldn't admit it," he said as he claimed the seat next to her and stretched out his legs.

"Ah, come on, Eric, admit it. You look forward to my visits."

"I admit to nothing," he said.

She noticed he was smiling, and she couldn't contain a smile of her own. "I'd offer you a glass of wine, but I only have the one."

"Thanks anyway."

"It's good to see you outside of your condo."

"Yeah. I come up here most every night that the weather permits. It frees me . . . if that makes any sense."

Carrie understood perfectly. "It does. It's like I can breathe in what's good and exhale the frustrations of the day."

"Exactly," he murmured.

"It's surprising we haven't bumped into each other before now."

"You come up here often?"

Carrie wasn't sure what to make of the question. She feared he was hinting that he hoped this was a one-off. Then, too, it could simply be a question. "Every now and again. Would you rather I didn't?"

"Not at all. It's kind of nice catching you here. Working from home, I don't often have human contact—well, other than over my computer screen."

Carrie had wondered about that. Once Eric started to relax, she found him to be good company. He explained that he owned his own business, how he was the tech support for a number of small companies around the country. He'd started out with computer support for one business, but as his reputation grew, he added more employees and other staff, all who worked remotely. Carrie couldn't help being impressed. He was an entrepreneur. He then explained that the company had grown fast and demanded more and more of his time, causing stress to mount as he struggled to meet those demands. No wonder he visited the rooftop.

He paused when he seemed to realize he'd been doing all the talking. "Sorry, I didn't mean to go on like that."

"No, really, I'm interested."

"I should go." He looked ready to leap off the lounge chair.

"Please don't," she pleaded, and she meant it.

"I need to get back to work," he insisted, as he stood.

"You know, there's more to life than work," she said, hoping that would convince him to stay.

He stared at her for a long moment, seemingly at a loss for words. When he finally spoke it was as if he couldn't say what he wanted fast enough.

"I'm a geek, Carrie. I don't know how to do relationships. I have a lot of acquaintances and only one real friend. I don't date . . . don't know how to date. I like you, and that makes me uncomfortable, because sooner or later you're going to discover I'm boring. I'm far more comfortable behind a computer than with people, especially women." He paused, exhaled, and added, "Especially beautiful women, so if you're looking to me like I'm some romantic hero, I'll be a sorry disappointment."

With that, he fled as if the roof had caught on fire.

It felt as if all the air had escaped from the roof when he left. After a moment, Carrie leaned back and sipped her wine. Eric thought she was beautiful. He might not think he had a romantic bone in his body, but he was wrong. So wrong.

Chapter 9

Julia woke from a bad dream and sat upright in bed, breathing hard. The nightmare had been vivid. In her dream, she'd been sobbing, heartbroken, when Heath announced he could no longer see her. His explanation was vague, and she tried to reason with him, unable to understand what had gone so dreadfully wrong. He repeatedly mentioned how sorry he was, and then before she could stop him, he walked out the door. She'd been crushed and brokenhearted, hardly able to absorb what had happened or why.

The deep sense of loss, the crippling emotion, was the same as the day she'd signed the divorce papers that ended her marriage.

Nonsensical as it seemed, ever since she'd started routinely dating Heath, she'd been waiting for the proverbial other shoe to drop. He was everything she had hoped to find in a companion.

It had been years since she'd laughed as much and as hard as she did with Heath. And his kisses. Wow. He stirred a part of her she had long considered dried up and dead, like a sun-wilted flower.

A couple nights earlier, he'd cooked her dinner and they'd shared a bottle of wine. The evening had been perfect. Overwhelmed by how wonderful their time together had been, she'd been far too keyed up to sleep. She was falling for Heath, and she was falling hard. How hard frightened her. Her fear was that anything this good would never last, and that had been the crux of her nightmare.

Heath was perfect for her. They'd both come through their divorces and survived their partners' infidelity. Like Julia, he didn't hash over the details of his divorce or trash-talk his ex-wife. She appreciated his determination to put all the unpleasantness of a dead marriage behind him. For her own part, Julia had mentioned Eddie only the one time, shortly after Hillary announced her engagement. They both seemed eager to let go of the past and look forward with happy expectation and hope.

Awake now, Julia dressed for her workout, although the dream hung on. It helped knowing she'd soon be with Heath. She needed the reassurance after that dreadful dream.

Like always, he was in the exercise room ahead of her. She'd long since given up bringing her earbuds. The music helped pass the time, or had before her friendship with Heath had blossomed. These days, they chatted, spurring and encouraging each other on to better times and distances. Once finished, they met for coffee at the Busy Bean, forming a new habit before returning to their individual schedules and wherever the day would take them.

Two or three times a week, Heath went into his downtown

office, and Julia did as well. She continued as a consultant, working about twenty hours a week, although she arrived later than before, having adjusted her schedule to accommodate coffee time with Heath. Mornings with him were the best part of her day.

On the afternoons when they were both free, they'd taken to touring local wineries, sampling Washington State wines and the tasting rooms all around the Seattle area. They often stopped for appetizers on the way home, letting the wine settle before getting back on the road.

For the last couple days, Heath had plans with a visiting college friend. The only time they were able to share was in the mornings before Heath left to meet his friend. She missed him, and strongly suspected his absence had been what had prompted her dream.

"Morning," Heath greeted warmly, when she joined him.

"Morning," she answered, responding to his smile.

"Did you sleep well?" He frowned a little, as if he guessed something had upset her. That he would detect anything after such a short acquaintance surprised her.

Heath didn't only look at her. He *saw* her.

She shook her head. "I was good until a nightmare woke me."

He arched his brows, confirming that he'd sensed she was troubled. "Do you want to talk about it?"

She didn't, preferring to put the dream behind her. Stepping onto the treadmill, she shook her head. She started her fast-paced walk, and he sat on the bike, pedaling at a relaxed speed, all the while keeping an eye on her.

Julia felt his scrutiny. Glancing at him, she had to wonder. "Can I ask you a silly question?"

"Of course."

"Do you sometimes think us finding each other is—"

"The best thing to happen since man walked on the moon?" he completed for her, grinning broadly.

She smiled back. "Well there's that. But doesn't it feel a little too perfect?"

"How do you mean?"

"Well, for one thing, we both had basically given up on relationships."

"With cause," he reminded her.

"With cause," she agreed. "We even share similar backgrounds. Your wife left you for another man, and my husband fell in love with another woman. We were each the innocent party."

"I can't speak for you; however, I accept at least part of the blame for Lee leaving me. We'd drifted apart. I knew it, only I didn't take it seriously. I was content and didn't take into consideration that Lee wasn't."

Julia admired his willingness to see his own part in the breakup of the marriage. It hadn't been like that for her.

"I loved my husband. I did everything I could to save my marriage. I was determined to do whatever it took to get my husband back. If the divorce went through, I wanted the reassurance I had done everything humanly possible to save what we had together. Only . . . only . . ." She paused, as the familiar pain struck her like a kick in the solar plexus.

"It doesn't do any good to look back now," she continued, after composing herself. "I did what I could, and when it didn't work out, I knew I had to let go and move forward." She remembered the good-bye letter she'd written as closure, and how that had helped her to look to the future without the regrets of the past.

Heath had stopped bicycling and was closely studying her. "Can you tell me what any of this has to do with the two of us?"

Explaining it would seem ridiculous. "It's like I said. Our relationship has come together so easily. So perfectly." Her biggest fear was that something was about to happen that would drive them apart. This giddy happiness wouldn't last. It couldn't. Before either of them were ready, it would come to an end.

Heath considered her words. "It's hard to believe you were close all these months and it took until now to find each other."

"I feel the same."

"You should know, Julia, I'm crazy about you. These last couple days with Steve, my buddy from college, have been great. We had a good time reminiscing and catching up. And yet, it felt as if a part of me was missing because I couldn't be with you."

Julia's heart felt as if it was going to melt at his words. "I feel the same about you. I'm afraid, Heath. Afraid everything is coming together too quickly."

"Does this have anything to do with your dream?"

Reluctantly, she nodded.

"Tell me about it," he said, "and then let us reason it out together."

"Okay. The condensed version goes like this: We were together and ecstatically happy, then something happened. Don't ask me what, because I don't know. What killed me was watching you walk away. I was left sobbing and heartbroken."

He listened and shook his head. "No way. That's never going to happen."

"I . . . I sometimes have prophetic dreams," she said. This

wasn't anything she had encouraged and rarely mentioned. Only two people in the world knew about this. It didn't happen often, and it always seemed to forecast bad news.

Before Eddie confessed that he'd fallen out of love with her, she'd dreamed about it. The day before Hillary had gone skiing, Julia had dreamed her daughter would break her leg. And she did. It was while she was undergoing physical therapy that she'd decided to specialize in physical rehabilitation. And it had happened plenty of other times while growing up. The worst had been dreaming about the death of her grandmother a week before she died of a stroke.

"No matter what, I'm not going anywhere, Julia. I can't imagine anything that would make me want to walk away from you. It took me nearly six years to find you, and I am not letting you go. I learned my lesson with Lee. You're too important to me to even consider such a thing."

"You're right. Time to let it go."

They finished their routine and reunited later over coffee. Heath's reassurances helped. Still the dream lingered, and she feared it would be like other nightmares she'd had over the years. She was experiencing the same feeling now as she had so often before, and did her best to ignore it.

"Do you have plans for tonight?" Heath asked, sitting across from her, sipping his coffee.

She shook her head.

"Let me cook for you again," he suggested.

She knew what he was doing. Bless him, Heath was offering a way of distracting her from her anxious thoughts.

"Dinner would be lovely, only it's my turn. You cooked last time."

"Fine, only I have the larger kitchen."

"Then fine, I'll use your kitchen and you can provide the wine." They never seemed to leave a tasting room without at least one bottle, and had put together a small but nice collection.

"Perfect. I need to go into the office this afternoon, so putting you in charge of dinner works best for me. What are you serving?"

"I was thinking about a Caesar salad with homemade croutons, topped with either barbecued shrimp or chicken, whichever you prefer. How does that sound?"

"Like a date."

"Deal," she said, eager to move past the nightmare.

By the afternoon, Julia's mood was lighter. She looked forward to their dinner and showing off her culinary skills. Knowing Heath had a busy afternoon, she walked down to the Pike Place Market and bought everything she needed for that evening's dinner. The romaine lettuce was fresh and crisp; the bread, when she purchased it, was hot from the oven. Walking past the bakery, she spied a lemon tart and remembered Heath mentioning that lemon was his favorite. She purchased the rich dessert as a treat for later.

Once he was home, Heath sent her a text and said he had everything ready for her. Julia carted her purchases from her condo to his.

Heath opened the door even before she could ring the bell. Automatically, he took the supplies off her hands and set them aside. Then, without a moment's pause, he reached for her.

Tucking his hand around her nape, he brought her mouth to his and soundly kissed her to the point that her toes curled.

"Missed you all day," he whispered, pressing his forehead against hers.

Julia released a breathy sigh. This man. Wow. Life didn't feel like it could get any better.

"I got us a bottle of my favorite sauvignon blanc from the Yakima Valley," he said, breaking away from her. "It's on ice. Should I open it now, or would you prefer to wait for dinner?"

"Now, I think."

"I was hoping you'd say that."

While Julia unloaded the lettuce and other ingredients, lining them up on the kitchen counter, Heath opened the wine. After pouring them each a glass, he turned on the music, classic hits from the 1970s. The Bee Gees were staying alive, and the beat of the music vibrated around the room. Soon Julia was bobbing her head to ABBA's "Dancing Queen." It was hard to hold still. It was as if her feet refused to stay in one place.

Twirling around the kitchen, Julia unloaded the salad ingredients and set the dressing aside to add just before they were ready to eat.

Now that the wine was poured, Heath handed her a stemless glass and then they touched the lips of the glasses together before giving it the first sample.

The white wine was crisp and cold, exactly the way Julia liked it best.

"The Sound of Silence" by Simon and Garfunkel played next. Heath set both their glasses aside and brought her into his embrace. "Let's dance," he said, slipping one arm around her waist and bringing her close. He gripped hold of her free hand and pressed it close to his heart, as if to say she had taken up residence there.

Leaning in to him, Julia closed her eyes as they swayed to the music. This was like a dream, and nothing resembling the one she'd experienced earlier.

For the next half hour Julia worked on their meal, in between chopping vegetables and dancing. Heath tied an apron around her waist, and she removed her shoes. Dinner was almost ready when the doorbell rang.

Julia glanced at Heath. "Expecting anyone?"

"No." He set his wineglass aside and headed toward the foyer to open the door.

Julia went about setting the table when she heard Heath greet his son.

"Michael." He sounded surprised.

"Hey, Dad. I stopped off to see Eric and . . ." He paused when he saw Julia. "Sorry, I didn't know you had a hot date tonight."

"Yes, this is Julia. She's the woman I mentioned who helped decorate the condo."

Julia remembered Health telling her that his son had recently stopped by and had admired the changes. The condo had turned out great and she was pleased with how much a few decorator pillows, collectibles, and paintings had improved the appearance of his home. Heath seemed to like her additions and told her his son had been equally impressed.

"Michael," Heath said, coming to stand next to her. He slipped his arm around her waist and smiled down at her. "This is Julia."

"Hello, Michael," she said, smiling at the man who was a

younger version of Heath. He was as tall as his father, with the same color eyes, which seemed to lock on her. And narrowed.

Frowning, Michael glanced from her to his father. For longer than seemed comfortable, he ignored her outstretched hand before shaking it.

"Michael?" Heath asked, and seemed stunned by his son's rudeness.

"Dad," he said tightly, dragging his eyes away from Julia. "I can see I came at an inconvenient time. I'll come back later."

Heath followed him to the door. "Michael, what's wrong?"

"We can talk later."

"Is it about Julia?" he asked.

Although Heath and Michael had both lowered their voices, Julia could still hear them.

"Not now, Dad." Before Heath could object, Michael was out the door.

The sound of it closing echoed through the room, sounding ten times louder than the music.

"What was that about?" Julia asked. "Did I do something wrong? Should I not have been here?"

Heath looked as perplexed as she was. "I don't know, but I'm going to find out," he said emphatically.

Julia wasn't sure what was happening. What she feared, though, was that her nightmare was about to become real.

Chapter 10

After Michael left Heath's place, the atmosphere between Heath and Julia changed. Earlier, Heath had been laughing and dancing around the kitchen island with Julia, acting like a man thirty years younger. She made him feel young again. And then his son had arrived, and everything changed. The shock of it had yet to wear off.

Heath didn't understand it. Didn't know what to make of it. Since he had been seeing Julia, he'd excitedly mentioned her several times to both Michael and Adam. When they'd come to see the changes in his condo, they'd been impressed, and rightly so. Julia had worked her magic. Both boys seemed genuinely pleased Heath had found someone for companionship. They'd never had a problem with him dating. In fact, they had encouraged him to try again, even after the disastrous results of his earlier attempts.

Something was very wrong, and Heath was determined to find out what it was.

Julia finished putting together their dinner. They ate in near silence, the mood altered, as if a dark cloud hung over them. Heath knew Julia was upset and did his best to reassure her.

It didn't help that she'd had that silly dream. As she described it, he could see how much it had upset her. The nightmare that predicted he would walk away from her. When she'd mentioned it, he'd nearly laughed. He couldn't think of a single thing in the world that would cause him to leave this incredible woman.

Heath hadn't been looking for love, hadn't sought out another relationship. Julia was a precious gift he'd been given, and by all that was holy, he refused to let her go without putting up one hell of a fight.

Even before Heath could get in touch with his son, he woke up to a text from Michael.

Dad, can u meet for lunch. Noon at Mama Sofia?

Heath sent back a thumbs-up. He was grateful Michael took the initiative, as he was anxious to clear the air. Whatever it was that had caused his son to react negatively to Julia needed to be settled, and the sooner, the better. After lunch, he'd seek out Julia and reassure her, confident whatever it was could be easily fixed.

Julia arrived for her workout, and it looked like she hadn't slept the entire night. He yearned to tell her not to worry, but hesitated, unwilling to speak too soon before talking to Michael. It distressed him to see how concerned she was, and he again blamed that dream.

"If you don't mind, I'd like to skip coffee this morning," she said when she'd completed her routine.

"Sure," he said, and then, because he couldn't resist, he gave her a reassuring squeeze. "Don't worry, Julia. I'll settle this with my son. We're good. Nothing is going to change the way I feel about you."

She responded with a weak smile, and he could tell by her expression that she didn't believe him.

He hated knowing this dream she'd had continued to upset her. Heath was confident everything would work out for the best. Really, what could Julia have possibly done to earn Michael's ire? She was a gentle soul, honorable, kind, generous, forgiving, and so much more. Not a day passed when he didn't thank God for sending her into his life. She was far more than he deserved.

At noon, Heath arrived at his favorite Italian restaurant, the very one he'd taken Michael to for his birthday a few weeks earlier. It was close to his office, and convenient for Michael, as well. To his surprise, he saw that both his boys were seated at a table, awaiting his arrival.

Michael and Adam! This made Heath increasingly curious as to what they had to tell him.

He didn't look at the menu, as he nearly always ordered the same entrée. The restaurant's gnocchi was by far his favorite, and he didn't see any reason to sample another dish. As soon as he was seated, the server arrived for their drink order.

"You might want a whiskey sour for this, Dad," Michael suggested.

Heath frowned. He never drank anything heavier than wine

for lunch. He shook his head and ordered a glass of the house red. His sons asked for a bottle of sauvignon blanc, as they had chosen the special of the day: octopus salad. Once their drinks were served and their luncheon orders placed, Heath looked across the table at his sons. He was proud of his boys and was grateful they'd maintained a solid relationship, despite the fact that Heath and their mother were no longer together.

"All right. Give it to me," he said, bracing himself.

Both boys appeared stiff and uneasy, as they looked to each other. Adam nodded toward Michael as if to suggest his brother start.

"Dad," Michael said, his dark brown eyes round and serious, "do you have any idea who Julia is?"

"You mean other than the woman I'm falling in love with?"

Again, his sons shared a look.

"Does the name Edward Jones, the pro golfer, mean anything to you?" Adam asked him.

A chill shot down Heath's spine. "Edward is your mother's husband," he said cautiously not understanding how this had anything to do with Julia.

"Dad, Julia is Edward's ex-wife."

Shock rippled through him. Julia had been married to Edward Jones, the man his ex-wife had left him for. The man Lee had had an affair with, long before Heath was aware his wife wanted out of their marriage.

"I should have ordered that whiskey sour," he murmured, as he struggled to absorb what his sons were telling him.

"How do you know Julia?" he asked. To the best of his knowledge, she had never met his sons.

Michael was the one to answer. "After their house sold, I

helped Ed move his desk and some other keepsakes he wanted. Julia was there. I only got a glimpse of her, and from her reaction last night, she must not have seen me. If she did, she didn't remember me. It doesn't matter because I recognized her."

"When you mentioned you were dating a woman named Julia, we didn't make anything of it. I mean, Julia's a common name. It wasn't until Michael saw her last night that he connected the dots," Adam said.

Yes, this information was a jolt. No denying it. But it wasn't the end of the world. So Lee had married Julia's ex. That was nearly six years ago now. It didn't mean he couldn't have a loving relationship with Julia.

"I'll admit this came at me out of the blue," Heath said. "I had no idea. What I don't understand is your reaction to Julia. She did nothing wrong. Edward was the one who stepped out on her. She's the innocent party in this." He didn't mention he was also the innocent party, despite his willingness to admit he contributed to Lee's unhappiness.

"You don't understand," Adam said. "Before the divorce was final, Julia sent a series of nasty texts to Mom."

Michael nodded. "Mom showed me what Julia wrote. She spewed hate on Mom and called her names you wouldn't want me to repeat."

Heath found this hard to believe. The Julia he knew would never resort to this kind of malicious behavior.

"Julia put Mom and Edward through hell. For one thing, she spitefully refused to sign the divorce papers. She did everything she could to make life miserable for Mom and Edward. Even when she knew he wanted the divorce, she refused to let him go and forced him to promise to wait six months."

Heath remembered Julia mentioning she had done everything she could to keep her family intact.

"Did it ever enter your mind that Julia was fighting to save her marriage?"

"There was nothing to save," Michael insisted.

"Dad," Adam protested, "you need to seriously think about what she did. This woman you're so hot for had our mother in tears with the things she said and did. Can you honestly say you're comfortable associating with someone who does those sorts of things?"

"We have all done things we regret," Heath countered. "Besides, this happened a number of years ago now. Emotions were running high—"

"It isn't only Julia, Dad," Michael said, cutting him off.

"What do you mean?"

"Have you met her daughters yet?"

He hadn't, although Julia spoke of Hillary and Marie frequently. It was clear she was close to them and treasured their relationship.

"Don't tell me you forgot what those girls did to Mom?"

Heath had a vague recollection of some altercation between the two families. All he recalled was his sons' outrage when Julia's daughters had openly confronted Lee at Lake Sammamish.

"Refresh my memory," he said, leaning back and crossing his arms over his chest. Their meals had been delivered, though now his appetite was gone.

Michael leaned forward with narrowed eyes. "The oldest one verbally attacked Mom."

"In public," Adam added.

"We were there," Michael said, his voice rising to the point that he attracted the attention of diners at nearby tables.

"Mom was mortified. Both her daughters said some horrible things."

"Thank goodness we were with Mom," Michael said. "No way were we going to let anyone talk to our mother like that."

His children had been raised to respect Lee. It didn't surprise him that the boys had come to her defense.

"We had to defend her," Adam said, "and soon we were all shouting."

"Unfortunately, it got loud and angry. But we weren't the ones who started it."

Heath had the urge to bury his head in his hands. "Did the police get involved?"

"No, Edward did."

That couldn't have gone well. Heath could imagine how difficult it was for Edward to be pitted against his own daughters, defending Lee and the boys.

"Edward stepped between us and told Adam and me that he would handle the situation," Michael explained. "He did his best to quiet down his daughters; however, they were having none of it. They were angry and belligerent."

"They continued to call Mom names and said some unforgivable things to their father," Adam went on, his voice rising.

"These aren't people you want to associate with, Dad. It's best to avoid Julia and her daughters. The thought of you getting mixed up with them is bound to cause trouble for us as a family."

Heath had heard enough. "That was years ago, and during a difficult and stressful time for everyone. I'm sure Julia's daughters are as eager to put that unpleasant incident behind them as you are. Let the past stay where it is. Dragging it into the future will solve nothing."

His sons stared back at him as if he were speaking a foreign language.

"Dad, Adam and I want you to seriously reconsider this relationship. Of all the women in the world, why did you have to fall for Julia? She's bad news."

Heath didn't see it that way and said as much. "Situations change," he insisted. "People change."

"Not Julia's daughters," Michael said emphatically.

"We told Mom you were dating Edward's ex-wife, and she was understandably upset."

He raised his hand, stopping them from saying anything further. His ex-wife's feelings toward whom he dated was none of his concern.

"Not my problem."

"Maybe not," Adam readily agreed. "But you need to know what Mom told us she did recently."

Leaning back, his meal practically untouched, Heath waited for what was sure to be even more negativity.

"I didn't realize until we spoke to Mom what Julia had done to Edward," Michael said.

Heath admired how Julia had moved on following the divorce. He found it hard to believe she'd given her ex more than a cursory thought. "All right. Tell me what horrible thing Julia has done now. I'm all ears. However, before you give me a list of her sins, let me assure you I'm going to have a hard time believing she has a malicious bone in her body."

Adam arched his brows as if to say his father had been brainwashed.

"Do you realize that Julia has kept her daughters out of Edward's life? Mom said he was nearly in tears the other night after she called to rub it in that Hillary is engaged. She had to tell him, because her daughter wants nothing to do with her own father."

Ah, so that was it. "Julia told me about that call," he said, relief filling him. "The reason she phoned was so Ed wouldn't be blindsided, should someone else mention the engagement."

"Julia has kept her daughters out of their father's life."

"They're adults," he countered. "If Hillary and Marie want a relationship with their dad, it's up to them."

Michael adamantly shook his head. "You can believe that if you want. Personally, I don't."

"Me neither," Adam added.

Michael's voice rose again as he pressed his point. "Julia has her daughters wrapped around her finger to the point they feel disloyal to her if they speak to their dad. Did you know that neither of them has had any contact with Ed since that awful scene at the lake?"

"Also," Adam added, "it's been nearly six years and Mom refuses to go to Lake Sammamish because of all the bad memories associated with that day."

Heath knew none of this.

"Dad," Michael said, his voice low and sympathetic. "I know you like Julia. We understand this news came out of the blue. I'm sorry to be the one to disillusion you about her, but we felt it was important that you know."

Adam agreed. "Michael and I felt you needed to hear the truth, so you know upfront the kind of people you're dealing with. There's a very good reason Edward wanted out of the marriage. Weren't you the one who said there are always two sides to a story? It might be hard for you to accept his point of view, seeing that he's the one Mom left you for."

His son had given him something to think about.

"Edward loves his daughters and they both refuse to have anything to do with him, despite the countless attempts he's made to open the lines of communication," Adam reminded him.

Michael looked hard at Heath. "Mom said it's breaking her heart to see him deal with one rejection after another. It's even worse now that Hillary is engaged."

Heath could understand how hard it must be to have his daughters reject him. As far as Julia was concerned, he chose to believe she had nothing to do with her daughters' treatment of their father. That behavior was on them.

"Dad?"

Heath looked up and realized his sons were both staring at him.

"You aren't saying anything," Adam said.

"What is there to say?" Heath asked.

The two exchanged another look, one filled with regret.

"We understand this is the last thing you wanted to hear. This isn't easy on us, either. It gives us no pleasure to be the ones to tell you these things."

Heath appreciated how difficult this conversation had been for his sons.

"Whatever you decide, Dad, we'll accept," Adam assured him.

"Not easily, though," Michael added, making sure Heath was aware of the consequences.

"After everything we've told you about Julia and her daughters, if you feel you want to continue with this relationship, you should know nothing will change between the three of us."

Perhaps he'd misread his sons' intentions; Heath was grateful for the reassurance.

"You should be aware that we would prefer not to have anything to do with Julia or her daughters, though."

Adam concurred. "Not after everything they said and did to our mother."

The sick feeling in the pit of his stomach intensified. "I'm going to need to think this through," Heath said, his head spinning.

"I'm sorry, Dad. I really am. No matter what your feelings, I'm going to avoid any contact with her."

"I understand," Heath returned.

The server came by to collect their plates. "Is there anything else I can get you?" he asked.

Health glanced up and nodded. "I'll take that whiskey sour now."

Chapter 11

Julia sat at the kitchen table with her sister, her hands warmed by cupping a recently poured mug of coffee. Her heart weighed heavy in her chest as she struggled to make sense of the last three days.

"It's over between Heath and me," she said, unable to hide how difficult this was to admit. Julia arrived unannounced at her sister's because she couldn't bear to remain in her condo a moment longer. It was torture not to hear from Heath. She needed to escape. Her sister was her best friend, her confidant, the one person who knew her better than anyone.

"You don't know that," Amanda insisted, taking her own mug to the table and sitting down.

Julia had come to Amanda at the lowest point in her marriage to confess what she'd held tight inside her heart for months. Eddie was involved in an affair. Amanda had held her while Julia had wept and cried with her. It was Amanda who helped convince her the divorce was inevitable, and it was time to quit trying to save her marriage and let go.

"Have you talked to Heath?" Amanda asked.

"No . . ."

"Then you can't say it's over until you two have worked out whatever the problem is."

"That's just it," Julia cried. "I don't know what's wrong. He's avoiding me completely and that tells me everything I need to know." Julia couldn't understand how everything they had shared, the laughter, the morning coffee times, the promise of finding that special someone, had gone south so quickly. The worst of it was that she hadn't a clue what had changed his mind or why. The fact that he'd left her completely in the dark was unacceptable. The last she'd heard, he was determined to connect with his son to ask about Michael's reaction when introduced to Julia. It appeared that whatever he'd had to say had changed Heath's feelings toward her. That he didn't have the courage or the heart to come to her about it was unacceptable. Pride insisted she not seek him out after two failed attempts. He was the one with the problem.

"Heath isn't exercising with you?"

"Not for the last two days," Julia said. Naturally, her imagination had gone wild. Three days ago, they were on top of the world, dancing around his kitchen with hardly a care. Now this intense, awkward silence.

"Maybe he's sick?"

Amanda offered a logical excuse, one Julia had considered herself.

"Too sick to answer a text?" she returned. She'd already sent him two texts, neither of which Heath had responded to. After being blatantly ignored, she refused to send another. Julia was determined to maintain her dignity. She got his message, painful as it was to accept.

Amanda shrugged. "Maybe he's traveling. He might have been unexpectedly called out of town. Who knows?"

"That's just it. I don't know." It seemed unlikely he would leave without telling her. No, whatever had prompted this silence had to do with something his son told him. Something he now chose to keep to himself, preferring to leave matters hanging rather than clear the air.

Amanda refilled her coffee. When she pointed toward Julia's mug, Julia shook her head. Over the last few days, she had downed enough coffee to keep a navy fleet afloat. She couldn't sleep, couldn't work. At this point, she was caught between angst and anger.

Just then her phone dinged, indicating she had a text. Amanda looked at her expectantly as Julia read the text.

"From Heath?" her sister asked.

Julia bit her lip and nodded, reading the note a second time.

"Well, don't keep me in suspense. What did he say?" She leaned closer, pressing her stomach against the edge of the table.

"He said he needed space and time to think."

Amanda released a sigh. "At least he had the courtesy to answer you, even if it took him this long."

Julia didn't share her sister's opinion.

"You know what?" she said, coming to a decision. "I don't care anymore. If he wants space, he can have it. I'm through."

She knew when she'd woken from that nightmare that it was one of *those* dreams. She'd felt it in her bones. Heath was going to walk away from her, and she didn't have a clue as to why.

"You know? Maybe *it's better this way*," Amanda said, straightening, stating the very motto their father had so often used.

"Maybe," Julia returned softly. It wasn't like she hadn't thought that herself over the last few days.

"I mean, if this is how Heath is going to treat you, then maybe it's time to move on."

Amanda was right. While Julia might claim she no longer cared, that was a lie. She did care, more than she wanted to admit.

"Meeting Heath has been good for you." Her sister had a way of looking at the silver lining of a situation.

Julia wasn't convinced. "I suppose it has." Since she'd started seeing Heath, she'd felt alive again. Young, and carefree in ways she hadn't been since Eddie had moved out of the house.

"Heath opened your eyes."

That he had. She heard music again. Not the songs that played over the radio or that she had on her playlist. The music had come from within. Her feet hadn't been able to hold still, her heart had beat to a strong cadence. She looked forward to each day with eager anticipation, knowing part of it would be spent with him. They hadn't known each other long; what set Heath apart was that he got her. He understood her in ways no man had since her ex-husband. And possibly even more than Eddie had.

"Before Heath, you'd given up on ever meeting anyone."

She couldn't deny it—Julia had given up, and with good reason. The memory of some of her dates was enough to make her want to smile.

"You know what I think?" Amanda asked.

Knowing her sister, Amanda was about to tell her. "Please," she said, gesturing across the table.

"I think you should meet Frank."

"Frank? The guy you wanted to introduce me to a few weeks ago. That Frank?"

"Yes, that Frank. He's a good guy, Julia. A really good guy."

Julia automatically shook her head. "I've already met the man you considered a really good guy."

Amanda held up her hand, stopping her. "I admit Joe was a mistake. I've already apologized. I blame Robert. Joe was his friend, so please don't hold that fiasco against me."

"What makes you think Frank is any better than Joe?"

"I know Frank personally, whereas I only knew Joe through Robert. I should have known better than to take my husband's word for it. His idea of a great guy is someone he can play poker with."

The experience had been a disaster from the start. "Joe thought a good idea for our first date was to take me deer hunting."

Amanda cringed. "I know."

"Then he invited me to watch him bowl. I learned he was in three bowling leagues, which only left a few nights in the week when he was available to do anything with me. And don't forget he entered his antique car in some show, and I was stuck, sitting in the hot sun, with him there all day."

"Please, don't remind me of what a failure that was."

"When I suggested a movie, Joe said he hadn't been to a theater since the original *Star Wars*."

"Like I said, Joe was a mistake."

"I forgive you."

"Which, in retrospect, is generous of you. I promise, Frank is nothing like Joe."

Leaning back, Julia crossed her arms. "Okay, I'm listening. Tell me about Frank."

Amanda beamed her a smile and, leaning forward, said, "He's part of my quilting guild."

"What?"

"That's good, right? He's artistic and creative and a lot of fun. He brings us girls homemade cookies. I mean, you can't fault a guy who bakes cookies."

"Widowed? Divorced?"

Amanda shook her head. "He's never married."

That should tell her sister something important. "Did he live with his mother until she died?"

"No. He worked as an underwriter for Pemco Insurance for over thirty years."

"He has an interesting choice of a hobby." Julia didn't know many men who were into quilting. It wasn't her place to judge, however.

"Are you sure he wants to meet me?" A man who'd remained single all these years would be set in his ways. He would be accustomed to being by himself.

"Yes," Amanda insisted. "He isn't looking to marry, which is something I thought you'd appreciate. All he wants is to meet someone with similar interests and companionship."

"I don't quilt."

"He knows that. You're creative, though. He was impressed when I told him about West Coast Interiors, and how you built that business from the ground up with your talent and drive."

Massaging her temples, Julia was confused. "I don't know, Amanda. If I hadn't met Heath . . ."

"Only you did meet Heath, and he opened your eyes to the possibility of there being someone out there to share the rest of your life with."

"Frank . . ."

"Frank is someone who will be a companion and friend. Isn't that what you really want? You're not looking for love eternal. You want someone to enjoy a movie with or go dancing."

"Or a pub crawl."

"Exactly," Amanda said, finishing her argument. "Won't you give Frank a chance?"

Julia could never doubt Amanda had her best interests at heart. Her sister meant well. What Amanda failed to recognize was that her heart was bruised, and she wasn't ready to leap into another situation that had the potential of bringing more rejection.

"I'll think on it."

"Don't hesitate," Amanda advised. "A couple of the widows in the quilting guild have their eye on Frank. They could easily swoop in and steal him away."

More power to those widows.

Chapter 12

Heath had spent two restless nights going over every aspect of his conversation with his sons. He didn't understand how he could have been oblivious to the fact that Laura had married Julia's ex. She had mentioned Eddie any number of times, and he hadn't made the connection, mainly because Lee always referred to him as Edward. Frankly, he hadn't paid much attention. Lee was out of his life, and he'd taken pains to move forward.

For the last three days, he'd been completely unfair to Julia. He should have sent her a text much sooner, rather than leave her in the dark. He hadn't meant to be insensitive. His only excuse was he needed time to think. Needed to sort out what all this meant for their future together, or if they'd be able to move past this.

His sons had made their position clear. For all Heath knew,

Julia might not want anything more to do with him if her daughters felt the same way that Michael and Adam did.

The following morning, he waited for Julia in the exercise room, needing to see her. She arrived the same time as usual, came into the room, and stopped cold, her eyes widening when she saw him. Without comment, she started to turn around and leave.

"Julia, wait."

She shook her head. "I'm giving you the space you wanted. I'll come back another time."

"Please," he said, softly, his heart in his throat.

"Please what?"

"Give me a chance to explain."

Julia cocked her head as if considering his request. "When?"

"Can we meet for coffee?"

"Not this morning. I have an appointment."

She wasn't going to make this easy, and he didn't blame her. He'd been an ass. "What about this afternoon. Say three, at my place?"

"I'd prefer the Busy Bean."

He paused and shook his head. "My condo would be better. You'll need to trust me on this."

After a brief hesitation, she sighed, nodded, and then, before he could stop her, she left.

Heath watched her go, his spirits sagging. He may very well have ruined the best thing to happen to him in longer than he could remember.

—

At three, Heath paced in front of the picture window, although he barely noticed the view. His nerves were on edge, and he didn't know what she would think or do once he told her what he had learned.

He'd had three days to ponder the situation. It had taken him that long before he was able to come to a decision. He was three days ahead of Julia. She was sure to be as surprised as he'd been when she learned the truth.

It went without saying that he would grant her whatever time she wanted to assimilate the information. What was important to Heath was that she needed to know he was determined not to give her up. It had taken him nearly six years to find a woman he could love, and he wasn't letting her go. His sons would need to accept that Julia was part of his life, and if they refused, then he'd do whatever was necessary to change their minds.

His doorbell rang, and Heath's heart hammered hard against his chest. Inhaling a calming breath, he opened his door to Julia. One look at the dark shadows below her eyes and he felt like the biggest jerk who'd ever lived. Wordless, he brought her into the condo and into his arms, hugging her close.

For a long time, she resisted, and he feared his heart was about to break, and then gradually her arms looped around his middle. Heath closed his eyes and breathed in the special scent that was all Julia. Roses and vanilla. He regretted every minute they'd been apart. He had no intention of letting anything like this happen again.

"I'm sorry, so sorry," he whispered into her hair.

"Just tell me what Michael said."

They sat on the sofa, side by side. He placed her hands in his and looked into her beautiful eyes. How he'd managed to stay away from her this long, he'd never know. The instant he saw her that morning, he knew he'd made the right decision. No way was he losing this incredible woman.

"Before I say anything, you might need a glass of something strong," he said, remembering what Michael had said to him when they met for lunch.

"I don't want alcohol. All I need is the truth," she countered, her gaze boring into his.

"Okay." He inhaled, held her look, and started. "Michael and Adam met me for lunch on Wednesday. I'd only been expecting Michael. When I joined them, Michael suggested I might want to order a whiskey sour. I rarely drink anything stronger than wine, and when I do, it's a whiskey sour or scotch."

She nodded, and he hoped she realized he was preparing her for what he was about to tell her.

"Please, just tell me what happened."

His fingers tightened around hers. "Michael recognized you from when he helped Eddie move his desk out of your house."

Frowning, she narrowed her gaze. "Why would Michael help Eddie move furniture?"

"He was lending a hand to his stepfather."

A moment passed before Julia made the connection. When she did, her eyes widened with shock and astonishment. Her voice was barely more than a whisper when she spoke. "Are you telling me that Laura is your ex-wife?"

Heath nodded. "Yes. Your ex-husband is married to my ex-wife."

Shaking her head as if that was impossible, Julia argued, "I thought you said your ex's name was Lee."

"That's what I called her. My mother's name is also Laura, so I called her Lee from the time we started dating."

She nodded, as if barely able to absorb what he was saying.

"You called your ex Eddie, and Lee always refers to him as Edward. I didn't put two and two together. I can see you're stunned, which is exactly how I felt."

"I . . . hardly know what to say."

"I understand. What I didn't know about," he said, and raised her hands to his lips, kissing her fingers, "is the antagonism and hard feelings between our children."

Julia's eyes slowly closed, as if remembering all that had gone before. Tugging her hands away from him, she straightened. "Hillary and Marie got into it with your two boys . . . They should never have confronted Laura. I told them so as soon as I heard what they'd done. I'm sorry, Heath. It was a bad time. They knew how deeply their father's betrayal had hurt me, and when they ran into Laura, they let loose. They were in the wrong."

"It's understandable."

"So many negative consequences came about because of that confrontation," she said, as if mentally reviewing the events of that awful day.

"Nothing happened that should make it impossible for us to be together, Julia. I can't bear to lose you. I won't."

"I need to think." Scooting off the sofa, she paced the rug, the same way he had done earlier before she'd arrived. Her arms hugged her waist, as if she'd suddenly grown chilled and needed all the warmth she could muster.

"That was the day Eddie drew a line in the sand with our girls. Nothing has been the same between him and our daughters since."

"What do you mean?"

Pressing her hand against her forehead, she continued. "When our children were shouting at each other, Eddie interceded. He told Hillary and Marie they needed to treat Laura with respect. That she was soon to be his wife, and if they couldn't accept her, then he didn't want to be part of their lives any longer."

Heath released a low whistle. "Did he mean it?"

"At the time, I'm sure he did. I know he's lived to regret it, because he's made multiple attempts to bridge the gap, without success."

"Hillary and Marie must feel that he made his choice?"

"Yes, unfortunately." Julia continued to pace.

He waited in the silence, wondering if he should drag another issue into their conversation. "I need to ask you about the text messages you sent Lee," he ventured, watching for her reaction.

Julia went still, and the color drained out of her face. "I . . ." She paused before starting again, leaving the impression there was something she wasn't telling him.

"It wasn't my finest moment, that's for sure. I regretted it and wish I'd risen above such behavior, but I'm guilty as charged."

He appreciated that she didn't make excuses and took responsibility for her failings. As he'd reminded his sons, at the time tempers were volatile and emotions ran high. He found it easy to forgive Julia, knowing how hard she'd battled to save her marriage.

"Your sons mentioned those texts?"

Heath nodded. "They brought it up along with . . . a few other things."

"Such as?"

Heath hadn't meant to get into anything else. What transpired between him and his kids would remain with him.

Julia turned toward him and let her arms fall at her sides. "Michael and Adam don't want you to see me any longer."

This wasn't a question, but a statement of fact—one he didn't bother to deny. "I've made my decision. I love my sons, but this is my life. After taking a few days to mull over possible ramifications, I'm determined not to lose you."

"No," she cried automatically. "You're doing the very thing that caused a wedge between Eddie and our girls. I refuse to be a party to this."

"Julia, I am not going to let my sons dictate whom I love. I'm not severing my relationship with them because I'm choosing to be with you. They assured me this wouldn't change our relationship."

"They want nothing to do with me."

Again, he didn't deny it.

Burying her face in her hands, Julia looked as if she was about to break into tears. Eating up the distance between them, Heath drew her into his arms and held her tightly.

"Oh Heath, what are we doing?"

"We're falling in love, that's what we're doing."

"But your boys."

"It was a shock. Deep down, I know they want me to be happy. And you, Julia Jones, make me extremely happy. They were willing to look the other way when their mother sought her own happiness. In time, once they've grown accustomed to us being together, they will come around."

Julia trembled in his arms and he kissed the top of her head.

"You need to realize this is only the first hurdle," he whispered.

She looked up. "How do you mean?"

He closed his own eyes and exhaled sharply. "You have yet to tell Hillary and Marie."

Julia went silent.

Heath had a sickening feeling in the pit of his stomach that the worst was yet to come.

Chapter 13

This was supposed to be a happy occasion. Instead, Julia's stomach had twisted into knots tight enough to dumbfound a sailor. Hillary had asked her, Marie, and Carrie to meet her at the bridal shop to help her choose her wedding dress.

Afterward they planned on lunch at Alice's, a local seafood restaurant that was a longtime family favorite. Julia knew she couldn't delay telling her girls that Heath's ex-wife had married their father, especially knowing how strongly they disliked Laura. Julia prayed Eddie had taken her advice and reached out to Hillary when he learned of her engagement.

They all met at ten, the appointment time Hillary had been given by the shop. They were seated in a private room and offered champagne before Hillary was ushered into a dressing area. Before they arrived, Hillary had previewed several dresses online and selected five within her budget.

"This is exciting," Carrie said, as Hillary followed the sales representative into the dressing room.

Julia sat between Marie and Carrie and shared her niece's enthusiasm. This was a happy day, or would be, once she was able to clear the air about Heath's relationship to the stepmother they refused to acknowledge.

"I'm happy for Hillary," Marie said, crossing her legs and settling back in the comfortable chair. "Did she tell you she heard from Dad?"

"She didn't." Julia was pleased to hear it, hoping that Eddie had taken her words to heart.

Looking surprised, Marie said, "I wonder why not."

Julia sighed, and was admittedly surprised. "I'm sure she has her reasons."

Marie shrugged. "It's no big thing. Dad called me first."

That would be just like Eddie. He had a habit of going through the back door when he wasn't sure what would greet him if he was direct.

"He believes I'm less stubborn than Hillary," she explained. "I guess I must be, because I decided to talk to him."

Carrie bent forward to look at her cousin. "So what happened? Don't keep us in suspense. What did he want?"

Marie shrugged, indicating it was no big deal. "Unfortunately, it was the same song, different verse."

"What does that mean?" Carrie asked, pressing for more details.

"You know," Marie said, as if bored with the subject. "He's more interested in us accepting Laura than anything else. He couldn't keep her name out of the conversation. It was Laura this and Laura that, as if I was eager to hear the updates on their wonderful life together."

Julia had a hard time understanding how her ex-husband could continue to be this insensitive.

"To be fair," Marie added, "he asked how Hillary and I were doing and if I was seeing anyone. He said he heard that we were both enjoying our jobs, you know, that sort of thing." She turned to Julia. "You must have said something?"

"I did." She didn't make a habit of contacting Eddie. In their last conversation, she'd filled him in on both girls, letting him know how well they were doing.

"Then Dad asked me to relay his congratulations to Hillary."

That was a step in the right direction, and hearing it encouraged Julia, although she wished he would have reached out to Hillary directly.

Before she could say anything more, Hillary stepped out of the dressing room in a gorgeous wedding gown that suited her beautifully. She stood on a small platform and looked at them expectantly, silently seeking their opinion. Her gaze automatically went to her mother first.

Julia couldn't take her eyes off her daughter. Hillary, with her shoulder-length dark hair, was as regal as a queen. She was taller than Julia by several inches, which came from Eddie's side of the family. Her blue eyes were all Eddie. Hillary was simply stunning. Julia found it hard to believe this beautiful young woman was her precious daughter.

"What do you think?" Hillary asked when no one spoke.

Julia had a hard time answering past the lump that formed in her throat. "Oh my," she breathed, in a raspy whisper.

Hillary's eyes widened. "You don't like it?"

"No, I love it. It's perfect; you're perfect."

Marie nodded. "I like it."

"Me, too," Carrie added.

The problem was, each one of the five dresses Hillary had preselected were equally gorgeous. Then the sales rep brought out another dress. One several hundred dollars above Hillary's budget. It was by far the most beautiful of all the dresses, making it even more difficult to choose one over the other. After a lengthy discussion with the sales rep offering her advice, they were able to narrow it down to two: the first one Hillary had tried on, and the last, most expensive, one. Both were the same style, sleek and elegant, and suited Hillary's slender frame beautifully.

"I'm going to think about it," Hillary announced, before the end of their appointment time. Julia knew the price difference between the two was a major factor. Her own wedding dress had cost less than five hundred dollars, but that had been nearly forty years ago now. Times and prices had changed. She recalled when she and Eddie bought their first home and worried if they would be able to make the nearly four-hundred-dollar-a-month house payment.

"Whichever dress you decide on will be perfect," Julia assured her daughter.

"I like the more expensive one," she said, biting into her lower lip. "It's six hundred dollars above my budget, though."

"Ask Dad for it," Marie advised. "He said he wanted to contribute to the wedding costs. You should let him."

They'd arrived at the restaurant and had been seated. Their orders were in, and they sat sipping a crisp white wine, chatting about the wedding arrangements. The wedding date was set now for early November, and the perfect venue had been found for the reception.

"I'm not asking Dad for anything," Hillary said, with more than a hint of defiance.

"I heard your father called Marie and wanted to congratulate you," Julia said. She probably shouldn't have mentioned she knew about this. This matter was between her daughters and Eddie.

"Dad called me," Hillary admitted with some reluctance.

"If you'd rather not talk about it, I understand. Whatever was said is between the two of you."

"I don't mind," Hillary said, as if it didn't matter to her one way or the other. Julia suspected otherwise. From the time she was born, Hillary had had her dad wrapped around her tiny hand. While she was growing up, they'd been especially close. This estrangement had badly hurt them both, and because it did, Julia felt that pain, and sincerely wished for them to go back to the good relationship they'd once shared.

"Sweetie," she said gently, "by offering to help pay for the wedding, your dad's doing what he can to bring the two of you together again."

Hillary snorted softly. "Then he's not trying hard enough."

"He did offer to get the country club for you," Marie inserted.

Hillary tossed her sister a smoldering look.

Eddie had hinted the same thing to Julia. It was a generous offer, and because he was a member and had worked as a pro golfer for the club for many years, he was sure to get a discount. Weddings were expensive, and his offer was one Hillary should consider.

"He did?" she asked, as if this was news to her. "That was generous of him."

"It was," Carrie added, and sipped her wine.

"Hey," Hillary said, and flashed her cousin the same look she had given her sister earlier. "Whose side are you on?"

"Do there have to be sides?" Julia asked.

"In this instance, yes," Hillary shot back. "While I'm willing to admit it was nice of him to offer, I refused."

"Hillary!" Julia was disappointed that her daughter hadn't taken hold of the hand her father had extended.

"I'll admit at first I was tempted, because at the time Blake and I hadn't found a place for the reception."

"Then why didn't you?" Carrie asked, just as their orders were delivered. "It would have made sense."

"I agree," Hillary said nonchalantly, as if discussing some mundane subject, like an ice-cream sale at the local Fred Meyer store. "Then he ruined it all by inserting how eager Laura would be to help me with the menu for the wedding reception, if we held it at the country club."

Groaning inwardly, Julia bowed her head. Once again, Eddie had blown it. Her ex-husband apparently had not learned the painful lesson that demanding the girls accept his new wife was not a good game plan. It astonished her that Eddie could be this oblivious.

"Well, that was just plain stupid," Carrie said, digging into her crab cakes with creamy lemon sauce.

"Tell Mom what you said," Marie urged.

Hillary shook her head. "Mom doesn't like to hear me swear. I do believe Dad got the message, though."

"I'm sure—" Julia started, but was cut off.

"Mom, Dad is the one who insisted he didn't want to be a part of our lives unless we welcomed Laura with open arms. I can't ever see myself doing that, not after everything she said and did to you."

"Oh honey, I've forgiven her. You need to do the same."

"I can't. Not after how she treated you. Dad wasn't any better, the way he lied and misled you when he was involved in an affair all along. I can't respect a man with no honor and integrity. It's worse when that man is my own father."

"All this happened a long time ago," Julia gently reminded her girls. "And remember, it was said in the heat of the moment. He never meant to completely sever his relationship with you."

"Oh yes he did," Hillary countered. "An entire year passed before he even tried to talk to me."

Julia recognized how difficult it was for both Eddie and the girls to let go of their pride. They shared more in common than any of them were willing to admit. "Your father gave you both time and distance to let emotions cool," she offered, hoping Hillary and Marie would take her words to heart.

"Uncle Eddie phoned me a couple times to ask me how you were both doing," Carrie added. Her niece tended to be a peacemaker. Julia appreciated her efforts.

Over the last month since Carrie had started her new job, Julia had seen a change in her niece. She'd quickly grown into the position, and was well liked by the residents. She had a cheerful disposition, and a generous heart when it came to offering the residents assistance. One of the condo board members had thanked Julia for recommending Carrie. She'd also learned that her niece had developed a friendship with Eric Hudson, often spending time with him on the rooftop in the cool of the evenings. Maybe there was more to do with the change in her niece than just her position as concierge. And that made Julia happy. When she questioned Carrie about Eric, her niece had claimed there was far more to him than met the eye. She didn't elaborate, which left Julia curious as to the budding relationship. On the outside they appeared to be polar opposites. However, to her way of thinking, their personalities might perfectly balance each other. Eric needed someone like Carrie to draw him out of his shell.

"I'd be willing to give a relationship with Dad a try," Marie said, abruptly taking Julia's thoughts off her niece, "but he still refuses to see us unless we include Laura. That's the issue."

"I doubt we'll hear from him again," Hillary said. "I made my wishes known. It's up to him what he decides."

"Dad insisted he should be part of the wedding, seeing that he's Hillary's father," Marie added.

"And I told him it's my wedding and I'm the one writing out the guest list. I made sure he understood Laura's name isn't on it and won't be. Dad has a choice. He's welcome to be part of the wedding, only Laura can't attend with him."

Julia started to speak. Hillary stopped her by holding up her hand.

"Don't say it, Mom. Nothing you can add is going to change my mind. Dad's the one who drew the line in the sand, and he's going to need to be the one to step over it first."

The way Julia saw it, Eddie had stepped over it by being the one to reach out to his daughters. She couldn't understand why he couldn't start with something easy, like taking Hillary and Marie to coffee and talking. It wasn't like Laura was attached to his hip or should be. If Hillary's heart didn't change, she feared that one day, her daughter would grow to regret not letting her father back into her life.

"Enough about Dad," Marie said. "This is a day to celebrate. Hillary is choosing her wedding dress."

"And paying for it myself," she added, before anyone else could suggest she accept Eddie's offer to pay the difference above what she had budgeted.

"And I'm enjoying lunch with my favorite women in the world," Carrie added.

The girls were right. Discussing Eddie had put a damper on what should be a happy day.

Hillary reached inside her purse and grabbed a pad. "This is my list of everything I need to arrange before the wedding," she said, and put a check by where she had listed the wedding dress.

"Blake and I need to order the save-the-date cards next. We plan to do that the first of next week and order the invitations at the same time. Which means we have to decide exactly what we want printed. Blake is leaning toward the traditional, with our parents' names listed. Personally, I'd rather not."

Julia swallowed down another groan. If Blake got his way, then it went without saying Hillary would leave her father's name off the invitation. That would be another slight toward Eddie that was sure to widen the gap between them.

"You're both old enough to make your own decisions," Julia said. "You haven't lived at home since you started college."

Her daughter gently shook her head. "Mom, stop. I know what you're doing. You think it would be best if we kept our parents' names off the invite because you want to spare Dad's feelings. It's sweet of you, but unnecessary. Blake and I are discussing this and will likely compromise."

"Understood."

The girls chatted among themselves while Julia's stomach clenched as she braced herself for what she would tell them next. She had barely touched her food. It was now or never. She knew Heath was anxiously waiting back at the condo to hear her daughters' reaction to her news.

"Hillary, Marie," she said. "I need to tell you something."

Her tone must have alerted them that whatever she was about to say was important. As soon as she spoke, all three girls reverted their attention to her.

Julia's mouth went completely dry.

"Mom," Hillary said, her eyes widening with concern, "what is it?"

Chapter 14

Julia's daughters continued to stare at her. Carrie, too. For the life of her, she couldn't find the right words or even where to start. She had thought it best to simply explain the truth. However, now, when she had their full attention, she discovered her tongue had grown thick, and she was hardly able to speak.

"Are you sick?" Marie asked, reaching across the table to take hold of Julia's hand and tightly hanging on to it. "Is it cancer?"

"No. No," she whispered, shaking her head. "It's nothing like that."

"Mom, you're scaring me." This was from Hillary, who was almost always unshakable.

"Aunt Julia, you know there isn't anything you can't tell us. We love you."

"I know . . ." She straightened and looked at the beautiful

faces of these three women who were in possession of her very heart. "I've fallen in love," she whispered.

All three of the girls broke into huge smiles as relief relaxed their shoulders.

"Mom, did you seriously think you finding love would upset us?" Marie asked, laughing softly.

"That's wonderful, Mom," Hillary added, her relief evident.

"It's Mr. Wilson, isn't it?" Carrie said knowingly. "I've seen the two of you together having coffee every morning at the Busy Bean. Then you went on that pub crawl together."

"How did you know that?" Julia was surprised word had gotten around the building, until she remembered she'd run into Kennedy, and then later a couple of the board members, at the event.

"It wasn't a secret, was it?"

"No, not at all." The pub crawl had been the turning point in their relationship. That was the night Heath had first kissed her. The night she felt the thick wall around her heart crack open with the possibility of falling in love again. Love had deeply wounded her before, and she'd been afraid until Heath had kissed her. That first kiss had changed everything.

"It is Heath," she agreed. "We've been spending a lot of time together, and it's been wonderful. Neither of us set out to care for each other the way we do. It simply happened. We share a lot in common. Until Heath, I didn't believe I would ever find someone again. It's like my whole world has opened up since we've been together."

"That's great. When do we get to meet him?"

"Anytime you want . . . only . . ." She couldn't make herself do it.

"Only what?" Marie asked, as her face sobered.

"Does he have a criminal record? Is he dying? Is he married?" Hillary injected.

Julia shook her head. "Heath is a good person. He's healthy. And he was married, but is now divorced."

"So what is it you're afraid to tell us?"

"It's about his ex-wife," she said, carefully easing into the subject.

Both girls leaned back in their seats. "Is she making your relationship impossible?" Carrie asked, concerned.

"Is she a witch the way Laura was?" Hillary added another question.

Julia held their gazes for several seconds, before she lowered her eyes and whispered, "She *is* Laura."

The admission was met with complete silence, while the three made the connection.

"Heath was married to Laura . . . the same Laura who is now married to our father?" Hillary asked, speaking first.

Julia nodded. "We only discovered this recently, and it was as much of a shock to us as it is to you. When Heath spoke of his ex, he called her Lee, and when I mentioned Eddie, he had no clue Eddie was the Edward who had married his ex."

"When did you make the connection?"

"Heath's son Michael recognized me."

On hearing Michael's name, both her daughters instantly stiffened. "I bet that didn't go well," Hillary muttered, her jaw tightening with distaste.

"I can only imagine what he said." Marie shook her head as if she'd bit into something sour and repugnant. "You might be fond of Heath, but you need to know his sons are a piece of work."

"You do realize that it's because of Michael and Adam that Marie and I will never have a relationship with our dad again."

"Oh Hillary, don't say that."

"It's true, Mom."

"What did his sons say when they learned Heath was involved with you?" Carrie asked.

"Yes, Mom, what did they say?" Both Hillary and Marie crossed their arms defensively.

Carrie asked the one question Julia had hoped to avoid. "They weren't happy about it, although Heath assured me our relationship isn't going to change anything between him and his boys."

"They don't want anything to do with you, though, right?"

Slowly, reluctantly, Julia nodded.

Hillary and Marie's faces tightened until they each wore pinched looks.

"Like you ever did anything to hurt them," Marie huffed.

"Mom, are you sure you're in love with Heath . . . I mean, there are plenty of other eligible men. Why does it have to be him?"

"You want me to break up with Heath?" she asked. This was her biggest fear. She'd prayed her girls wouldn't react the same way Heath's sons had.

The three shared an unreadable look.

"Aunt Julia, we want you to be happy."

"I am happy . . . or I was until this information came to light. It's a complication Heath and I never anticipated. You need to know this has shaken us both. After talking to his sons, Heath needed a few days to mull it over. In the end he decided he wasn't going to let what happened between Laura and Eddie stand between us."

"And I suppose he naturally assumed you would do the same?" Hillary repeated, raising her voice. "Does he have any idea of the awkward position that puts you, and Marie, and me in?"

Julia had to agree it was awkward. "I believe he does."

"I doubt it."

Julia didn't know what to expect when she shared this news with her family. Like her, they were stunned. It would take time to fully absorb all the implications. "The thing you need to understand," she said, hoping to add clarity, "is that this doesn't change the way Heath and I feel about each other."

All three girls were quiet. Finally, it was Marie who spoke. "Maybe it should, though."

For one wild moment, Julia felt certain her heart had stopped. "What do you mean?" she asked, once she found her voice.

"Laura is poison. Why Dad would choose to leave you for that witch says everything I need to know about the kind of man my father is," Hillary said.

"And it isn't only Dad Laura has poisoned," Marie added. "She's infected the entire family. Her sons hate us, and because they are loyal to their mother, it sounds like they won't even give you a chance."

From what little Heath had said, Julia knew this was likely true.

"I know this isn't what you want to hear, but, Mom, please,

you need to seriously think about not continuing in this relation-ship."

Hillary was right; this wasn't what Julia wanted to hear. Still, as painful as it was, she was grateful for her daughters' honesty.

"It isn't that we don't want you to be happy," Hillary ex-plained further. "I'm sure Heath is great, only you should know there are plenty of fish in the sea. All you have to do is keep your eyes open to new possibilities.

"Our relationship with you has always been our safe place. When Dad left, you were the one who held everything together. We knew you would always be there for us. Dad was gone, and he made it clear he no longer wanted to be part of our lives."

The divorce had been emotionally hard on her daughters. Eddie seemed to feel that, because they were older and basically on their own, breaking up their family wouldn't hurt them, as they had their own lives now. How wrong he'd been. How naïve.

"I know how you feel about Heath," Hillary continued, "but, Mom, you can't seriously ask us to deal with his family? Can you even imagine what the holidays would be like? And what happens when there are grandchildren? Can't you see what an impossible situation you're putting yourself and Heath in?"

"And us?" Marie added.

Julia felt the sudden need to cry. Tears filled her eyes, and she blinked them away. "Nothing will ever change between us, that I can promise you," she whispered. Still, she needed to seriously consider what Hillary said.

Before lunch, her mind had been set. She'd been determined to work this out with her family so she could be with Heath. Seeing how upset this news made her daughters, Julia realized she needed to do as they suggested and carefully consider her options.

Back at home, Julia sat in her condo, gazing out her window with its limited view of the blue-green waters of Puget Sound. She couldn't face Heath, even knowing he was anxiously waiting for her return. For a solid hour she remained motionless, reviewing the lunchtime conversation. Before today, everything had been clear in her mind. Now she wasn't sure about anything. About Heath. About the future. About her daughters' reaction.

Her doorbell chimed, and without answering she knew it was him. Her feet felt as if she had strapped on weights as she slowly approached her door.

As she suspected, it was Heath. Wordlessly, she stepped aside so he could enter. As soon as she closed the door, he brought her into his arms and held her tightly against his chest; so close she could feel the solid beat of his heart. His heart that was her very own. Julia didn't know how she would ever be able to give him up.

The same thought repeated itself when he kissed her. In all her life she'd never been kissed with such passion, with such incredible need. It was as if the only reason he drew breath, the only reason he lived, was because it meant he could be with her.

Tears filled her eyes. "I don't know how I am going to learn to live without you," she whispered brokenly.

"That's because you will never need to find out. I can guess what your daughters said, Julia."

She looked up at him, his handsome features blurred by the tears that swam before her. "You can?"

"I heard the same from Michael and Adam. It shook me, and I figured once your girls learned who I was, it would rattle you. I stayed away for as long as I could, before I realized I couldn't allow Laura's infidelity and my children to rule my life."

She understood, she really did. Hillary and Marie were everything to her. They had remained faithfully by her side throughout the divorce, and afterward, had become her staunch supporters. They claimed all they wanted was for her to be happy. But, and it was a big but, they hoped she would find that happiness outside of a relationship with Heath.

"Until I started seeing you, Julia, I had no idea how lonely I'd become," he continued. "I went through each day like a robot without emotion, without laughter, without sunshine. You brought all three back into my life, and by all that's holy, I'm not letting anyone take what we have away. Not my children. Not yours. Definitely not Lee or Eddie."

Julia so badly wanted to believe their love was possible. She leaned her forehead against his chest, knowing that if she gazed into his eyes, she would never have the courage to leave him.

"I need time to think about all this," she told him.

"No," Heath insisted.

"No? You took three days," she reminded him. "Am I not allowed that same grace period?"

He hesitated. "You're right. I did take those three days and I left you hanging, not knowing why—something I regret. But I needed that time to realize how precious you are to me and find the courage to fight for us. And that's what I intend to do, Julia. I'm determined not to lose you."

She looked up, and her eyes met the intensity in his.

"I love you, and I'm not letting you slip away from me without one hell of a fight. You take all the time you need, but realize one thing."

"What's that?"

He grinned down at her and kissed her again with enough soul and passion to set her heart racing.

"My love, I fully intend to win your heart, and I refuse to let our exes or our children stand in the way."

What Heath had failed to realize, she mused after he left, was that he already had possession of her heart.

Chapter 15

True to his word, Heath refused to let her give up on them as a couple. After a week, she realized she didn't have it in her to let him go, either. They would stand together and prove to their children that despite everything, they were meant to be together.

So Julia and Heath began to practice a don't ask, don't tell policy. They wouldn't hide their relationship, but at the same time, they wouldn't refer to each other in front of their children, in the hope that would maintain the peace. While they had no intention of sneaking around and hiding their relationship, they wouldn't make the same mistakes Eddie had and insist their children accept that they were together.

Saturday, ten days after the lunch, Heath invited Julia to sail Lake Washington with him. It was a perfect August day, and according to Heath, the wind was perfect. Never having been on a sailboat, Julia wasn't sure she would know what to do. Heath assured her the only thing necessary was to sit back and enjoy herself. Earlier, he'd let it slip that Laura had rarely gone on the water with him. While he sailed, she'd headed to the golf course. It made sense that Eddie would connect with a woman who enjoyed golf, seeing that Julia's sport was tennis. She played occasionally even now.

Her doorbell rang. They'd agreed to meet at eleven. Heath must be anxious, as he was nearly fifteen minutes early. With a hop to her step, she headed to the door and was stunned to find her ex-husband standing on the other side, wearing a dark frown.

"Eddie? What are you doing here?" she asked, taken aback, hardly believing she was seeing him. It had been two years or longer since she'd last set sight on her ex. He'd gotten heavier, and his hair was nearly all silver now. It looked good on him, she was willing to admit. He'd always been tall and good-looking. He was well aware that even though he was close to sixty, he still had the ability to turn heads.

He noticed her shorts, hat, boat shoes, and the sweater she had tied around her neck. "Looks like you're going out?"

"I am." She didn't enlighten him as to where or with whom.

He frowned. "This will only take a few minutes."

Stepping aside, she allowed him into her condo. This was his first visit to her home and he looked around, eyeing the area. Julia was proud of it and the way she'd used her design skills to make this place her own.

"You like living here?" he asked, rubbing his fingers through his hair. It was a nervous habit she remembered well. "I never thought you'd be happy living in a condo."

"I love it. The Heritage is perfect for me. I can walk to work and to the market. It's convenient to everything." She wasn't going to defend her choice, and wondered at his small talk. He must have a reason for this unexpected visit, but she wasn't going to ask. He'd get to it sooner or later. Julia was sure Hillary's wedding plans were what had prompted him to stop by. Her daughter hadn't enlightened her to any new developments in regard to her father. The next move, she believed, had to come from Eddie.

With his hands stuffed in his pockets, her ex-husband paced in front of the window, looking down at the floor. She'd covered the hardwood with Oriental rugs she'd purchased at a discount, from a well-known company. They were of the finest quality. She loved the feel of them against her bare feet and often went without shoes while home.

"I'm assuming you stopped by for a reason," she said, growing impatient. She didn't want to keep Heath waiting.

He shrugged. "Is it true?" he asked, looking up and glaring at her. "Are you dating Laura's ex?"

So that was it. She should have realized Eddie would have gotten word of her involvement with Heath. "Not that it's any of your concern, but yes, it's true."

He snorted as if amused, and clearly he wasn't.

Julia clasped her hands in front of her. "I suppose Michael told you."

Eddie shook his head. "He told Laura and she told me. Neither one of us is happy about this."

Julia laughed outright. This was rich. "And I should care what you and Laura think?" How ironic and ludicrous that they would assume their opinion mattered one way or the other.

"You're doing this on purpose," he said.

"On purpose?" she repeated, not following his line of thought.

He glared at her. "It's your way of getting back at me."

This was Eddie at his most self-absorbed, egotistical self. "In case you've forgotten, our marriage ended six years ago. You moved on and so have I. Whom I date is none of your concern."

"Normally, I'd agree. I really couldn't care less. But Heath Wilson? Julia, please."

"Please what?"

"Do you think I'm stupid?"

Julia crossed her arms and shook her head. "You should know by now how unwise it is to ask a question when you already know the answer."

"Very funny. I'm onto your game."

It amazed her that she had been married to this man for thirty-one years. The Eddie standing in her home was a stranger.

"It might surprise you to learn I'm not playing games, Eddie."

He snickered with disbelief. "How do Hillary and Marie feel about this?"

She maintained her distance, letting the sofa separate them. He remained on one side and she on the other. "You should ask them."

"Like they'll talk to me," he answered, frowning.

"And whose fault is that? Or are you going to blame me for that, as well as everything else that's wrong in the world?"

His mouth tightened into a thin line. "You've changed, Julia."

"Really? Then it's for the better."

He wore a hurt, puzzled look, as if she'd surprised him. "You never used to be this flippant."

She shrugged. "I can't imagine what happened to make me that way," she said, smiling.

Eddie ignored this. "I know our girls can't be happy that you're dating Heath. Michael and Adam are upset about it, and consequently, Laura is, too."

"I'm sorry to hear that, although it changes nothing. I'm not breaking up with Heath because Laura is upset."

Julia's doorbell chimed again, and she knew it could only be Heath. She checked her watch. He was right on time.

She opened the door, and he leaned forward and kissed her softly on the lips. "Come on, girl, the wind is up and . . ." He paused when he saw Eddie standing on the far side of the room. He slowly straightened and came to stand at her side, placing his arm protectively around her waist.

"In case you haven't met," she said, gesturing toward her ex-husband, "Heath, this is Eddie."

Heath stiffened and nodded before he looked at her. "You okay?" he asked.

"She's fine," Eddie snapped.

Heath's head came back at Eddie's abrupt response.

"I believe I can answer for myself, thank you, Eddie," she said calmly. "As you can see, Heath and I are ready to leave."

"Hold on for two seconds," Eddie said. "I'm glad Heath is here. I'd like to talk to him man-to-man."

"Anytime," Heath said. "I suggest we meet later and leave Julia out of this."

"Oh no you don't. Julia needs to hear what I have to say. You both do."

"Eddie . . ."

"Julia, please," he insisted.

Heath gestured toward him. "Have at it, old man."

Eddie snorted. "Old man? I'm younger than you."

"Stop," Julia said, growing impatient with her ex and Heath. The testosterone level rose every time one of them opened his mouth.

"Fine." He glared at Heath. "I want to know your intentions toward my wife."

"Ex-wife," Julia and Heath corrected simultaneously.

"Yes, my ex-wife. It's all very convenient how the two of you met. You sought her out, didn't you? You learned where she lived and purposely purchased a condo in the same building."

"Sure, I did," Heath said, as if finding the question ridiculous. "I knew the best way to get your goat was to sweep Julia off her feet." He smiled as he said it, leaving no doubt he was joking.

Eddie didn't appear amused. "It was the best way you could think to rub the divorce in Laura's face."

"Unfortunately, you give me far more credit than I deserve," Heath said. "The truth is, Julia and I were both stunned to discover our connection."

"I'll bet," Eddie returned sarcastically.

"What brought us together is all we found in common," Heath continued. "You're happy with Lee, and I don't begrudge you or her. Get over yourself, Eddie, and leave the two of us alone."

Eddie blinked several times. If he'd hoped for a physical confrontation, Heath wasn't going to provide it. He was unperturbed and sensible, refusing to take Eddie's bait.

"Now, if you'll excuse us, Julia and I have a hot date on my sailboat. I would normally say it was a pleasure to meet you, only that would be a lie."

"It would be for me as well."

"Fair enough."

Heath reached for Julia's hand, and they stepped aside as they waited for Eddie to leave.

He paused to stand in front of them. "I hope you know what you're doing," he said to Heath, ignoring Julia.

"I do," Heath confirmed.

"You treat her right or you'll have me to answer to."

"I know the treasure I found in Julia and have no intention of letting her go."

Eddie frowned. "Is that a dig?" he asked.

"No, it's a fact."

Eddie glanced toward Julia, and offered a weak smile and a nod before he walked away.

Chapter 16

The monthly book club meeting was well in progress. Carrie had checked in with the group and saw that both her aunt Julia and Heath were among those discussing the latest read—a mystery by Jana DeLeon. Carrie had made sure coffee had been set up and had baked peanut-butter cookies herself.

As she settled into her position as concierge, Carrie had grown to love her job and the variety of activities that she oversaw; the book club was one of several. The meetings were held in the library room, adjacent to the lobby, and was the location for the yoga and wine groups as well. The card players set up in there also. Most of these activities took place in the evenings, and it was almost always the same people. She heard from newer residents that these sorts of arranged events were unusual in most condo buildings. For Carrie, it seemed just what made The

Heritage above and beyond. Overseeing these gatherings added variety and fun to her duties, and she enjoyed adding a personal touch to make them special, like baking cookies.

Although Eric claimed he wasn't good at relationships, to her delight he continued their nightly meetings on the roof. He'd relaxed considerably and they had grown comfortable with each other. After a few weeks she'd learned his father had died when Eric was young, and of his mother's financial struggles simply paying rent and putting food on the table. Eric did whatever he could to supplement her income, getting a paper route when he was twelve. It helped explain his drive to succeed and the long hours he spent cooped up inside his condo.

One evening she'd casually asked him about why he said he didn't do relationships. It took him a long time to answer, and what he told her broke her heart.

"In high school, I had a crush on a girl in my calculus class. My friend Michael encouraged me to ask Ellen to the senior prom. I was shocked when she agreed to go with me. I don't think I'd ever been more excited. It was my first official date."

"It took you until your senior year to go out on a date?" she asked.

"You have to understand, Carrie, I was working two jobs to help my mom. As the oldest with three younger siblings, there was never enough. I should have known taking Ellen to the prom was a mistake. Instead, I'd foolishly held on to the belief that I could pull it off."

Just from the way his voice dipped, she knew his date hadn't gone well. "What happened?" She reached for his hand and he gripped hold of hers so hard she nearly cried out.

"The afternoon before the dance I learned I was expected to bring Ellen a corsage. Michael's mom let me borrow his brother's suit. I was in a panic not knowing what to do. No way could I afford flowers for Ellen. Then my mom had an idea. She had an arrangement of plastic flowers. She cut up one and tied a ribbon around it, making it as pretty as she could. I figured it would be fine. It was the best we could do on the spur of the moment. But when I gave it to Ellen, this horrified look came over her face. Once we were at the dance, she couldn't get away from me fast enough. She had all her friends gathered around her and they looked at me like I was a scumbag for not buying her a real corsage. The evening was a disaster from start to finish."

"Oh Eric, I'm so sorry." She could imagine what life must have been like for him, during and following the prom. No doubt his date had viewed him as a cheapskate. Word must have spread around school through Ellen's friends about the disastrous night. The little of the fallout he did mention was probably the tip of the iceberg.

Eric exhaled slowly. "I've never told anyone about that disastrous night. Not even Michael knows all of it."

"You trusted me enough to share it," she said, and leaned toward him, bracing her head against his shoulder. "It means a great deal that you would."

"I've shied away from relationships ever since, letting school and then work consume my time and energy. I don't know how to do them."

"You seemed to be doing just fine with me."

He grinned then, his look shy and expectant. "Are we in a relationship?" he asked.

"Do you want us to be?" she countered.

He turned and studied her for a long moment. "More than I should admit . . . What about you, Carrie? Would you like to be?"

She started to answer, when he cut her off, "Before you say anything . . ."

"Yes," she returned, eager to reassure him. After Justin, Eric was a diamond in the rough. A prince, as far as she was concerned.

"Yes?"

"Yes, I'd like that more—"

"To be clear," he said, butting in again, "I'm a geek. And a workaholic; I rarely go out."

"Would you be willing to . . . go out?" she asked.

"With you?"

She smiled. "Is there someone else you'd rather spend time with?"

"No, no way," he rushed to tell her. "I'd only go out with you."

"Good," she said, and squeezed his hand. "There's a movie I've been wanting to see, and I'd love it if we could go together."

He didn't hesitate. "I'll need to check with my team about the time away."

"Of course."

He leaned back and seemed to relax. "This would be a date, right?"

"Yes, it will, and I won't require a corsage. All I need is you."

Eric wrapped his arm around her elbow, dragging her closer to his side. "You have no idea how firmly you have me, Carrie."

———

She'd done her best to encourage Eric to attend at least one of these events at The Heritage, hoping to draw him out of his condo for more than their evening chats.

Laughter echoed from the book club discussion as she returned to her desk, and Carrie smiled. Everyone seemed to be enjoying the chat and the refreshments. Her personal phone rang, and she reached for it, irritated to be interrupted while working. It could only be Justin.

Justin had contacted her every day for the last week, wanting to get together. He seemed oblivious to the fact that she was no longer interested in maintaining their relationship. That was a decision she'd made, following their last outing, when they cycled around Green Lake.

Her eyes had been opened. This was a dead-end relationship. As Carrie and her mother had discussed, Justin was like Peter Pan. He would forever be chasing his shadow, searching to find himself, taking advantage of others, and taking his mother's generosity for granted, sponging off her.

As she suspected, the call was from Justin. "Carrie," he greeted her with enthusiasm, as if he'd been waiting all day to hear the sound of her voice. "How about a movie later?"

"I'm working."

"You work, like, twenty-four hours a day. Don't you get time off for good behavior?"

Carrie didn't find his humor amusing. Since he didn't seem to be getting the message, she decided to spell it out for him. "I appreciate you asking," she said, although she strongly suspected she would have ended up paying for him as well as herself. "I believe it's better if we don't see each other again."

"You mean you're moving on? Are you breaking up with me?"

"We aren't actually a couple, you realize. We've had some good times and it's been fun. But I have other interests now and feel you should look for someone else to pay for your lunch or movie ticket. I'm busy."

He seemed to have trouble believing her. "Come on, Carrie, you don't mean that."

"I do. And I'd appreciate it if you didn't call me during work hours." Something she'd already repeatedly mentioned. Or contact her at any other time, for that matter, although she didn't say it.

"Okay, if that's the way you feel. No biggie. The sea is full of fish, if you catch my drift," he said stiffly.

"Then you best get fishing. Good-bye, Justin," she said, and disconnected, glad to officially put the relationship behind her.

Not five minutes later, her personal phone rang again. It would be like Justin to try to talk her out of this, and she answered abruptly. "What now?"

"Carrie?"

She'd snapped without looking to see who called and realized it was her cousin Hillary. "Oh Hill, sorry," she said, "I thought you were Justin."

"Is he still calling?"

"Unfortunately, yes, but I made sure this time he understood I'm moving on."

"Good for you. Did you tell him about Eric?"

"No way. The last thing I wanted to do was prolong the conversation. What's up?" Carrie had casually mentioned Eric to her cousin, looking for feedback on this new, promising relationship. Hillary had listened and encouraged her, not that she needed much. The time she spent with Eric was often the highlight of her day.

"Can you sneak away and meet me at the hospital tomorrow for lunch?" Hillary asked.

"Sure. Is everything all right?" Her cousin didn't sound like herself.

"Not really," she whispered. "I saw my dad."

This was news. Big news. Neither Hillary nor Marie had had much to do with their father in the last six years. In all that time there'd been only an occasional phone conversation, none of which had been pleasant or lasted more than a few minutes.

"I'd appreciate it if you didn't say anything to your mom or mine."

"Of course." The three girls often shared confidences, which had made them as close as sisters. "I'll see you at noon in the hospital cafeteria."

"Great. Thanks." The line went dead.

Whatever had transpired had upset her cousin, and she apparently needed a sounding board. Carrie was happy to be the one Hillary had reached out to, and she sincerely hoped she could help her cousin and best friend make sense of whatever had taken place.

Seeing that the book club didn't seem to be needing her for anything more, Carrie made her way to the rooftop and was pleased to find Eric waiting for her, although she was several minutes beyond the time they usually met.

He glanced at his wrist as if to say she was late, which made her smile. She'd meant to tell him the night before about the book club gathering for that evening.

"Did you miss me?" she teased, taking her seat in the lounge chair beside him.

He grinned, shrugged, and reached for her hand, wrapping his fingers around hers. She noticed he'd brought up a bottle of wine and two glasses.

"Come on, admit it! You thought I wasn't going to show."

He grinned and conceded. "Okay, fine, I was beginning to have my doubts."

"Eric," she said, serious now. "I enjoy spending time with you. Being with you is what I look forward to most in the evenings."

"Me, too," he confessed. He hesitated, looked at her intently, and then looked away. "The movie was fun. Would . . . Would you consider having dinner with me next?"

He was asking her out on a date. She more or less did the asking about the movie. This was big for him, and it thrilled her that he was willing to step out of his comfort zone on her behalf. "I'd like that more than just about anything, but not in your condo, right?"

"Right. A restaurant. I'll make the reservations."

She did her best to hide how pleased she was. "I can do that if you like, it's part of my job."

"Thanks, but I'll take care of it."

His smile grew, and so did Carrie's.

Hillary had a table outside on the patio and was waiting for Carrie once she arrived. Carrie quickly collected her lunch and joined her cousin. The hospital cafeteria food wasn't half bad. The two occasionally met at the hospital, as Hillary had only an hour's break. To make the most of their time, Carrie generally joined Hillary there. At first she'd had her doubts about finding any cafeteria food appetizing, but she'd been pleasantly surprised.

The sun was out and several hospital staff were also taking advantage of summer on the patio. Carrie slid her tray onto the tabletop and claimed the seat across from her cousin.

"Thanks for coming," Hillary said, as she unwrapped her sandwich.

"You said something about your dad." Carrie didn't mean to leap directly into the conversation; however, time was slipping away.

Hillary nodded. "Dad showed up uninvited at my apartment the day before yesterday. I hadn't seen him in nearly six years, so it was a shock."

"I bet."

"He asked if we could talk," she said, lowering her gaze. "Seeing that he was at my front door, I couldn't very well ignore him." She shrugged, as if it was hard to admit how eager she was to talk to her father.

"Of course not."

"He congratulated me and said he was excited for me and Blake and wanted to talk about the wedding."

The engagement was exactly what was needed to get Hillary, Marie, and their dad talking again. While neither of her cousins would admit it, they missed him. If the situation were reversed, Carrie knew she would miss her father terribly. It was stubborn pride that had kept them apart this long. Carrie knew Hillary had the stronger personality, and Marie would follow her sister's lead. Eddie had made a terrible mistake early on and had paid a price. The entire family had.

"He said it had been wrong to say what he did . . . you know, about Marie and I accepting Laura."

"He actually apologized?" Wow, this was unexpected. "That's great."

"I thought so. He asked for a hug, and I gave it to him."

"I know how hard this separation has been for all of you," Carrie said. "I couldn't be happier for you." To have Eddie finally admit he'd been in the wrong was colossal. It changed everything. However, if he had patched things up with his family, then it didn't make sense that her cousin had asked her not to say anything to their mothers.

"What happened?" Carrie asked.

"I should have known," Hillary said, and her voice wobbled as she struggled to hold back emotion. "I should have known."

"What?" Carrie pried.

"Dad offered to help with the wedding expenses. I put money down on the wedding dress and asked the shop to hold on to both, in case I could squeeze an extra six hundred dollars out of our budget for the more expensive one. When I mentioned the dress, Dad offered to make up the difference so I could have the one I wanted."

Carrie waited, knowing there was more to come, and whatever it was had deeply wounded Hillary. Her cousin had tears in her eyes as she fiddled with the plastic wrap from her sandwich.

"Then he said he wanted to pay for the wedding invitations."

She swallowed tightly. "He went so far as to write out the way he wanted them to read, and wouldn't you know, he listed Laura's name."

Carrie shook her head, angered at her uncle's blatant attempt at manipulation. "In other words, he'd pay, with several strings attached to his generosity."

Straightening her shoulders, Hillary continued. "I explained that given the circumstances, Blake and I had decided we weren't going to list either set of parents on the invites. Blake and I were the ones paying for most of the wedding costs, and we were the ones sending out the announcements, not our parents."

"That makes sense."

"But Dad insisted that if he was putting money into the dress, then he was contributing, and therefore his and Laura's name should be included."

Oh boy, Carrie could see where this was going, and it didn't look promising.

"Then I said he could keep his money. I made sure he realized I couldn't be bought, and furthermore, I had no intention of ever inviting Laura to the wedding."

So Hillary had thrown down the gauntlet.

"At that point, Dad blew up at me," she continued, "and said I was being vindictive and unreasonable."

This was what Carrie had feared.

"Then he blamed Mom and said she was the reason, which we all know isn't even close to the truth. I made sure he knew Mom had been after us to mend fences all along, only I doubt he believed me.

"He needed to know the only one keeping us from him was himself. I told him he couldn't shove Laura down my throat and reminded him that in all the time he's been married, not once has she made an effort to reach out to either Marie or me, and frankly, I was glad. I wanted nothing to do with her, and if his apology was his way of forcing me to accept her, then he had wasted his time and he could keep his money."

How quickly their meeting had disintegrated. Not only were Hillary and her dad both stubborn, they both had a temper. "So that was it?"

"Oh no, he was only getting started. Dad and I got into a shouting match. It was awful. Before he left, he went off on Mom again, claiming she's dating Heath to hurt him and Laura, which is totally ridiculous. I ended up practically shoving him out the door."

"Oh Hill, I'm so sorry."

"I am, too," she whispered brokenly. "Blake said he'd never seen me more upset. It was over an hour before I could even speak coherently. I was hurt and angry and . ." She paused, swallowing back a sob. "I feel dreadful. I . . . had so hoped, you know, that Dad and I could have a relationship again. I've missed him and I think he's missed Marie and me. I don't know why he keeps insisting on forcing Laura into our relationship. I mean, I could probably tolerate the woman if she made even the smallest effort. She hasn't, and so why should I? Since Laura's the one who robbed us of our dad, she should be the one to make the first move."

"Does Marie know?"

Hillary nodded. "She told me Dad reached out to her after he cooled down. He asked her to tell me he regretted stopping by and I should make plans for the wedding the way Blake and I wanted, only he wouldn't be part of it."

Carrie felt sick at heart for her two cousins. She could only imagine how painful this situation was for them.

"*It's better this way*, I guess," Hillary whispered.

Carrie didn't believe that for a minute. Although they had never said it out loud, she knew both Hillary and Marie had hoped the wedding would be the road that would lead their father back into their lives.

Chapter 17

Julia and Heath walked hand in hand at the Washington State Fair in Puyallup, a growing community southeast of Seattle. The fair was one of the largest in the country and attracted more than a million people in the three weeks it ran. On the opening day, admission was free for everyone who arrived between ten-thirty and noon.

It'd been a couple years since Julia had attended, and she had always gone with her sister, as Eddie had never been interested in the fair. The year before she'd been tied up in a project from work and couldn't get away. The year before that, Amanda had been on vacation with Robert.

When Julia casually mentioned to Heath her disappointment that Amanda couldn't attend opening day with her, Heath had volunteered. Her sister was off on a quilting adventure with friends in Ocean Shores. Nothing stood between Amanda and her quilting friends. She hauled her sewing machine with her, and enough fabric to clothe the entire Grays Harbor area.

Exploring the fair had always been one of her favorite events of the year. Spending the day with Heath made it even more fun. As soon as they entered the grounds, Julia paused to breathe in the sights, sounds, and smells. This was everything she'd remembered from when she was young: the rides, the cotton candy, and onion burgers. Viewing the farm animals had always been a fun time for her.

Although it was still early in the day, the crowds were thick, which was why Julia made sure she stayed close to Heath's side. Being with him seemed natural. Even now, after all these weeks, it amazed her how easily he had fit into her life and she into his. They did nearly everything together. That week alone they'd met each morning to work out, attended the book club discussion, played tennis, gone out for dinner one night, and cooked for each other two of the last three nights.

Walking through the arcade, the booth attendants called out, enticing Heath to try his hand at winning a prize. He paused and asked Julia, "See anything you like?"

Surely, he was joking. "Not a single thing."

"You sure? I played baseball in high school. The star pitcher."

"You still got it in you, old man?" the guy taunted, bouncing a ball up and down in his hands, eager for Heath to hand over his money.

"Now, there's a challenge, if I ever heard one," Heath said, laughing good-naturedly.

"Three balls, three dollars. Show me your stuff."

Heath grinned. "I'm thinking you'd enjoy that stuffed teddy bear," he said to Julia.

"And I'm thinking I'd like a raspberry scone instead," she returned.

"Sorry, buddy," Heath called back at the carny, "perhaps another time. I'm going to feed my girl."

The scones were one of the highlights of the fair. Already, the queue was twenty people deep, but to the credit of the enthusiastic servers, the line moved quickly. It wasn't long before they both were enjoying warm, jam-filled scones.

They walked through several of the exhibitions, and then ate greasy hamburgers piled high with grilled onions and cheese. "This is a heart attack on a plate," Heath teased.

"It's a rare treat." They both usually ate healthy food, choosing fresh fruits and vegetables with lots of chicken and fish.

After they'd finished lunch, Heath asked, "How about a ride on the Ferris wheel?"

Julia couldn't remember the last time she'd been on a carnival ride. Being with Heath made her feel like a kid again. "That sounds like fun."

"You know, the tradition is for the couple to kiss at the very top, so be prepared."

Julia had never heard of such a tradition and wasn't about to say so. She welcomed Heath's kisses. He was by far the best kisser she'd ever met, and she'd never grow tired of the taste and feel of his lips on hers. Patiently, they waited their turn before climbing onto the seat, sitting close together. Heath wrapped his arm around her shoulders, keeping her tucked against his side.

Sure enough, when they reached the very pinnacle, Heath captured her mouth in a searing kiss that lasted nearly all the way to the bottom of the ride. By the time they broke apart, Julia's heart was racing at a furious pace. To the point that she had trouble catching her breath.

"Listen, old man," she teased, "no matter what that guy had to say, I can personally verify that you haven't lost your touch."

He chuckled and gave her shoulder a gentle squeeze. "Nice to know."

After the rides, they wandered through multiple buildings, viewing farm animals and the crafts displayed. By the time they left the fairgrounds, it was late in the afternoon. Julia was tired and exhilarated at the same time. She enjoyed seeing the fair with her sister, but viewing it with Heath was an entirely different experience.

"I had a wonderful time," she told Heath as they neared Seattle. Being it was Friday afternoon, the traffic was at a near standstill. "Thank you," she said, leaning her head against his shoulder as he navigated his way back into the city.

"I should be the one thanking you. This was the best day I've had in ages, and I'm talking about more than the greasy hamburger, scone, and cotton candy."

Julia felt the same. She'd had a perfectly lovely time, and although she was worn out from all the walking, and bloated from the notoriously unhealthy fair food, this was a day she would long remember and hold dear.

Back at The Heritage, Heath walked her to her front door and kissed her once more before returning to his own condo. Anxious to put her feet up, Julia hadn't been home for more than a few minutes when Marie arrived.

"Hi Mom," she said, after Julia let her inside the condo.

"Hey." Having her youngest daughter stop by on a Friday night was a rarity. Marie liked to go out with her friends and let loose on the weekend. Of course, it was early yet. "This is a surprise," she said, leading her daughter into the living room.

They sat across from each other, and right away Julia noticed how nervous her daughter seemed to be.

"Honey, what's wrong?"

Her daughter paused, as if unsure where to start. "I'm breaking a promise to Hillary, but there are extenuating circumstances."

Julia frowned. "If you're doubting yourself, then perhaps you should take a day or two to think it over."

"I already have. I'm not sure what to do, and you're the only one who will know what's best."

Thinking this might be something that required a drink stronger than coffee or tea, she poured them each a glass of white wine. After handing one of the stemless wineglasses to her daughter, she gestured. "Okay, I'm ready."

Marie held on to the glass with both hands and steadied her gaze on the pinot grigio. "Dad came to see Hillary."

That was actually good news. If Marie thought she'd be upset by this development, then her daughter was wrong. Eddie had made the first step, which was something he needed to do. She also knew how difficult it was for him. Perhaps now healing could take place.

"He apologized for saying he would have nothing to do with us unless we accepted Laura into our lives."

This was far and above what she had hoped to hear. As stubborn as Eddie was, to have him express regret for his thoughtless words was a big step in the right direction.

"Hillary said this was what she'd been waiting all these years to hear." At this point, Marie paused and swallowed hard. To cover up her emotion, she took a drink. "And then . . . he had to go and blow it."

Julia felt her entire body tense with frustration and anger. "Tell me what happened."

Marie leaned forward and braced her elbows on her knees. "He offered to pay for part of the wedding. He said he would help Hillary get the dress she wanted. And the invitations. Then, as if it was understood, he added that since he would be contributing toward the expenses, both his and Laura's names needed to be included on the invitations."

It appalled Julia that Eddie would attempt such manipulation and somehow believe that bribery would get him what he wanted. It didn't take much of an imagination to guess Hillary's reaction.

"Hillary was furious. She made it clear she had no intention of having Laura attend the wedding in any capacity, which, naturally, angered Dad."

How one man could screw up an apology any worse than this was hard to imagine. "Oh dear."

"Then they both said a lot of things I know they'll regret."

Legendary tempers were something father and daughter had in common. The years apparently hadn't eroded Eddie's volatile nature.

"Afterward, Dad got me involved. He wanted me to let Hillary know that he regretted stopping by, and that she should go ahead with her wedding plans. Only now he said we should leave him out of it."

Julia felt like crying. This was even worse than she had imagined. If it was in her power, she'd like to slap some sense into Eddie. He knew better than to force Hillary to bend to his will, or he should.

"That was Sunday. Dad called me again on Wednesday and asked me to do him a favor."

"Now what?"

"This is why I need advice, Mom," Marie explained. "Dad wanted the name of the wedding shop where Hillary was buying her dress. When I asked him why, he said he was going to make sure Hillary got the dress she wanted. I gave him the name of the shop, and then he made me promise not to tell Hillary."

"Surely she'll find out when she goes to pick up the dress."

"I said the same thing. If Hillary discovers Dad paid for the dress she wanted, especially after their argument, then she would refuse. Dad explained that he would talk to the shop and have them tell her the dress had been discounted, and she could have it for the same price as the alternate dress."

Julia hadn't been married to Eddie all those years not to recognize what he was doing. This was his way of saying he regretted their argument. He refused to let Hillary know, because she was as stubborn as her father was. If she discovered what he'd done, she'd refuse the very thing she wanted most.

"You said you wanted my advice," Julia reminded her.

Marie sipped the wine, as if gathering her thoughts. "I've been thinking about this for the last two days. Hillary didn't say anything about the wedding dress when we last talked, so I have to believe the bridal shop hasn't connected with her yet. The thing is, Mom, Hillary hasn't been herself since the argument with Dad. I know she has her own regrets. I feel like, given time, someone should tell her what Dad did and why."

"And you believe that someone is me?"

"Of course. You'd know what to say."

"She hasn't mentioned seeing your father to me, and, more important, I've made it clear I am uncomfortable standing between you girls and your dad."

"I know, but, Mom, Hillary needs to know."

This was not a decision Julia cared to make on the spur of the moment. "I'll think on it and get back to you. That's the best I can do for now."

Marie looked vastly relieved. "Thanks, Mom. I know you'll know what's best."

Julia wished she shared her daughter's confidence.

Chapter 18

Julia carefully weighed her options before making her decision, knowing that Hillary was hurting, and because she knew him, Eddie had to be hurting right along with their daughter. Putting herself in the middle was something she had promised she would avoid at all costs after their divorce. Only now the price was too high, and she felt she needed to step in and do what she could to untangle this mess.

Both sides were obstinate and foolish. As adults, they should be able to solve this discord themselves, without her leaping in to negotiate. The sad truth was that it was unlikely either her daughter or her ex-husband would be willing to step forward to resolve this.

After two days of thoughtful consideration, she contacted Eddie and asked if they could meet for coffee. He reluctantly agreed, as if he was doing her a favor. Julia had to look past his attitude and swallow her own pride. After a bit of back and forth, they set a time for late morning at the Busy Bean. Heath had booked the tennis court for later that afternoon, so that would be her reward for getting through this conversation. He'd asked her what she wanted for her birthday and she'd made a simple request: tennis and later dinner at Canlis, her favorite restaurant.

Julia arrived early and bought her own latte. Eddie joined her ten minutes late to be sure she realized she was putting him out. When he approached the table, she noticed how haggard he looked. Shadows beneath his eyes told her he hadn't been sleeping. Even his steps seemed sluggish, as if it demanded more energy than he could muster to walk across the room. Clearly this argument with Hillary had beaten him, both emotionally and physically. The extent of it surprised her, validating her decision.

After a brief greeting, he glanced down at his hands. "I suppose Hillary came running to you with tales of what a horrible father I am," he said stiffly.

He seemed ready for her to berate and criticize him, which she had no intention of doing. Her one desire was for there to be reconciliation between Eddie and his daughters. Nothing would please her more than helping her girls and their dad find a way to mend their differences.

"As a matter of fact, Hillary didn't tell me anything."

He briefly looked up, as if he wasn't sure he could believe her.

"Marie did," she enlightened him.

A brief smile came and went. "She always was a bit of a tattle-tale."

Julia didn't confirm or deny his statement. "Marie told me about you working with the bridal shop to pay the difference on the more expensive dress that Hillary wants."

He shrugged, indicating it was nothing, and seemed embarrassed that she knew.

"Marie wants me to be the one to tell Hillary the truth."

His eyes shot up to her. "Don't. If you do, Hillary won't accept the gift. I want her to have that dress."

"You're probably right, although it might be better if I do."

"It isn't," he insisted.

"She should know you regret the argument, and it would give her the opportunity to express her own part in this falling-out between you two."

"It doesn't matter. She said Laura isn't invited to the wedding, and if she isn't invited, then I'm not going, either. Nothing you say will change my mind. If the girls disrespect my wife, then they are disrespecting me and—"

Raising her hand to stop his tirade, Julia said, "Honestly, Eddie. Haven't you ever heard of baby steps? You can't force your daughters into a relationship with Laura—especially not with the bad blood between them and her and her sons."

"What do you mean by 'baby steps'?" He cocked his head to one side and seemed genuinely curious.

"How about starting with a birthday card signed by both of you. Perhaps a short note from Laura alone. Introduce her a little at a time, instead of forcing the girls into a relationship with her. I know you regret that dreadful scene at the lake."

"Do Hillary and Marie?"

"That's not for me to say. Ask them yourself. Frankly, I'm uncomfortable standing between you and the girls. I needed two days to think this through before I was comfortable enough to suggest we meet. This isn't a role I'm happy with, or even one I want."

Her words were met with a tense silence.

"Once I learned Hillary and Blake were engaged," Julia continued, "it seemed the perfect opportunity for healing between you and the girls. Why is it always one step forward and two back with you?"

"What do you mean?"

"Don't be obtuse. I couldn't have been more pleased to learn you'd apologized to Hillary. She badly needed to hear you regretted that day as much as she did. We both know you spoke in the heat of the moment."

"You weren't there. You didn't hear the horrible names your daughters called the woman who was soon to be my wife."

He thought rubbing in the fact that Laura was his wife now, and not Julia, would hurt her. But now the jab ricocheted off her. Still, she didn't miss the fact that he referred to Hillary and Marie as her daughters.

One step forward, three and four back. Would he never learn?

"You're right, I wasn't with them that day. I'm grateful not to have been part of that horrible, embarrassing scene. Even if it did take nearly six years, you were honest enough to take the first step toward reconciliation when you sought out Hillary."

"It wasn't easy."

"I'm sure it wasn't. Really, Eddie, was it necessary to call Marie and tell her you wanted nothing to do with the wedding?"

He let her words soak in for a few awkward moments. His eyes filled with remorse as he admitted, "You're probably right.

I was angry . . . I should have cooled down first. I guess this is what you mean by taking two steps back?"

She arched her brows because that was answer enough.

He shrugged it off. "All right, I'll admit it wasn't my smartest move."

She agreed. Rubbing it in wouldn't help, so she kept her mouth closed. "Now to the reason I asked to see you. As I mentioned earlier, Marie thought it would be a good idea if I told Hillary what you'd done for her. She believes hearing it from me would help her understand this was your way of apologizing."

"I can't say I disagree. I suppose, deep down, I want Hillary to know I will always love her. If letting her have the wedding dress she wants relays the message, then all the better."

"Excellent, because I've decided not to tell her."

Eddie's mouth thinned before it sagged open. "What are you getting at? Why not?"

"Because, Eddie, I feel you need to do it yourself."

"What? I can't. You and I both know Hillary won't talk to me."

"You found a way around her stubborn pride before; do it again. This is your daughter; she's hurting the same way you are. You're the only one who can take this pain away. I didn't say it would be easy, but what I do know is that you both desperately need this. It's slowly eating you up, and Hillary isn't doing much better. She needs her father, and she wants a relationship with you. Not you and Laura. You. Once she believes that you love her, then maybe she'll open her heart to Laura."

"You don't know that."

"Perhaps not, but I know my daughters. Marie's already halfway there, and if given the chance she'd run to you with open arms." Their youngest was by far the most forgiving. Hillary took after her father and was quick to anger and struggled with forgiveness, unwilling to let go of past hurts.

Silence hung over them as Eddie mulled over her words.

"Will you talk to Hillary?" she asked gently.

His gaze connected with hers. "You won't do it for me?"

His question caused her to emit a short laugh. "No. That was a joke, right?"

"No." His shoulders trembled with a deep sigh.

"Eddie?" Julia wasn't about to let him off lightly.

"Okay. I'll think about it."

This was all he was willing to give her. Julia had no choice; she had to accept his decision. "Don't wait long, Eddie." If he dallied, it could well be too late, and he'd forever lose both his daughters.

Standing, he looked ready to leave before he paused. "You still seeing Laura's ex?"

"Yes, Heath and I do well together."

He snorted as if thoroughly amused, and then shook his head as if he found it hard to believe. "You know Laura and I think this is all a bunch of bull."

She ignored the jab. "As I mentioned before, Heath and I share a lot in common." Biting her tongue was difficult. How badly she wanted to remind him they had both been betrayed by the one person they loved and trusted most in the world.

Eddie knocked his knuckles against the tabletop. "I bet you do." Once again, he started to leave. "Oh, one last thing."

"Sure."

"I'd appreciate it if you didn't contact me again outside of anything to do with the girls. It distresses Laura."

"Then I won't," she said with a saccharine-sweet smile. "The last thing I would want to do is distress your wife."

"How'd your talk go with Eddie?" Heath asked when they met in the lobby before heading out to play tennis.

Julia wasn't sure how best to answer. "About as good as it could, I suppose. Eddie is, well, Eddie. It's hard for him to admit when he's in the wrong, and even harder to make amends." She didn't mention the final dig. He'd acted like she made excuses to contact him, when nothing could be further from the truth. She'd done what she could to help him and their daughters. What happened next was up to him.

Heath gave her shoulder a gentle squeeze. "I know this was hard for you."

She appreciated his understanding. It had been difficult, and she was grateful it was over. Time to move on and shake off the unpleasant meeting. Playing tennis to work out her frustrations was exactly what she needed now.

"Did you tell him what you decided?"

"Yep, and then I suggested this might well be his last chance with the girls. What he does now is up to him. If he chooses not to act, then he'll need to learn to live with the regrets."

"Those are strong words."

"They are," she agreed, but she meant everything she'd said.

"Hey, you two," Carrie said as they walked toward the concierge desk. "It looks like you're off to Wimbledon."

Heath laughed. His hand remained on Julia's shoulder, a gentle reassurance that he was by her side. Julia had talked about her decision with him and had appreciated his words of wisdom. He didn't advise her, didn't try to persuade her one way or the other. He had simply listened and encouraged her.

"I didn't know you played tennis," Carrie said, directing the comment to Heath.

"Your aunt is much better than I am. The real reason I'm willing to make a fool of myself is so I can see her in a skort."

Julia smiled. "Don't let him fool you. He's a fine tennis player."

Heath led her into the basement parking garage. "Did you know Michael's friend Eric and Carrie are dating?"

Julia had heard rumors along those lines. "I haven't heard much. What do you know?"

"Michael thinks it's great that Eric has finally found the incentive to get outside of his condo. Supposedly, Eric's become a workaholic and is shy by nature, but smarter than anyone Michael knows."

"Carrie would be good for him."

"I think so, too. Eric took her to a movie last week and a dinner this week. They seem to get along great. He doesn't know Carrie's related to you and I didn't mention it."

"Probably a good idea." Later, Julia would make a point of asking her niece more about this budding relationship.

Heath drove, and they arrived five minutes before their scheduled court time. Over the last few weeks, they'd managed to get in a match or two about once a week. When they'd first started playing, Heath had been rusty and Julia generally bested him. It'd taken three or four court times for Heath to keep up with her and become a worthy opponent.

The first game they played went to Heath. "Hey," he called across the net. "You're losing your edge. This match is mine."

She snickered. "In your dreams, smarty-pants. I was going easy on you."

Bending forward, her racket in hand, Julia bobbed in a standing position, balancing on one foot and then the other, waiting for Heath to serve. The ball bounced just inside the line, but she reached it in time to return it toward the far corner. Heath raced across the court and then abruptly stopped.

The ball flew past him as his racket fell onto the court.

Heath dropped to his knees.

"Heath?" she cried, wondering if he might have stumbled.

Then he looked at her and she knew.

He hadn't tripped. This was serious.

Frantically, Julia screamed for help as she raced around the net to reach him.

He looked up at her before his eyes rolled back, and he collapsed facedown onto the court.

Chapter 19

"Nine-one-one, what is your emergency?"

Julia's voice trembled so violently that she was barely able to speak. A man from another court over had rushed to Heath's side, reaching him almost at the same time as Julia. Immediately assessing the situation, he started CPR while Julia hurriedly located her phone to call for help.

Within minutes, she heard the sirens and raced to meet the paramedics who came to tend Heath. Everything happened so fast that she barely had time to absorb what was going on before Heath was taken away, sirens blaring.

Collapsing onto the bench on the side of the court, she buried her face in her hands. Her knees were shaking so hard she was in danger of slipping off the edge of the seat.

A woman she didn't know came to sit down beside her. She

gently touched Julia's arm. "Are you okay?" she asked softly, as if afraid of alarming Julia.

"I . . . I don't know." Tears rolled down her cheeks as she drew in a deep breath, hoping to ease the frenzied beat of her heart so she could think clearly. Her greatest fear was that she was about to lose Heath. It crippled her mentally, to the point that she found it difficult to move. The look in his eyes right before he collapsed was branded in her memory. It seemed, in those last seconds, before he lost consciousness, like Heath was saying good-bye. A giant sob shook her entire torso.

"Is there someone you can call?"

Julia couldn't think clearly enough to figure out what was necessary, what she should do next. Then she noticed Heath's bag sitting at the end of the court. His phone was inside.

She should let Heath's sons know.

Later, she decided. It was more important that she get to the hospital and find out his condition. If she contacted Michael and Adam without any details, it would freak them out worse.

"I have to get to the hospital," she said, desperately needing to know if Heath had survived before she contacted his family.

"Here." The man who had given Heath CPR handed her a bottle of water. "Drink this first."

She nodded, not realizing how dry her throat had become. Guzzling down the liquid, she paused for a moment to calm herself. Her own heart raced at an alarming pace. All she could think about, all that mattered, was getting to Heath. Getting to the man she loved.

Searching inside his bag, she located his car keys. Although she didn't feel she was in any condition to drive, she wasn't willing to wait for an Uber to get her to the hospital. She'd chance it, also knowing Heath wouldn't want his vehicle to remain in the parking lot at the tennis court, unattended.

Shaken as she was, Julia was grateful to make it to the hospital without an accident. She was fortunate enough to find parking and literally ran into the emergency entrance, arriving breathless at the information desk.

"I'm Julia Jones. My . . . friend"—she didn't know how else to explain their relationship—"was brought in by an ambulance . . . I believe he's had a heart attack . . . We were playing tennis. Can you please tell me his condition?" she pleaded.

"Name?"

"Oh yes, sorry. Heath. Heath Wilson."

"You're not a relative?"

"No." She knew what that meant. The medical facility would update only a family member.

Stumbling into the waiting area, Julia was sure the receptionist must think she'd been drinking. Her knees had yet to recover and the shaking continued.

Collapsing into a chair, she reached inside Heath's tennis bag and retrieved his phone. Guessing his passcode was his birthday, she tried that, and sighed with relief when it worked.

Searching his contact list, she quickly located Michael's name and called him first.

Heath's son answered on the fourth of what seemed to be endless rings. "Hey, Dad, what's up? I'm a little busy now. Can we connect later?"

"This isn't Heath," Julia said, forcing herself to sound calm, although she wasn't sure she succeeded.

"Julia? Why do you have my dad's phone?" he demanded, sounding none too pleased to hear from her.

"I'm at Seattle General. Your father's here . . . I believe he's had a heart attack."

Stunned silence followed before Michael raised his voice, nearly shouting at her. Not knowing what else to do, she started to explain what had happened as best she could.

"Is he okay?"

"Oh dear God, I . . . I don't know," she said on the tail end of a sob. "The staff will only talk to family, so I don't have any information."

"I'm on my way."

"Thank you," she whispered, and then added, "Do you want me to call Adam, or will you?"

"I'll let my brother know," he said, and abruptly ended the call.

Because Julia was barely holding herself together, she texted Hillary, who thankfully happened to work at Seattle General. Within minutes, her daughter joined Julia in the waiting area.

"Mom, what happened?" she asked, sitting down next to Julia and reaching for her hands, taking them both in her own.

Not until she felt her daughter's warm hands did she realize how cold she was.

"Talk to me," Hillary said encouragingly, when Julia found no words. Once more, she was on the verge of breaking down, her heart pounding as if looking for a way to break out of her chest. When she was able, she explained watching Heath collapse on the tennis court. Once again, the panic and fear of seeing him go down was almost more than she could endure, and she broke into sobs.

"Oh Mom. I'm so sorry." Hillary hugged her, and Julia let her, soaking in her strength and calm, desperately needing it.

When she found her voice again, she whispered, "I'm afraid, Hill, so afraid he isn't going to make it."

Her daughter tenderly rubbed Julia's back as she remained with her. "Weren't you the one who told me to not cross a bridge until I get there?"

Julia sniffled and nodded. With tears streaking her face, she bit into her lower lip and whispered, "I love him. I didn't believe I would ever love anyone as much as I once did your father. Heath proved me wrong. Falling in love at my age wasn't anything I expected to happen . . . I thought that part of my life was over and . . . and I accepted it and . . . and then I met Heath."

Hillary hugged her tighter. "I'm going to call Aunt Amanda. She can sit with you."

Julia nodded, aware that Hillary had to return to work. Amanda would come right away. Julia would need her sister, especially if the news about Heath was bad.

Hillary left her, and no sooner was she gone from the room than Heath's two sons arrived. Ignoring her, they stormed into the emergency room and went directly to the receptionist to ask about their father.

Julia couldn't hear anything that was said other than the doctor would be out to talk to them shortly. Both boys were upset, and she wished she had some words of reassurance to offer, but she didn't.

Turning away from the receptionist, Michael glared at Julia. Slowly he walked over to her. "You can go now that we're here."

Several people around them looked up at the gruff way in which he spoke. Julia chose not to react and kept her voice low and serene. "I'm here because I care about your father. I'm not leaving until I find out Heath's condition," she said. Not wanting to cause a scene, she was determined to remain where she was, despite his sons.

"You're the reason my dad is here," Michael said with malice. "Dad should never have been playing tennis, and certainly not with you."

Julia didn't have it in her to argue. She could appreciate that Heath's sons were upset; so was she. Rather than explain that she had as much right to be at the hospital as they did, she simply shook her head, letting them know she wasn't leaving.

"Aunt Amanda is on her way and she—" Hillary stopped speaking when she saw Michael and Adam standing over Julia in what must have looked like a threatening stance. Joining her mother, Hillary placed her arm around Julia's shoulders.

"Your mother should go," Michael insisted again. "Her being here isn't helping."

"My mother is staying right where she is. It's not up to you to say who can and can't be in this room."

Again, the stares from those sitting in the area were focused on all of them. Julia was embarrassed but unwilling to leave. Michael and Adam would need to accept that she wasn't going anywhere until she knew Heath's condition.

"We don't need her here." Michael's voice was raised.

"Too bad, she's not leaving," Hillary returned in equal volume.

The two were practically nose to nose, glaring at each other, waiting for one or the other to back down. The scene reminded Julia of gunslingers facing off.

"Hasn't your family done enough?" Adam said, speaking for the first time.

"What do you mean by that?" Hillary demanded, turning her attention away from Michael. "It was your mother, the cheating bitch, who ruined our family."

"Hillary, please." Julia gasped and grabbed her daughter by the arm. "Stop. Arguing isn't helping."

"Your dad—"

"Keep my dad out of this," Hillary retorted. "No, don't. You can have him. He doesn't know the meaning of honor or fidelity. You want him, he's all yours."

"That's fine with me," Michael countered. "We think the world of Edward. In return, I want you to keep your mother away from our father."

"Both of you, please stop." Julia pleaded, as she buried her face in her hands. She couldn't deal with this now, not when her fears ran rampant, and it felt as if she was about to lose Heath forever.

"Just stay away from our father and we'll call it even."

"Fine by me," Hillary said with a laugh. "My sister and I aren't happy with their relationship, either. As far as we can see, there isn't a single decent member in the entire family."

"Stop!" Julia cried once more. "Please, just stop."

"Keep your dad away from my mother," Hillary went on to say. "I'll do my part and you do yours."

"Deal."

The emergency room doors opened and Amanda appeared. Seeing her sister, Julia rushed toward her, desperately needing to escape.

"Julia?"

"Get me out of here," she cried. "I don't care where you take me, just get me out of this hospital."

———

It had been a crazy day, with the news of Heath's heart attack. Carrie was more than eager to escape to the rooftop with Eric. As soon as she arrived, she found him standing waiting for her. He immediately met her and drew her into his arms, hugging her.

"I heard about Heath," he said. "Is there anything we can do?"

"Not at this point. Wait," she said, "how did you know?" Eric had little contact with anyone in the condo other than her.

"Michael. We were scheduled to have a business call when his assistant postponed it. Later, Michael phoned to update me from the hospital."

"Did he happen to mention how Heath is doing?" Carrie knew her aunt was beside herself for information. Her one hope was that with Hillary working at the hospital, her cousin might be able to get some insider information to relieve her aunt's mind. One thing was certain, neither Michael nor Adam would be inclined to do so.

"He was in surgery the last I heard," Eric said. "Your aunt isn't with him?"

Carrie sadly shook her head. "Michael and Adam didn't want her there. From what my mom told me, there was something of a scene, and Julia left."

"A scene? Why wouldn't Michael and Adam want Julia at the hospital? Heath is crazy about Julia. If he knew this, it would upset him."

It dawned on Carrie that Eric didn't know about the connection. Both Hillary and Marie weren't psyched about Julia being with Heath and hoped the relationship would burn itself out. That didn't seem to be happening, though. If anything, the two had grown closer. Seeing how good they were together made Carrie happy for them. In time, she believed her cousins would come to accept Heath.

"Carrie?" he pressed, when she didn't immediately respond.

"You know Julia is my aunt, right?"

"Yes, you mentioned that before."

Carrie hesitated, unsure this would be welcome news, knowing Michael was Eric's best friend. "Her ex is married to Michael's mother."

Eric frowned as he processed this news. "Let me get this straight. Michael's mother is married to Julia's ex-husband and now Heath and Julia are dating? How did that happen?"

Unsure, she shrugged. "All I know is that they seem perfect for one another and they're happy."

"Then more power to them." Eric easily accepted the information.

Relieved, Carrie leaned her head against his shoulder. "I'm glad you feel that way. I wouldn't want their relationship to stand between us."

Eric's arms tightened around her. "Can't see that happening, Carrie."

Closing her eyes, she whispered, "Good to know."

Chapter 20

Heath heard mumbled voices. One he didn't recognize, but the other was familiar. Straining to make out the words, his mind was clouded, and it seemed as if they were speaking in a foreign language. Slowly opening his eyes, he blinked against the bright light. It was as though he was staring into the sun. He quickly closed them again and rolled his head to one side.

"Dad, are you awake?"

That familiar voice belonged to his son. "Adam? Where am I?"

"You're in Seattle General."

"The hospital?" The last thing Heath remembered was being with Julia on the tennis court.

"You had a heart attack. They had to operate and you now have three stents. You're going to be okay, but you sure gave us all a scare."

Heart attack? Three stents? Suddenly his entire world was

spinning. His heart was perfect at his last physical. He didn't know how that could have changed overnight. It made no sense. His physician had given Heath a clean bill of health. He ate the right foods, drank red wine sparingly, and religiously exercised. In fact, the doctor had claimed he wished all his patients were as dedicated as Heath was.

"I need to let Michael know you're awake," Adam said.

He heard his younger son talking and realized he was on the phone. "Dad's awake." This was followed by a pause. "Yes, I'll tell him."

"Tell me what?" Heath asked. While his thoughts remained muddled with questions, he was able to hear only one side of his son's conversation.

"Michael is on his way," Adam explained.

Now that his vision had cleared, he looked around the room and was surprised not to find Julia. "Where's Julia?" he asked.

Adam hesitated. "I have no idea."

"She was with me earlier." Now that his memory had returned, he remembered her stricken, horrified expression as he collapsed. Her fear had matched his own.

"Yes, she was," Adam confirmed. "She was the one who called nine-one-one and made sure you got to the hospital."

Knowing Julia, she must be worried out of her mind. "I need to talk to her," he said, eager to reassure her. Eager to have her close to his side.

"That's not a good idea, Dad." Adam looked uncomfortable as he walked over to the window and looked outside.

"Why not?" Heath asked, finding the words thick on his tongue. He fought back the need to sleep, refusing to give in until he could connect with Julia.

"You need to rest. Michael and I will talk to you about her later."

"No, I want Julia here. If you won't call her, then I will."

"Dad, please, that isn't a good idea."

No way was Heath willing to let his sons deter him from talking to Julia. He wanted her with him, needed her. No one could convince him she wouldn't be here now, unless someone had prevented it. Instinctively, Heath knew his sons were the ones responsible.

Despite his best efforts, he fell asleep, waking again when he heard Michael and Adam whispering. He kept his eyes closed, because they were talking about Julia, and he wanted to hear what they had to say.

"Dad insisted he wanted Julia," Adam was telling his brother. "Did you let her know he's out of surgery?"

Michael snorted. "After what happened, are you kidding? The less we have to do with that family, the better."

Heath wanted to know exactly what had happened. From the sound of it, it wasn't good.

"You won't be able to keep her away," Adam returned, "and Dad's determined he wants her at his side."

"Not if I have anything to say about it."

Heath had heard enough. "What did you say to her?" he demanded, angry now and impatient.

Both his sons looked surprised when they realized he had heard them talking. "We thought it best if she left the hospital," Adam explained. "She was crying and worried. Her daughter was with her, and then Michael and Hillary got into a shouting match."

Heath groaned, well able to picture the volatile scene.

"That daughter of hers is evil," Michael inserted, frowning.

"As you might have guessed, Michael and I were upset and worried. Julia was, too, and then Hillary got into the mix. It wasn't pretty."

"What did you say to Julia?" Heath needed to know what had taken place so he could fix this.

Michael shrugged, as if that would explain everything. "She demanded that we stop shouting."

"Then some woman I've never seen arrived, and Julia left with her," Adam added.

"It must have been Amanda," he said, closing his eyes. The thought of what she must have endured upset his stomach.

"It wasn't like she introduced us, Dad," Adam said. "It could have been her sister. They sort of looked alike, I guess."

"What about Hillary?"

Michael looked uncomfortable as his gaze moved around the room, avoiding Heath's. "She had a few choice words to say after her mother was gone, and then she left like she couldn't get away from us fast enough."

Heath breathed deeply and waited until his temper had cooled before he spoke. "Listen, you two, I understand there is bad blood between our families. That's unfortunate. What you need to remember is that Julia and I are separate from what happened between you and her daughters."

"Dad—"

"No, you listen." He raised his arm without realizing it was connected to an IV pole, which set a buzzer off. When he lowered his arm again, the sound stopped.

"You're my sons and are a part of me. I love you. If necessary, I would die for you. What I won't do is let you stand between me and the woman who has changed my life. Julia means the world to me. Have you any clue how isolated I'd become after your mother left? Julia has given me far more than either of you realize. She's everything to me. I love her."

"Dad, no," Michael said, and his face tensed. "Don't do anything rash, like marry her. You barely know this woman."

"How can you trust her?" Adam asked.

Arguing wasn't going to convince his sons that Julia was the woman for him. Their minds were set, and nothing he said would convince them otherwise. His strength was waning, and he closed his eyes. Later he'd have more to say—for now, for now, he needed to sleep.

Heath woke when Hillary Jones entered his room. She stood stiffly, just inside the door, as though this was the last place she wanted to be.

"You asked to see me?"

He nodded, nearly desperate, since he hadn't been able to reach Julia, after repeatedly trying. "Thank you for coming."

"I'm on break and only have a few minutes," she said gruffly, having no qualms about letting him know she was eager to be on her way.

"I appreciate that you're here. I wanted to apologize for the way my sons treated you and your mother yesterday."

She lowered her gaze, avoiding eye contact. "You don't need to apologize; I gave as good as I got."

He was tempted to smile. "So I understand. Good for you."

She looked up then, as if surprised. "Mom was badly shaken. If your sons owe anyone an apology, it's my mother. They were horrible to her, insisting she should leave. They made it sound as if she was responsible for your heart attack, which we both know is ridiculous."

This was exactly what Heath feared. "That should never have happened. How is she now?"

"She spent the night with my aunt Amanda."

"I haven't been able to reach her." That worried Heath more than anything the heart specialist had told him earlier.

"She wasn't able to sleep after she left the hospital. I spoke to her this morning, and she said she was going home to nap. I suggested she turn her ringer off. She probably forgot to turn it back on."

That helped explain her silence and eased his mind. "I'd feel better if I was able to talk to her, reassure her I'm alive and well."

"I let her know you were recovering from surgery. She wanted to come to see you herself, only I discouraged it for fear she'd run into one of your sons. I assured her you would be back home soon."

Heath had gotten the same news from the heart specialist, along with a list of new medications he would need to take for the foreseeable future.

Hillary came farther into the room. She held his gaze for a long moment before she asked, "Do you love my mother?"

Heath welcomed the question. "With all my heart. What makes you ask?"

Julia's daughter crossed her arms as she stepped closer to the bed. "My mother is everything I hope to be one day. She's the most loving person I know. She is thoughtful and generous. She does everything she can to show us how loved we are. Even when she knew Dad was cheating on her, she was willing to swallow her pride and pain and look past his betrayal to keep our family together."

Heath agreed, Julia was the most loving, caring woman he had ever known. How any man could walk away from her was beyond him.

"That said, after Dad left, Mom struggled to find herself. She did an amazing job, but deep down I don't think she was happy. It was like a part of her heart was missing. Since she's been seeing you, I've noticed a change in her. Her smiles come easier now, and there's a glow about her that I hadn't seen in a long time."

He saw all that in Julia—that light was the same one that touched his heart and brought sunlight back into his life.

"When she told Marie and me she was dating you, I'll admit we were upset. We discouraged it and made sure she realized that we weren't on board with this relationship. Then yesterday, when she didn't know if you would survive, my mother lost it. I've never seen her this undone, not even after we lost our grandfather."

Heath hated how deplorably his sons had treated Julia. One day they would realize how they had wronged her and apologize.

"I know there's trouble between our families, and I regret that. I would welcome a way to bring us all together and end this animosity."

"I would welcome that, too," Hillary told him, "only the way things are now, it's highly unlikely. Your sons . . ." She paused and shook her head. "It's better I not tell you what I think."

"Thank you." Heath didn't want to be in a position where he would need to defend Michael and Adam.

"What I will say," Hillary continued, "is after seeing how Mom reacted yesterday, Marie and I talked. If Mom has your heart, then we won't do anything more to discourage your relationship."

"She is my heart," Heath said, and it was more truth than Julia's daughters would ever understand.

"She clearly cares deeply for you," Hillary said, dropping her arms to her sides. "Marie and I decided that it would be wrong for us to stand in your way, especially if you shared her feelings."

"I do, heart and soul."

She smiled then, and Heath did, too.

"Thank you," he whispered, overwhelmed and grateful.

Her eyes narrowed. "You hurt her, and I'll make sure you regret it."

"It will never happen," he promised her. He thrust out his hand.

Hillary stepped forward and shook it.

This was a start, Heath mused, as she left the room.

The beginning of the healing for their families.

Chapter 21

For fear of running into one of Heath's sons, Julia stayed away from the hospital even when every beat of her heart urged her to find a way to be with him. Because Hillary worked as a physical therapist at Seattle General, her daughter was able to update Julia on Heath's condition following his surgery. A dozen times or more since she'd walked out of the hospital with Amanda, Julia was tempted to call him, but hadn't, for fear of disturbing his recovery. Her one consolation was the brief text messages he'd sent, assuring her he would be home soon and eager to see her. He thanked her and claimed her quick action had saved his life.

She nervously waited for word when the hospital would release him. She was told he was unlikely to spend more than a couple days recuperating from his surgery. She was certain one of his sons would escort him home and impatiently waited for the chance to see him herself. Not until she could hold his face and look into his eyes would she believe, once and for all, that he had truly survived.

Hillary had been good about keeping her updated; without knowing Heath's condition, Julia would have been lost.

Her doorbell rang. Because she was waiting for Hillary's call, she was irritated and in no mood for company. When she saw Heath standing on the other side of her threshold, she burst into tears.

Immediately she was in his arms. Heaving huge, gulping sobs, she clung to him, holding on as if she never intended to let him go.

"Sweetheart. Julia. I'm okay . . . only I should probably sit down."

Julia instantly brought him into the condo.

Heath sat on her sofa while she searched for a tissue and blew her nose. She had never been one of those women who looked beautiful while crying.

"It looks like you missed me," he teased. He patted the place at his side, and she sat next to him.

"I was so worried," she whispered, still having trouble believing he was here with her.

"Me, too," he said, and placed his arm around her shoulders, tucking her close against his warm body. He tilted his head so it rested on top of hers.

"I thought I'd lost you," she said, struggling not to dissolve into tears a second time.

"It isn't going to be that easy to be rid of me, my love. I have a lot of incentive to live. I only just found you, and I fully intend on sticking around for a good while longer."

"Tell me what the doctor said." She didn't mention that no one would update her on his condition because she wasn't family. What she had been able to learn came from Hillary and her contacts within the hospital. She'd never let anyone know, for fear of getting her daughter in trouble.

For the next ten minutes, Heath relayed what the heart specialist told him. He had a follow-up appointment scheduled for the next week. He listed the new medications he would need to take. Julia made a point of remembering each one, so she could research the drugs on the Internet. The more information she had about his heart and the problems associated with this attack, the better she would be able to watch for signs. She wanted to be sure there wouldn't be a repeat of what had happened, at least not if she could help it.

"If you don't object, I'd like to go to the doctor with you," she said. She felt it was important that she know his limitations and was afraid Heath would either forget to tell her or purposely leave something out.

Surprise showed in his face at her request. "You'd do that?"

"Of course. I want to support you."

He tightened his hold on her and kissed the top of her head. "I don't know what I ever did to deserve you."

"Oh, stop," she said with a soft laugh.

"Do you think I'm joking? I thank God every day that we're together."

She could see how serious he was and wondered if he realized that she felt the same. "I thank Him for you! Oh Heath, you can't imagine how frightened I was that you weren't going to survive this."

"Like I said, I'm still aboveground, and I intend to stay that way for a long time to come."

"I'm holding you to that," Julia told him.

His eyes grew dark and serious before he lowered his mouth to hers and kissed her. It'd been years since anyone had kissed her with the passion and intensity Heath did. By the time he lifted his head from hers, it felt as if her insides were melting.

He was home and recovering, and that was what mattered most.

That evening, Julia cooked dinner for Heath. Michael called to check on him, and after dinner Adam did, too. It did her heart good to know how close Heath was with his sons. She prayed that at some later date, his sons would accept that she loved Heath and wanted only the best for him.

Earlier, when Heath mentioned his conversation with Hillary, Julia knew she had to make an effort with Michael and Adam, the way Heath had with Hillary. Unsure how it would play out, she decided not to tell him in advance.

Julia felt it was her duty to give Heath the same peace of mind Hillary had given her after talking to him. If she could convince Heath's sons that she had only their father's best interests at heart, then perhaps there would be a way for them to forget the distance between the two families. The fact that she was willing to make the effort should tell Michael and Adam she was serious and sincerely cared for their father.

"That was Adam," Heath said, once he was off the phone.

"Your sons love you," she said, stating the obvious.

Heath's eyes grew wary and he looked down. "I heard how rude they were to you at the hospital, Julia, and I'm genuinely sorry. They should never have spoken to you the way they did. One day, they will apologize, that I can promise you."

She came to him and slipped her arms around his middle, assuring him as best she could that all was forgiven. "It's fine. I understand. Your heart attack frightened them as much as it did me. They didn't mean it. And I refuse to take offense."

"You're far too generous."

"Besides," she said, smiling up at him, "nothing was going to keep me away from you much longer. I didn't care if I had to sneak into the hospital in the dead of night, I was determined to be with you." She would have if the hospital had kept him any longer than the two days. Without Heath's texts, brief as they were, she would have surely gone mad.

"Speaking of nights, I've been working on a little birthday surprise for you."

"Oh?" He certainly had piqued her curiosity. "Tell me more."

"I'm not going to ruin the surprise. Because of my recent setback, I've had to delay it."

"Just as long as we aren't returning to the tennis court anytime soon."

"This has nothing to do with what you wanted for your birthday, my love. This is actually something else I'd arranged earlier. I had to do a bit of rescheduling while I was in that hospital bed. We will go out for dinner the way we originally planned, just not yet."

That he would be thinking about her birthday following heart surgery nearly brought tears back to her eyes. Knowing how badly he wanted to do something special for her, she did her best to hold the emotion in check. "You could give me a hint."

He shook his head. "Don't worry, you'll find out as soon as I can get everything put in place again."

Two nights later, Heath arrived to pick her up for her birthday surprise. When she reached for her purse, he stopped her. "You won't be needing that."

"No purse?" This was all rather mysterious. "Okay." Unsure what to think, she followed him to the elevator.

Instead of heading to the lobby, they rode up to the rooftop. Lights were strung across the space, shading the area in warmth. Carrie stepped into view, her hands held together in front of her. She looked to Heath and said, "Everything is arranged the way you asked."

"Thank you." He reached for Julia's hand.

"Heath." Julia paused, looking around at the table set up with a bottle of champagne, crystal flutes, and a beautifully decorated birthday cake with her name written across the top.

"Are you ready for your surprise?" he asked.

"You mean the cake and champagne aren't it?" It seemed Heath had something more up his proverbial sleeve.

Kennedy and her friend moved from the shadows in the corner. "Happy birthday, Julia," she said.

"Thank you." Kennedy was young, around the same age as her daughters, if Julia were to guess. She was a member of Seattle Women's Chorus. Last Christmas Julia and Amanda had attended a performance and she'd recognized Kennedy.

Kennedy introduced her friend, and then Carrie started the music as the two women in beautiful harmony sang Julia's favorite song from Frankie Valli, "My Eyes Adored You." Their voices blended melodiously, clear and vibrant, wrapping their way around Julia's heart as Heath opened his arms to her.

"Shall we dance?" he said.

"Here? Now?" she whispered, self-consciously.

"Come on, Julia. Don't you know my eyes adore you?"

No way could she refuse him. Walking into his arms, she tucked her head beneath his chin and let him gracefully lead her around the rooftop. They danced together, as if they had spent a lifetime matching each other's steps, not once faltering.

This was above and beyond the most romantic birthday gift Julia had ever received.

When the song ended, Heath reluctantly broke away from her. "Champagne?" he asked.

"Please."

While he poured it into the flutes, Julia thanked Kennedy and her friend. "Frankie Valli himself couldn't have sung that any better," she told them. "Thank you."

"Anytime," Kennedy said. "Heath gave our choral group a donation. He didn't need to do that, as we would have been happy to sing to you for free."

"Please stay for cake."

"How about we take some and leave you two alone?" she suggested.

Carrie dished up the cake—coconut, Julia's favorite—and the two women left. Heath handed her a flute along with Julia.

"You arranged this?" she asked her niece.

A smile lit up Carrie's face. "All part of the concierge service. Happy birthday, Aunt Julia."

It was by far the best birthday surprise of her life, and Heath had made it happen.

Chapter 22

Julia had rarely been this nervous. She hadn't told anyone where she was headed, least of all Heath. He would do his best to dissuade her if she had been foolish enough to mention what she intended. Nor was she tempted to tell Hillary or Marie, knowing they would strongly disapprove. After the confrontation at the hospital, she knew she had to do whatever was necessary to find a way to reach Heath's sons and end this tension between their families.

The office building was walking distance from The Heritage, and the fifteen-minute hike gave her time to sort through her thoughts of what she would say. By the time she arrived, her hands were moist and her mouth was dry. Her throat already had a lump and she wasn't sure she'd be able to swallow past it to talk.

After entering the high-rise, she approached the receptionist desk and announced herself as if she were a long-standing client.

"Julia Jones for Adam Wilson."

The man behind the desk reached for his phone and called up to the office where Adam was employed. Heath had casually dropped the information weeks ago, proud that his sons had followed in his footsteps and gone into the investment field.

The man at the reception desk jerked his gaze to her. "You don't have an appointment?"

"No. Will you please ask Mr. Wilson's assistant if he has time to see me?"

Julia was instructed to wait. Walking over to a lobby chair, she sat on the edge of the seat while she awaited Adam's response. She chose to approach Heath's younger son, hoping he would be more amenable to hearing her out than Michael would be. She was left to wait for five minutes.

Five of the longest minutes of her life.

Five minutes in which she wondered at the wisdom of what she was about to do.

Five minutes in which she debated walking away and forgoing the hope that she might reach an understanding with Heath's sons. But she knew the best way to accomplish this was likely through Adam.

The receptionist motioned to her. As Julia rose, she noticed her knees were as unsteady as her resolve. With her head held high, she walked back to his desk.

"Mr. Wilson will see you."

"Thank you," she said, and hoped none of her apprehension showed in her voice. After giving him her identification to copy, he handed her a badge that read VISITOR and a code for the elevator.

Security was tight. It might have been easier to visit Fort Knox, and certainly less stressful!

A woman stood by the elevator when Julia stepped off. "Hello, I'm Tamera from Mr. Wilson's office. Please follow me."

"Thank you," Julia said, as Tamera led her to double glass doors. She entered a code at the small panel on the wall, which allowed them to enter.

As his assistant escorted Julia down a long hallway, she glanced into the offices of men and women working at their computers and phones.

Adam had one of the smaller offices. His desk was massive, with two oversized monitors. He looked up when she entered. Only it wasn't Adam. Instead, she faced Michael.

When she hesitated, he motioned for her to take a seat. "Adam asked me to meet you," he explained. Seeing that Julia had come this far, she wasn't going to back down now. She'd hoped to speak to Adam, but it seemed she'd been outsmarted. This was the first time she'd had the chance to get a good look at Heath's oldest son. He was a younger version of his father. They even wore their hair in the same style.

"I'll admit this is a rather unexpected surprise," he said, looking none too pleased to see her.

"I imagine it is." She was well aware neither of Heath's boys would welcome her with open arms. Knowing this hadn't stopped her; she felt she had to try.

"I'll admit I'm curious."

That was what she'd been counting on.

"Why are you here? Because if you're looking for an apology for what I said at the hospital—"

"I'm not," she said, cutting him off.

"Okay, then kindly fill me in?"

Looking down at her hands, Julia nervously smoothed her skirt. She'd dressed professionally, as if she was headed to work, wanting—no, *needing*—to look her best.

"I would like to clear the air between us . . . between our families."

"And you think the two of us talking will help achieve that?" He made the question sound laughable.

"That was my hope." She glanced up, laying aside her pride and wishing he would recognize how difficult coming to him had been for her.

"Before you say anything, you should know I doubt anything you have to say is going to change the way I feel about you or your daughters. As far as I'm concerned, you're wasting your time, but have at it." He leaned back in his leather chair and knotted his hands over his chest, as if waiting to be amused.

Inhaling a calming breath, she offered him a weak smile. "First off, I know how close you are to your dad. Your relationship means the world to him."

Michael didn't deny or affirm her statement.

"As you know, when your father and I met, we had no clue there was any connection between us. Of course, we both were aware that the other had been previously married, but neither of us knew who our former spouses were."

Michael's mouth thinned. "And?" He made a circular movement with his hand, indicating she should get on with it.

"It's been six years since the divorce," she reminded him. "Heath had moved on, and so had I. Neither of us was expecting to find anyone else, and we both had settled into a solitary life."

"You didn't move into The Heritage because of my father?" he asked.

How cynical of him and utterly ridiculous, although she didn't say it. "I moved to The Heritage first. Your father moved in after I did. I couldn't possibly have arranged our meeting."

That didn't seem to convince him, as he steadily regarded her.

"Dad said you changed your workout schedule and that was how you supposedly met." He mentioned this as if it was all the proof he needed that she'd somehow manipulated the relationship.

"You're right. I sold my business and only work as a consultant now. Because I had more free time in the mornings, I shifted my exercise regimen from the afternoons to earlier in the day."

He raised his eyebrows, as though he still remained skeptical.

"For a week or longer Heath and I didn't say a word to one another. He was the one who introduced himself. We soon learned how much in common we shared. Our spouses had both fallen in love with someone else. We both had two children. Heath had sons and I had daughters. We bonded over our disastrous dating experiences."

"Fine. You enjoy my father's company. That doesn't change anything."

"Michael, please. Is there anything I can do to assure you I genuinely care for your father? And I know he cares for me. It hurts us both to have our children oppose our relationship, when it means the world to us."

"I'm not here to judge if you do or don't care for my father. I don't like that he's with you, especially when there are plenty of other worthwhile women who would welcome his attention."

Her pleas hadn't appeared to move him.

"If it reassures you any, I promise I won't get in his way. If he wants a relationship with you, that's on him, only you should know I have no desire to have anything to do with you or, God forbid, your daughters."

His attitude made reconciliation between their families seem less and less likely. "I realize you have reasons to resent me. I made a terrible mistake before the divorce was final when I sent those text messages to your mother, and for that I apologize. To you and to her. It happened a long time ago, but I instantly regretted letting my emotions get the best of me. My hope is that you can understand what led me to do something I knew was wrong." She didn't mention Laura was the one to initiate the exchange. Julia accepted responsibility. All she could do was hope Michael realized his mother had been the one to tear apart Julia's marriage and her life.

"You made my mother's life miserable."

She wanted to ask if he realized Laura had done the same to her. "I never meant your mother any ill will, Michael. It's unfortunate because there were wrongs on both sides."

"More so on yours," he insisted. "Furthermore, it's ridiculous that you won't allow your daughters to have a relationship with their father. Clearly this has been your revenge. You wanted Edward to suffer for leaving you for my mother. As far as I'm concerned, that is unforgivable. Nothing you say is going to change my mind. I can only imagine what you'd do to destroy my father, should he dare have a change of heart about you."

She closed her eyes and let his harsh words pass over her like a forceful wind capable of toppling a strong oak tree.

"I've heard what you have to say. I have an appointment I need to keep," he said, standing and walking over to the door and holding it open for her.

Julia had trouble finding her balance as she rose to her feet. Every part of her being wanted to defend herself, wanted to explain that Eddie's estrangement with Hillary and Marie was on him, not her. Only any defense she offered would be for naught. Michael would choose not to believe her.

He continued to stand at the door, holding it open.

She walked out, her throat thick, realizing her visit had accomplished nothing and quite possibly had done more harm than good.

"Thank you for your time, Michael. I appreciate you listening. I'm more sorry than you know that we couldn't come to terms."

He nodded. "I understand, and I'm sorry, too. Like I said, we won't stand in the way of Dad's relationship with you, if that's what he chooses, but we'd rather you weren't part of his life. I don't mean to be cruel or uncaring, but it would serve us best if you agreed to no longer see my father."

Julia swallowed hard at his words and left, making her way to the lobby. Once there, she collapsed in the chair she'd sat in earlier. Several minutes passed before she was able to stop the shaking. Coming to see Heath's son had been a terrible mistake. She should have known better, should have accepted that anything she said wouldn't change matters. The future stretched before her: Heath and her balancing their love for their children against their love for each other.

—

When she returned to The Heritage, Carrie was at the front desk. Her niece immediately sensed something was wrong.

"Aunt Julia? Are you feeling ill?"

"I'm fine," she lied. "Or I will be . . ." She wasn't sure herself what that meant.

Once in her condo, she felt the strongest need to get away for a few days and think. A trip to the coast strongly appealed to her. Time spent by the ocean always had the power to calm her. When Eddie had finally admitted to the affair, it was to the ocean that she'd gone. Booking a hotel room in Oceanside, Julia had walked the beach for days. She'd grieved and prayed for a way to save her marriage. She hadn't returned since, and knew it was the one place she needed to be now.

Walking into her bedroom, she grabbed a suitcase and packed a few items, sent a text to Hillary, telling her where she was going, and then left. She didn't want to talk to Heath, not even by text, knowing he would ask too many questions. She needed to think, and he would be a distraction she needed to avoid.

Chapter 23

Heath hadn't been able to reach Julia for two days. He didn't understand why she wouldn't answer her phone. At first, he assumed she'd put it on mute and forgotten, as she'd done before when she'd gotten busy. Then, the following day, after several tries, he decided he would seek her out.

She hadn't shown up at the gym in the mornings, which surprised him. He was on restricted physical activity. He'd been amused when Julia had watched over him like a grade-school playground monitor, making sure he didn't overexert himself. She hadn't mentioned any work projects, either. To be on the safe side, he'd phoned the office and been told Julia wasn't expected anytime that week.

Usually, Julia filled him in on her plans for the day, and he'd tell her his. To not see or talk to her for two days running was highly unusual, and he had started to worry, more determined than ever to find answers.

When Julia didn't answer the door, his uneasiness multiplied tenfold. For a while now, he'd felt something wasn't right with her. She hadn't been herself. They'd taken in a Mariners baseball game, and she'd been distracted and unusually quiet. When he tried to draw her out, she smiled and assured him all was well and claimed she was tired.

Unwilling to leave her disappearance unanswered, Heath decided to check with Carrie. Being at the front desk eight hours or longer each day, Carrie was able to catalog who came and went from The Heritage. She might clue him in as to why he hadn't been able to reach Julia.

He strolled up to her desk and waited while she signed off on a delivery from UPS. When she'd finished, she greeted him with a smile.

"Hello, Heath. How can I help you?"

Leaning against the desk, he casually asked, "Have you seen Julia the last couple days?"

"I don't think so," she said. "Any reason you're asking?"

He shrugged. "I haven't been able to reach her."

"Oh?" Carrie frowned, as if mentally reviewing the last time she'd seen her aunt. "You know, come to think of it, the last time I saw her, she didn't seem quite herself. I asked if she wasn't feeling well, and she assured me she was fine."

"And you haven't talked to her since then?"

Growing thoughtful, Carrie shook her head.

Heath was growing more apprehensive by the minute. "Did she say anything else?"

Carrie shook her head. "No. Sorry." She reached for her phone. "Maybe my mother knows."

The sisters were close; if anyone knew, it would be Amanda. Heath waited for what felt like an eternity for Julia's sister to pick up.

"Mom," Carrie said, "Heath is here. He hasn't been able to reach Aunt Julia. Do you have any idea of where she might be?"

"No. Has he tried calling her?"

Heath could hear Amanda through the phone. *Try calling Julia?* As if that hadn't already occurred to him! "Would you mind if I spoke to her?" he asked, and held out his hand for Carrie to give him her phone.

Obediently, Carrie handed it to him. "Amanda, this is Heath. I haven't heard or seen Julia since yesterday morning. She didn't show this morning and now I'm concerned. Did she say anything to you about going away?"

"No. Come to think of it, I tried calling her myself yesterday afternoon, and she didn't answer. I left her a message."

"And she didn't return the call?"

"No. I'd forgotten all about it. That isn't like Julia."

"I've called several times and it automatically goes to voicemail."

"Has anyone thought to check her condo?" Amanda asked, a thin line of panic infiltrating her voice. "For all we know she might have fallen or—"

Heath didn't wait for her to finish. Setting the phone down, he asked Carrie, "Do you have a master key in case of an emergency?"

She nodded and was already reaching for it before he finished asking the question.

"Call me as soon as you find her." Amanda's faint voice echoed over the phone where Heath had set it down.

"Will do, Mom," Carrie yelled into her phone as she and Heath raced for the elevator.

By the time they reached Julia's condo, Heath's pulse was racing at a speed he knew wasn't doing his heart any good. He felt dizzy with worry. If anything had happened to Julia, he didn't know how he would find the strength to continue. Now that he'd found her, he didn't want to face life without her beside him.

Carrie was frightened and her hand shook as she inserted the key that would open the lock. The instant the door swung open, Heath raced inside.

He called out her name several times as he ran from one room to another, only to come back empty.

Carrie remained in the middle of the living room, and when she saw him, Heath shook his head. "She's not here."

Slumping onto her sofa, he ran his fingers through his hair. "Where could she be?" he asked with a low moan. It was essential he keep calm; however, he was finding that harder to do with every passing minute.

He reached for his phone while Carrie checked the condo herself, in case he'd missed some clue as to where Julia had gone. He intended to text Hillary, but before he found her name in his contact list, his phone rang. Because he had his phone in his hand, he answered on the first ring.

"Dad," Michael said impatiently, "I thought you said you were coming in to the office today."

The appointment had completely fled his mind in his concern

over Julia. "I ran into a bit of a snag," he said, rushing his words together in his eagerness to get his son off the phone. "Julia is missing."

"Julia? You know she stopped by uninvited yesterday morning, don't you?"

"She did what?"

"She had some idea that if she reached out to me we'd find a way to bring our families together."

Heath's blood went cold. "What did you say to her?" he asked, unable to hide his anxiety.

"I didn't say much of anything. I let her have her say and then basically told her nothing she said would change the way Adam and I feel about her or her daughters."

Heath groaned. Hearing this, he was convinced Julia's disappearance was linked to the visit with Michael.

"Dad, come on, you can't fault me for being honest," he said, and then added, on a teasing note, "She seemed to think we should form a circle and sing 'Kumbaya,' which is ridiculous. She has no understanding of what she put Mom and Edward through. I can forgive her, sure, but that doesn't mean I will have anything to do with her."

Heath's eyes slammed closed as he battled for control of his temper. "Do. You. Realize. What. You've. Done?" He enunciated each word between clenched teeth, with barely controlled anger.

"Dad, calm down. If you want to blame me that she's missing now, then fine. All I did was tell Julia the truth. Look how upset you are right now, thinking I have somehow offended her. Can't you accept that the anger you feel is happening because of her? You're upset with me and Adam because of her. If you continue in this relationship it will only build a wall between us. With each argument it will grow taller and thicker. I was honest with Julia and she was honest with me. Maybe she's taking time to assess what it means for the two of you to stay together. Adam and I feel it would be better if she moved on to greener pastures."

Heath didn't dare speak for fear his next words would likely damage his relationship with his son. Heath's stomach roiled, and for half a second he thought he was going to be sick. When he was able to speak, he managed to tightly control his voice. "Did you ever consider what your mother did to Julia?"

"I don't think it is a good idea for you to defend—"

"Did you?" he asked, louder this time. "Lee tore apart Julia's world. When she made a single request to wait six months to try to save her marriage, your mother made her life a living hell. Did you know anything about those ugly text messages Lee sent to taunt her?"

"No, but I read the ones she sent to Mom. How would you know about any of this anyway?" Before he could answer, Michael sarcastically said, "I suppose Julia told you, and naturally you believed her."

"No, she didn't. Julia never mentioned a word of this, not even when I confronted her about the texts she sent your mother. The only thing she mentioned was the regret she suffered for lowering herself to Lee's level."

"If she didn't tell you, then who did?"

"Hillary."

"And you believe that witch?"

"Yes, because she showed me a picture of the texts Lee sent Julia. Trust me in this, Michael, what I read, it was shameful."

"Dad, I hope you're hearing yourself. What did I just say?

Already Julia is coming between us. It will be like this as long as you insist on being with her. You need to ask yourself who's more important to you? Julia, or Adam and me?"

Heath had heard enough. "I refuse to answer that . . . not when I'm this emotional. I'm hanging up now, because I need to find Julia."

He disconnected before Michael had a chance to respond. As soon as Heath was able to breathe again, he sent a text to Hillary and another to Marie, knowing both of Julia's girls were likely at work and probably wouldn't see his message until they were on break. Having to wait to hear back was killing him.

Carrie returned and must have overheard his conversation with his son. She placed her hand on his shoulder. "Don't worry, we'll find her."

Not knowing who else to turn to, all Heath could do was wait. His condo felt bleak and empty, and his heart was heavy, especially after speaking to his son. Pacing his condo, he feared he was about to wear out an entire section of carpet. He saw Julia everywhere he looked. In the paintings that hung on his walls that reminded him of their time together in Gas Works Park. The colorful decorative pillows on his sofa that she hand-picked for him, along with the lamps on the end tables. She'd even added a pitcher he used as a utensil holder next to his gas stove. It wasn't only in his home, either—Julia had left an indelible mark on his heart. He didn't know what he would do with himself until he could hold her and reassure her.

Just before noon, Hillary called. When his phone buzzed, he jerked it so fast and hard, it nearly flew out of his hand.

"I got your message," she said. "Don't worry, Mom is fine."

"Where is she?"

"She asked me not to tell you if you called, only I don't want you to worry. She went to the ocean. She finds peace there."

"Where, exactly?"

"Sorry, Heath, I think you should give Mom time to sort all this out by herself. She needs to clear her head and think through everything."

"But . . ."

"I know it's hard. Heath, trust me, it's best to leave her be. Mom will return when she's ready. It's best if she doesn't see you right now."

They spoke for a few minutes longer, and eventually Hillary was able to talk him off the proverbial cliff. She managed to convince him, despite his persistence, that seeking out Julia now wasn't the right thing to do.

Patience and *waiting,* Heath decided, were the two worst words in the English language.

Chapter 24

Julia spent three days at the beach. On the one day it rained, she found a cute coffee shop, called Bean There, on the main street running through town. As the raindrops bounced against the large window, she sat and enjoyed a vanilla latte and a home-made cinnamon roll. While she was there, a man arrived, and the lovely young woman behind the counter immediately brightened. Her name tag identified her as Willa. She came around the counter, and Julia could see she was pregnant. The young man, clearly her husband, ordered a coffee and the two of them sat together, their heads close, whispering animatedly. Seeing the love they shared nearly brought tears to her eyes. She'd felt that same devotion and love from Heath . . .

Once she finished her breakfast, she strolled down to a quaint bookstore and purchased a book by one of her favorite authors, C. S. Lewis. The rest of the day was spent reading on the hotel balcony, tucked back from the wind and the gloomy gray clouds. While enjoying the book, she stumbled upon a passage that connected with her heart, something that wasn't unusual when she read C. S. Lewis.

He wrote about his time at the ocean, and she suspected it must have been after the death of his wife, Joy. He spoke of how he viewed the sea as a lifeline that connected him to things that were temporal. Julia was sure this comfort, the solitude and silence, the steady pulse and current of the waves, was exactly what he'd needed. What she needed now.

Spending time at the ocean with only the sounds of the wind, the rain, and the water filled her heart. It offered her strength to face the future. This calming connection she felt with nature reminded her that this pain in her heart would pass in time.

The morning of the fourth day, she packed her bags, checked out of the hotel, and loaded up the car for the drive back to Seattle. While at Oceanside, she'd turned off her phone, not wanting to be distracted. Before leaving the hotel parking lot, she checked her messages and found several from Heath, a couple from her sister and her two daughters, and another from Eddie. Rather than deal with any of them right then, she decided to wait until she was back home.

The drive out to the ocean had passed in a haze; she'd badly needed to get away. She hadn't reached any earth-shattering decisions, nor did she have clarity on how best to proceed with Heath and his family. The wasplike sting of Michael's determination to never accept her was a constant reminder of what the future would be like between him and his sons. The one positive that came with their meeting was the assurance that she had done what she could to heal the rift between their families.

As she walked into The Heritage from the basement parking garage, she found Carrie at her desk. When her niece saw Julia, she leaped from her chair and raced around to hug her, as if Julia had been away far longer than those three full days.

"Aunt Julia, you're back!" she cried.

Julia returned the hug. "Did anything happen I should know about?" she asked. Carrie was always full of information.

"How can you ask me that, Aunt Julia? Heath has hardly been himself since you've been gone," Carrie said. "I certainly hope you're going to put that poor man out of his misery."

"I'll let him know I'm back right away."

"Good. I don't think Hillary would be able to hold him back another day from setting out to find you."

"They're talking?"

Carrie nodded. "Every day, and more than once, I suspect. Heath met with both Hillary and Marie one night and treated them to dinner. He invited me, too, but I was with Eric."

Julia grinned, pleased to know the relationship between her niece and Eric seemed to be blossoming. Once she spoke to Heath, she'd find out more about what happened between him and her daughters. Hillary and Marie agreeing to have dinner with him was a positive sign and instantly cheered her. Hearing this gave her hope. Fragile as it was, still it burned inside her and lightened the burden she carried.

Once back in her condo, Julia unpacked her suitcase, set a load of wash going, and then called Heath.

He answered on the first ring. "Julia? Thank God. Where are you?"

"I'm here. I'm home."

"I'll be right there." The line was immediately disconnected.

By the time she got to the front door, Heath was stepping off the elevator. He waited until they were inside the condo and the door closed before he brought her into his arms and kissed her. His mouth nearly slammed against hers, as if he'd been dying without her. She tasted his hunger, his worries, his need to protect and shelter her from the wounds his son had inflicted. After several passionate kisses, his large hands framed her face, and he looked into her eyes before touching his forehead to hers and taking in several ragged breaths.

"I nearly went crazy when I heard you'd left."

"I should have—"

"No," he stopped her, and then, as if he couldn't help himself, he kissed her again and again.

Wrapped in his arms, she felt his love surround her, and in that instant she knew he was her heart and soul, and at the same time, she was his. They were meant to be together.

As her father had reminded her countless times: *It's better this way*. She wouldn't have believed it when she'd signed the legal document that had ended her marriage to Eddie. Brokenhearted as she'd been, she'd found herself unable to see past the blinding pain of loss. All she could see were the empty years ahead without the man she had thought she'd grow old with. The man she'd loved.

"I'm sorry," he whispered.

She smiled and gently kissed him before leading him into her kitchen, where she made them each coffee.

Heath sat at her kitchen table and held the mug between his hands. Julia sat across from him. He stretched out his arm and gripped hold of her fingers with his own. "I talked to Michael, and Julia, I am so, so sorry for the things my son said."

"You don't need to apologize, Heath, it wasn't you."

"I was sick at heart when he mentioned you'd gone to his office. Why didn't you tell me that was what you'd planned?"

In hindsight, she should have. "Because I knew you would try to talk me out of it."

He seemed to weigh her words. "You're right, I probably would have. Why did you think going to my son was necessary?"

"I had to try to make peace. I'd hoped if I apologized for my part in all this, we might be able to move past the tension between your sons and me. I knew it would be too much to ask Michael and Adam to become friends with my girls, but I'd sincerely hoped things could change with me and them." It hurt that her attempt had failed; she so wanted matters to be different. She hated that loving Heath would risk his relationship with his children. She couldn't bear it if it did.

"I love you all the more for trying, Julia. In time, I have to believe my sons will come around."

"Carrie mentioned that you went to dinner with Hillary and Marie?" This was a big encouragement.

"Hillary and I had a couple conversations while I was in the hospital. It was a rough start, but she recognized how important you are to me and was willing to listen. She reminds me a lot of you. She might be stubborn like her father, but she was willing to listen and willing to fill me in on a few details I didn't know. Your daughters have your back, Julia. Once they understood how precious you are to me, they were both willing to give me the benefit of the doubt."

The fact that her daughters were supportive of Heath being a part of her life meant the world to Julia.

Heath's eyes grew sad and weary. "I can only pray that one

day Michael and Adam will realize all you mean to me and accept that nothing is ever going to change the way I feel about you."

Julia bowed her head, fearing that might now be impossible.

"I've made a lot of mistakes in my life, but, Julia, you aren't one of them."

"We all made mistakes, Heath, you can't beat yourself up over the past. We have to let go of the things we cannot change and move forward."

"I've been thinking about when Lee decided she no longer wanted to be married to me." He paused and looked past her, as if he found it difficult to continue. "I let Lee have her way," he continued. "We'd grown apart and had different interests. When she decided she wanted to learn to play golf and signed up for lessons with Edward, I didn't give it a second thought. She wanted me to join her, and I refused. In fact, I encouraged her, so she could go out on the course with her friends. I had no interest in playing myself. She didn't want to sail with me, so why should I make the effort to take golf lessons with her? How different our lives would be if I'd agreed."

"Eddie gave lessons to countless women through the years. I don't see what you did that was so wrong."

"Don't you see?" he asked. "I figured, fine, she wanted out, then I wasn't about to fight her. If we split, I didn't feel it would have a negative effect on the boys, who were on their own by that time."

Julia knew what he was saying, as she felt the same thing when it came to Hillary and Marie. Their daughters had been in college, about to start their own lives. While she didn't want the divorce, and fought to save her marriage, deep down she felt her daughters would adjust without serious emotional consequences. Little did she understand what the divorce would do to their relationship with their father.

"Michael and Adam also, to some extent, needed someone to blame," Heath continued.

Julia had never thought of it in those terms. She realized Hillary and Marie had probably felt the same way.

"Michael had no idea Lee had sent you those distasteful text messages. If he did, he conveniently forgot about them. All he could see was the loss of his family as he knew it, and he found it easy to blame you for the ones you sent Lee. That gave him all the incentive he needed to focus his anger on you."

"And Hillary and Marie . . ." She had never thought of her daughters' anger toward their father in those terms. It embarrassed her that Heath knew about her part in this fiasco. But still better that he recognized her own role in this mess.

"Yes? What about them?" he prompted, when she didn't finish.

"They were hurt and angry at their father. He became the focus of their resentment. They saw my pain and were helpless to ease it. Deep down, I think they even might have believed their anger would somehow manipulate him to leave Laura and come back to me. Even as young adults, they wanted their family to remain intact."

"That sounds logical."

While Julia had been at the beach, her thoughts had drifted toward Hillary and the wedding. For weeks she'd held on to the hope that their daughter's marriage would be the bridge to bring her girls and their father back together. She'd done all she could to facilitate that happening, to no avail.

Instead, Hillary's engagement had lit off a series of pipe bombs. Her ex-husband's refusal to work toward reconciliation with small steps had led to one emotional explosion after another. Instead of easing them toward forgiveness, his attempts at manipulation had stoked the fires of their discontent and bitterness.

Julia no longer believed Eddie was capable of understanding their daughters' sense of pain and loss. She didn't blame him completely, because she hadn't truly accepted it herself until now, when she could see that their anger was as deep as Michael's was toward her.

Gently squeezing Heath's hand, Julia asked, "Do you think there's any way Michael and Adam will ever accept me?"

Heath shook his head. "I don't know. I wish I could look into the future and reassure you that sometime down the road our families will come together without all this anger and resentment. Unfortunately, I don't have a crystal ball."

"I know."

"I will tell you that no matter how my children feel, I am not losing you."

She closed her eyes, letting the love she felt for this man fall over her like a protective shield.

"Please tell me that while you were at the ocean, thinking over everything, you reached the same conclusion, because, Julia, I'm telling you right now, I will fight for you. When my marriage fell apart, I let it, but I won't make that mistake with us."

She had reached that same decision. While it was painful to accept that she might never have a relationship with Heath's sons, she would have him, and he was more than enough.

"I'm yours, my love."

His relief was obvious.

The doorbell rang and Heath looked to Julia. "Are you expecting anyone?"

She shook her head. They both rose to their feet, and Heath moved into the living room while she went to answer the doorbell.

As soon as the door opened, Eddie stormed into the room like an avenging angel. When he saw Heath he nearly exploded.

"Get out of my way." With his hands knotted into fists, he raced toward Heath, shoving hard against Heath's chest with both hands.

Shocked, Heath stumbled backward and fell against the sofa.

"Eddie?" Julia yelled. He was out of control.

He whirled around to face her. "Is it true?" he demanded.

"Is what true?" She didn't have a clue what he was talking about. "Eddie, for the love of heaven, what has gotten into you?"

"If you'd listened to the voicemail I sent, you'd know."

"I was away. What happened? What's wrong?"

Eddie's heated gaze remained locked on Heath. "Hillary asked Heath to escort her down the aisle."

Chapter 25

"What?" Julia said, too stunned to do anything more than look at Heath.

"Don't tell me you didn't know?"

"I didn't, Eddie, I swear."

"I don't believe you. Not for a minute. No doubt you put Hillary up to this—"

"That's enough," Heath said, cutting Eddie off. He stood protectively in front of Julia.

Heath's protective stance seemed to provoke Eddie even more as he continued to lambast her until Heath stepped forward, narrowing the distance between them. Eddie shoved him again, and to his credit, Heath didn't retaliate. He didn't defend himself, although Julia could see how much restraint it demanded on his part.

Eventually, Eddie said everything he intended, mixed in with swear words she had never heard from him while they were married. The shock of his attack left her badly shaken.

The silence, once Eddie slammed out of the condo, vibrated through her like a sonic boom.

"Well," she said, exhaling slowly. "That was . . . unexpected." Finding the best way to describe his interruption escaped her. Now that he was gone, she felt the sudden need to sit down. Heath joined her.

Every time Julia thought the situation between Heath's family and her own couldn't get worse, it invariably did. Eddie shoving Heath and yelling at her had been a nightmare. She would be forever grateful that Heath had kept a level head. It would have been easy to see the fight escalate to an all-out brawl.

"Did Hillary actually ask you to escort her down the aisle? You, instead of her father . . ." This was beyond anything she would have expected from her daughter. A shock. Then again, that must have been her daughter's game plan. Her goal was to use Heath to get to her father. Her heart ached at the extremes Hillary was willing to go to to punish Eddie. It deeply saddened her.

Heath reached for her hand and captured it between his own. "While we were at dinner the wedding came up. When Hillary talked about the ceremony and me taking the place of her father, I thought she was kidding. I brushed it off as an ill-advised joke. I don't believe that's what she wants. This is a ploy to get back at her father, and a foolish one at that."

Julia squeezed his hand, regretting that Hillary had put Heath in such an uncomfortable position. She wished her daughter hadn't used Heath to manipulate her father. The situation between Eddie and the girls was worse than ever because she had.

"Your daughters are a reflection of you, Julia," he continued. "The interactions we've had have given me an appreciation of the two of them. They both are fun, and thoughtful, and smart, and so much like their mother that it was easy to share my heart with them. That said I know you would never pit your daughters against Eddie.

"Hillary and Marie know how deeply I love you; they both said what they wanted most for you was to be happy. I promised I would do everything in my power to make sure you were."

"You do make me happy, Heath, more than you'll ever know."

He hugged her close and she relaxed against him.

"I need to talk to my daughter." If Hillary had been looking to get a reaction out of her father, then her plan had worked in spades.

"Talking this out with her is a good idea," Heath agreed.

The opportunity came the following afternoon. Julia sent Hillary a text to tell her she was back in Seattle and then added that she wanted to see her.

Hillary arrived still in her work clothes. She hugged Julia and asked about her time at the beach. While Julia brewed tea, they exchanged small talk. Bringing the tea into the living area, she set the tray down on the table and sat across from Hillary.

"How are the wedding plans coming along?" she asked, as she poured them each a steaming cup of tea.

Hillary stared down at the tea and then slowly raised her eyes to her mother. "What's up?" she asked.

"Why does anything have to be up?"

"Tea. You only serve tea when we're about to have a serious discussion."

Julia leaned back against the sofa and smiled to herself, surprised she hadn't recognized this in herself. It was her tell.

"Yes, well, this is an important matter. I heard you asked Heath to be part of the wedding party in a role that traditionally belongs to your father. Heath assumed you were joking."

"I sort of was, but why not, Mom?" Hillary asked. "The two of you are together now. Since I've gotten to know him, I've come to admire Heath. If Dad doesn't want a relationship with me, then I'm not going to spend the rest of my life pining after him."

"Oh honey, you're going about this all wrong. Your father is badly hurt that you don't want him with you. I'd only been back to Seattle two seconds when he thundered in here with the assumption I knew about this. Heath was here also, and as you might imagine, there was a huge blowup between them. If Heath hadn't kept his cool, it could easily have turned into a brawl."

Hillary had the good grace to look stunned. "Oh no." She covered her mouth with both hands. "Marie must have told Dad. I'm sorry, Mom, I never meant for Dad to know or put Heath in that position."

"What did you expect would happen?"

She shrugged. "I don't know . . . I certainly didn't think Dad would confront him."

"You had to realize how deeply this would hurt your father." Hillary couldn't deny the thought hadn't gone through her mind.

Hillary hung her head. "Even if Heath knew I was only partially serious, he made sure I understood it wasn't his place. It should never have gone any further. I don't know what Marie was thinking by mentioning it to Dad."

Marie had a lot of explaining to do. "Then what do you suppose prompted Marie to tell your father?" While grateful Hillary hadn't purposely set out to humiliate her father, she was curious what had led her younger daughter to tell Eddie.

Hillary reached for the china cup—Julia always served tea in her chinaware—and Julia noticed how her daughter's hand gently shook.

"Marie was terribly upset. We both were."

"What happened?"

Hillary stared down at the tea. "He showed up at my apartment and told me he had paid for the wedding dress. I thanked him and made sure he accepted the fact that he couldn't buy my favor."

"You didn't return the dress, did you?"

She shook her head. "No. I love that dress and was grateful Dad did what he did. I told him I appreciated the gesture, but I wanted to be sure he realized where I stand."

"How did he react?"

"He said he loved me and was sorry for the way things were between us."

This was progress, although she had a terrible feeling Eddie hadn't learned his lesson. He couldn't buy his daughters' favors or manipulate them, either.

"I told Dad I loved him, and how badly I wanted things to go back to the way they once were."

"And then?" Julia asked, knowing at some point the conversation had gone off course.

"I admitted how much I've missed having a father," Hillary said, and her voice was rife with pain.

"Oh sweetie, I know you have. And I know your father deeply misses having you and Marie in his life."

"At that point I started to feel hopeful. Dad asked to meet Blake and suggested we all go to dinner. Then I asked if he meant to include Laura, and you can guess what he said."

Indeed, she could. It seemed Eddie would never learn. "I can."

"He made it abundantly clear he and Laura are a team. She's his wife and belongs at his side. It was all the evidence I needed to confirm, once again, he loves Laura more than he does either Marie or me." Tears floated in Hillary eyes.

"Yes, he does love Laura, but you need to understand that the love your father feels for you and Marie isn't the same as what he feels for Laura."

Hillary smeared the tears across her cheek as she straightened. "I wish I could believe that, Mom. I really do, and I would if Dad didn't continually put Laura above Marie and me. I'd hoped we would be able to put the past behind us, and then it happened, the way it always does with Dad."

"What did he do now?" she asked, her patience at an end.

"Dad seemed to think that because he paid the six-hundred-dollar difference in the wedding dress, that gave him the right to tell me how the wedding would go."

"You mean with Laura?"

"Laura was part of it for sure. I mean, it's like the two of them are inseparable. Making sure I knew she would be included in the wedding was only part of his overall plan."

This was beginning to sound even worse than Julia had imagined.

"Dad had a seating plan drawn up to show me, with a lot of his golfing friends included. Blake and I have a limited budget, and I could see that Dad planned to use the wedding to boost his ego with his cronies. No way am I including all these extra friends of his and Laura's. Okay, to be fair, Dad offered to chip in for the added expense, but this is my and Blake's wedding."

Julia hardly knew what to say.

"Oh, that's not all," Hillary continued. "He spoke with someone, I think it must have been a pastor—not Pastor Rick, that's for sure. Dad went to great lengths to explain how these things work when the bride's parents are no longer married. He had the church pews drawn with little spaces for each of the families."

"Did you consider he was only trying to be helpful?"

"Mom, no. He was manipulating me again, or trying to. It wasn't only the seating chart for the wedding, either. He had another one for the reception, and the crazy part is he excluded Heath from both charts. And this is the killer. He included Michael and Adam; like I'd ever consider them as guests. Not a chance."

"Oh boy," Julia said and expelled a sigh.

"When I asked him about Heath, he said inviting him would be uncomfortable for Laura."

Clearly Eddie hadn't given a thought to her own comfort, Julia mused.

"That was when I lost it. I mean, I tried to hold on to my cool, I really did. I told Dad exactly what I thought about his seating chart and where he should put it and then I asked him to leave."

Julia felt terrible for Hillary, and Eddie, who couldn't seem to do anything right when it came to his daughters. She wanted to shake him, only she doubted it would do any good.

"I called Marie and told her what happened, and she was as angry as I was. I didn't know she called Dad; she must have. I never meant for Heath to get mixed up in this. It was that night that we went to dinner with Heath and the argument with Dad was fresh on my mind. I shouldn't have said anything. I regret it now."

Hillary left soon afterward, and Julia sat in silence, debating how best to respond or even if she should. She had never wanted to be put in this position, even though Eddie had repeatedly thrust her into the space between him and their daughters.

Her thoughts were heavy, and she almost didn't hear the phone ring. She reached for it and noticed it was from a number she didn't recognize. Thinking it might be one of those pesky robocalls, she ignored it until, a few minutes later, the same number called again.

"Hello," she answered tentatively.

"Julia?"

It was a voice she didn't recognize.

"This is Laura, Edward's wife . . ."

Julia gasped, completely taken aback to hear from the other woman.

"I'm sorry to ask this . . . Would it be possible for the two of us to meet and talk?"

Julia was stunned speechless. This was the very woman who had turned her life upside down. The woman who had destroyed her marriage and nearly destroyed her. The woman who had taunted and ridiculed her.

When she didn't immediately respond, Laura added, "I wouldn't ask if it wasn't important."

"Does Eddie know you're calling me?"

She hesitated. "No, and he wouldn't like it if he did know."

Julia had no desire to meet Laura. None whatsoever. In all the years since the affair, followed by the divorce, she had seen the woman only once, and then from a distance. She didn't want to have anything to do with her, and it hit her hard, right between the eyes.

In that moment, Julia realized she was more like Hillary and Marie than she'd ever realized. She had encouraged her children to resolve their anger, when clearly she was holding on to some of her own.

"All right," she said, and was surprised how hard it was to get the words out.

Chapter 26

Julia wasn't sure what she should wear to meet Eddie's wife. Before she left, she changed clothes three times. The first outfit she chose was a business suit, one she wore into the office when meeting an important client. Checking her reflection, she quickly changed clothes. Laura wasn't anyone important to her, nor was she a client.

Next, she tried an expensive pair of designer jeans and a blue cashmere sweater. Standing in front of the mirror to assess herself, she decided the outfit screamed success, as if she was hoping to impress Laura with how well-off she was. Like she cared how Laura viewed her. In the end she went with a simple pair of black slacks and a soft blue top. Simple. Classy. The perfect look for what she intended.

Laura had suggested they not mention the meeting to their children or to their partners. Julia wasn't sure what to make of the request, but reluctantly agreed. If she did happen to mention it to Heath, she wasn't sure what he'd say.

When Julia arrived at the Starbucks near Pacific Place, an upscale mall in downtown Seattle a short walking distance from The Heritage, Laura was sitting at a table by the window. Julia bought a cup of coffee and confidently approached the other woman. Or what she hoped looked like confidence.

Laura offered her a weak smile. Her gaze bounced to her coffee and back, and Julia could see she was nervous. Well, that made two of them.

Pulling out the chair, she sat and waited for Laura to speak. The other woman was the one who had asked for this meeting. Julia was patient and had no intention of initiating the conversation.

Eddie's wife paused for several uncomfortable seconds before removing her focus from her coffee to look at Julia.

"Thank you for meeting me."

She nodded, still waiting. If she was silent long enough, she figured Laura would eventually state her purpose.

"I know I was the last person you ever expected to hear from."

Since it was true, she nodded in agreement. Laura's call had stunned her, and she'd spent a sleepless night wondering what the other woman could possibly want.

"I imagine this is as uncomfortable for you as it is for me."

If she was looking to find mutual ground, then this was about as mutual as it was going to get. Julia didn't mean to be rude or standoffish; this woman wasn't someone she would ever consider a friend. She wished Laura would get to the point.

"I never thought I'd do anything like this," she said, breathing out a trembling sigh.

"Laura, I get that you're uncomfortable. I'd appreciate it if you would tell me why you wanted us to meet."

She stiffened and sat up straighter. "It's about Edward."

Julia was tempted to tell Laura that Eddie was her problem now, but held her tongue.

She exhaled slowly. "Hillary's wedding is tearing him apart. He'd hoped Hillary getting married would finally bring them all together again."

Julia had held high hopes for that herself.

"When Marie told him that Hillary had asked Heath instead of her father to escort her down the aisle, he lost it. I've never seen him that upset."

Julia knew exactly how upset he'd gotten. "Did you know that he came to me and basically attacked Heath?"

Lowering her head, Laura said, "I didn't . . . I'm sorry, although I don't know what I could have done. He left the house and didn't tell me where he was going. Seeing how angry he was, I didn't ask . . . I realize now I should have. When he returned, he went into the bedroom. I went to check on him, and, Julia, I found him with his face in his hands, weeping." Tears gathered in her own eyes. "I've never known Edward to cry. It . . . It broke my heart, and I knew I had to do something to fix this if I could."

Julia could identify. If Heath were emotionally hurting, she would do whatever she could to ease his pain.

"The problem is Eddie," Julia said, feeling bad for her ex-husband. "When it comes to the girls, he can't seem to do anything right. He might be a whiz on the golf course, but with his daughters, he's consistently stuck in the sand trap."

"It's because of me, isn't it?" Laura asked.

That seemed fairly obvious, but Julia refrained from saying

so. "The crux of the problem is his attempts to manipulate Hillary by insisting you attend the wedding and be part of it. And that's not all. Did you know he put together a seating chart for the wedding and the reception and gave it to Hillary along with a list of his buddies he wanted to invite? A chart which included you, Michael, and Adam. But not Heath, because he didn't want to make you uncomfortable."

Surprise flashed in her eyes. "He did what?"

"He seemed to believe the money he invested in Hillary's wedding dress entitled him to make his wishes known on how he wanted the ceremony to go. From what Hillary said, I'm surprised he didn't decide to write her vows along with everything else. He did offer to pay the extra for his friends, but it was too little too late, as far as Hillary was concerned."

Laura lowered her head and closed her eyes. "I'll talk to him."

"It's too late. The damage is done."

Laura looked up then and blinked a couple times, as if trying to hold everything inside. "Please tell Hillary I will stay away from the wedding if she'll allow her father to be part of her day. It means the world to him. Edward misses his daughters so much. I'll do whatever it takes to make things right for Edward and his girls."

Julia sincerely appreciated the effort. At this point, she didn't know what either of them could possibly do, and said so.

"Do Hillary and Marie hate me that badly?" Laura asked, turning her hands over, palms up, on the tabletop.

Julia decided to share the insight she'd had with Heath. "To the girls, our family as they once knew it was torn apart. I know Eddie felt, as I did, the girls were young adults, ready to start their own lives, and the divorce wouldn't necessarily negatively affect them. To complicate everything, the anger we all felt toward one another brewed in our children."

Laura nodded. "Yes, it was the same with Heath and me. Both boys were already on their own and it seemed if we were going to split, that was the time."

"Exactly, only we were both wrong."

"How do you mean?"

"I mean the children on both sides of this divorce were badly hurt. Not knowing what to do with that pain, they looked for someone to blame. The fight at Lake Sammamish certainly didn't help."

From the way her mouth twisted, Laura got it. "In the case of your girls, that someone was me?"

"Sending me those text messages escalated matters, and me returning with ones of my own was equally inflammatory."

Laura's face fell, and it looked once again as if she was close to breaking into tears. "I . . . I should never have sent those."

"I have my share of regrets, too." A minute or longer passed before she spoke again. "Did you know I tried to talk to Michael?" Julia asked.

Again, Laura looked taken aback. "You did? When?"

"Last week. I showed up at his office unannounced. I wanted to talk to Adam, but he sent Michael to meet me instead."

"How did it go?"

"Badly. If my girls were looking for someone to blame, they chose you. Your sons apparently blame me."

"You?"

"They told Heath if he wanted a relationship with me to keep them out of it. Like Hillary and Marie with you, Michael and Adam would prefer there be no contact between them and me."

"I'm sorry," Laura whispered. "I'm so sorry."

Julia nodded silently, accepting her apology.

"I know my boys have negative feelings toward your daughters."

Remembering the scene in the hospital, Julia said, "That's putting it mildly."

Laura looked genuinely miserable. "How did everything get so twisted and unpleasant?"

Julia was tempted to remind this woman it had started when she sought Eddie out for private golf lessons. However, mentioning it wouldn't help either of them. The past was behind them. What they needed now was a plan to make things right for all involved, and that appeared to be an insurmountable task.

Ever hopeful, Laura turned her focus on Julia. "Do you think it would help if you told Hillary I've agreed to not attend the wedding?"

"Probably not, and I'll tell you why. Eddie won't stand for it. He'll insist you be part of the wedding or he won't go, and then we're back right where we started."

"What could I have done differently?" Laura asked.

On hearing the question, Julia thought Laura couldn't possibly be serious. For the six years that the other woman had been married to Eddie, not once had she made a single effort to connect with Hillary and Marie. After this meeting, Julia was convinced there would be a spiritual award awaiting her for holding back her opinion.

"It would have helped if you had made an effort with the girls," she suggested. She had tried with Michael, and while the results weren't what she'd wanted, at least she'd made the effort. Given the chance, she'd try again.

"Yes . . . I suppose, only the girls have made it abundantly clear they wanted nothing to do with me. I'm the enemy."

"And they see you as heartless, caring nothing for them, because you haven't done anything to prove otherwise."

Laura agreed. "It's a weak excuse, but no one likes to be rejected."

"True. However, when you married Eddie, you married his children right along with him. If you tried, even now, I believe in time Hillary and Marie would come to accept you."

"That isn't going to happen in a few months, though."

"Maybe. Maybe not. All I can say is that it's never too late to start."

Laura looked completely clueless. "Where do you suggest I begin?"

Julia shrugged, unsure herself. "A card or a text congratulating Hillary and Blake on their engagement. Something small. I never could get Eddie to start with baby steps. I'm hoping you can. With him, it was all or nothing, and his tactics failed miserably."

Laura reached for her phone. "I'll do it. I'll do anything to clear the way for Eddie to have a relationship with his children, especially after finding him in tears."

"Don't expect Hillary to respond. Give it a day or two and try again. Perhaps suggest a florist. I know she and Blake have been searching for one and would appreciate the help."

Laura nodded eagerly. "My cousin has a flower shop, and I know she'd give Hillary a discount."

"That's a great start."

Laura released a deep sigh. "Julia," she said, and her eyes were sincere. "Thank you."

"You're welcome." To her surprise, she didn't choke on the words.

Laura hesitated, as if uncertain. "Would you mind if we meet again?"

Should she? It didn't take Julia long to see they had a far better chance of bringing all their loved ones together if they were on the same page.

"I think that might be a good idea," she said, and hoped she wasn't making a big mistake.

Chapter 27

"You're meeting with who?" Amanda demanded, as she carried a cup of coffee to Julia.

"You heard me."

"This is a joke, right?" Her sister sat down across the kitchen table from Julia and stared at her with her mouth sagging open. "You do remember this is the very woman who tore your marriage apart, right?"

"As horrible as it sounds, Laura may be the only option I have to move forward." Julia could hold on to the pain or she could let it go; she chose healing.

She needed to tell someone she'd been meeting with Heath's ex-wife. Her sister seemed the most logical person, and, frankly, she was surprised by Amanda's reaction. Perhaps she shouldn't be, remembering how conflicted she'd felt the first time Laura called.

"I didn't start out intending to have anything to do with her. Then, once we got past the awkwardness of the situation, I wasn't as put off as I assumed I would be."

Shaking her head, Amanda leaned forward and braced her elbows on the table. "You better start at the beginning. She contacted you?"

"Yes, and as hard as it is to admit, Laura did it for all the right reasons. She wants me to help her find a way for Eddie to reconcile with the girls." Seeing how badly her ex-husband had botched every attempt, it was going to take some creative thinking on their part.

Amanda rolled her eyes. "And how's that working for you?"

Julia wasn't sure how best to answer. "We've discussed a few ideas." They were making headway and taking it one step at a time.

"Oh, do tell."

"When did you become such a skeptic?" Julia teased. "Laura and I are joining forces to work toward a solution. Our goal is to have everything resolved before the wedding. We're never going to pal around together or be the best of friends. But I've learned we don't have to be enemies, either."

"Good luck with that, big sister. Eddie can't seem to keep his foot out of his mouth. How can you be sure anything the two of you do is going to help matters? The wedding is less than two months away."

Amanda knew Julia's ex-husband's last attempt to resolve matters with Hillary had caused far more damage than anything he'd done in the last six years since the divorce.

"I know it's going to be tricky to pull this off." Julia knew better than anyone how difficult this would be, and on such a short time schedule.

"That's an understatement if I've ever heard one."

"I know."

Amanda reached for her coffee and leaned back in her chair. "Does Heath know you're meeting with his ex?"

This was the negative aspect of her newfound relationship with Laura. "No, not yet."

Amanda arched her delicately shaped brows halfway to her hairline. "Do you think it's wise to keep him in the dark?"

Julia shrugged. "I don't know. I guess time will tell." This was the one drawback that she could see. Once Eddie and Heath learned what the two women were planning, it could blow up in their faces. Laura was as aware of this as Julia was; still, neither was willing to give up.

"I suggest you tell him, and the sooner, the better," Amanda advised. "Keeping it a secret is risking more than you should. Besides, did you ever consider that Heath might have a few insights of his own?"

Julia hadn't. Sipping her coffee, she mulled over her sister's words. "You're right, he needs to know."

The opportunity came sooner than she expected. Sooner than she was prepared for. They were sitting in the Busy Bean, enjoying a scone and coffee, following their morning workout.

"I stopped by the other day and you were out."

"Which day?" She well knew which one, and hedged for time to decide how best to drop this bomb in his lap.

He told her. "I thought you decided to step back from work."

Her hand cradled the disposable coffee cup a bit harder than necessary, causing the top to spring free. She reached for it and replaced the lid, all while avoiding eye contact. "I wasn't at the office."

He studied her, and his gaze slowly narrowed. "Can you tell me why you look incredibly guilty? Julia?" He looked away and stiffened, his features tightening with doubt. "You're making me nervous . . ."

She covered his hand with hers, needing to reassure him. Naturally, her meeting another man would be his first thought. It would be hers, in light of how their spouses had betrayed them with an affair. "I have my faults, Heath. However, I would never cheat on you. That is one promise I can categorically make."

He instantly relaxed. "Then why did you look like a kid caught with her hand in the cookie jar? Something's up, and apparently, whatever it is, you'd rather I not know."

"True enough," she admitted. "Amanda suggested it would be better if I told you, and I agree."

"Well, then perhaps you should."

Shifting uneasily in the chair, she drew in a deep breath. "I've been in contact with Laura."

His eyes widened with surprise. "My ex-wife?"

She nodded.

"Why? Hasn't she brought enough pain into your life?"

She found it heartwarming that he immediately mentioned her loss and not his own. It was almost verbatim what Amanda had asked.

"I'll admit the first couple times we talked it was uncomfortable, but it's gotten easier."

"You mean to say you've been meeting on a regular basis. What the hell for?"

He wasn't taking to this the way she'd hoped.

"Laura's concerned about Eddie and his relationship with the girls."

"Eddie," he repeated, as if even the name of her ex put a bad taste in his mouth. "He made his own bed and he can lie in it. You've done enough for him, far more than he deserves."

She didn't disagree. "True enough. He's put me in the middle, and I've repeatedly told him I wasn't comfortable standing between him and our daughters."

"Then why are you doing this?"

"It's not for him, Heath, it's for Hillary and Marie. As angry and upset as they are with their father, they continue to love him and need him. Can you imagine how difficult it would be for you if Michael and Adam wanted nothing more to do with you because of me? Can you imagine how miserable that would make you? It's a step in the right direction and might lead to a time when your sons are comfortable with me."

He had the good grace to take her words to heart. "I would do anything to make that happen."

"Eddie would, too, only his efforts haven't helped the situation. His pride has blinded him. He's eager, and thoughtless, and I'm convinced he doesn't mean to be. He so badly wants his daughters to accept Laura. Even his ridiculous taking over of the wedding was his misguided attempt to help. He actually thought his seating plan was offering a solution to a delicate situation." It was everything else he wanted that had upset Hillary, and rightly so.

"The girls are dead set against having anything to do with Lee," Heath commented, and unfortunately, he was right.

However, Laura had been making inroads. "Don't be so sure. Laura and I have been working on a few baby steps with the girls. She's been texting them with little things."

"Such as?"

"Quotes and little jokes, and while the girls haven't responded, they haven't blocked her, either."

"You've been advising Lee?"

Julia nodded.

Heath looked as if he disapproved. "Do the girls know about your involvement in this little plan of yours?"

"Heavens, no."

"That's what I thought."

They had made progress, though, and she was pleased by the small chips in the concrete wall her daughters had built up against the other woman. "Laura recommended her cousin who owns a florist shop to Hillary. Hillary still doesn't have the florist booked for the wedding, so I suggested it wouldn't do any harm to check it out, and even went with her when Blake had to cancel at the last minute. The florist specializes in wedding arrangements, and despite Hillary's willingness to dismiss the woman out of hand, she was impressed."

"Is she going with her?"

"I don't know. I've leaving that up to my daughter and Blake."

Heath didn't appear convinced. "You are playing a dangerous game, my love."

"I know, but one that's necessary for my girls and for their father, if Eddie's ever going to have a relationship with them again. It's not for him as much as it is for Hillary and Marie."

He accepted her decision, but she could see that he wasn't completely on board. Not that she blamed him. Heath had no reason to champion Eddie, although he seemed to understand why she felt joining forces with Laura would help.

She gave him a few minutes to process and then added, "No one is more surprised than me to learn that Laura and I have more in common than you would assume."

Heath locked eyes with her. "I doubt that."

"We both love the same men."

He snickered softly. "All right, I'll concede that point."

"We both want what's best for our children."

Heath hesitated. "Is this your way of telling me you want to get our children together and resolve their dislike of each other?"

"It would be ideal, if possible."

"Now you're really taking on more than either of you can handle."

"Oh ye of little faith. Perhaps individually it would be, but working together, Laura and I see potential for healing all around."

"I wonder if it's possible," Heath whispered.

"If we are going to stay together—"

"And we are," he inserted.

"Yes, we are," she agreed. "Then I would sincerely hope that I could at least be on friendly terms with your sons. If Adam accepts me, then I think in time Michael will, too."

Heath shook his head. "I'd like that, Julia. I haven't said much because I knew it would upset you. Since Michael and Adam found out about the two of us, my relationship with them has been strained."

This was what Julia had feared most, and she wished Heath had said something sooner, although she didn't know what she could have done.

"So you see this isn't only about Eddie. Laura and I realize this is for us and all our children. We all have wounds, and some of them cut deep. Until we find a way to heal, they will continue to fester."

Slowly Heath nodded. "I'm surprised at Lee. You said she was the one who contacted you?"

"Yes, and she did it out of love for Eddie."

"And she's willing to help forge a relationship with you and our boys?"

"Yes." That was something else they were working on making right. It wouldn't be easy; it wouldn't be overnight, either. But it was important.

"I'm surprised you're a willing partner in this, especially since Eddie cheated with her."

"Ah, but, Heath, if it hadn't been for Laura marrying Eddie, I would never have met you. To my way of thinking, I have a great deal for which to thank her."

He grinned and leaned close to kiss her cheek. "Leave it to you to find the positive."

"This is something I learned from my father. He was the one who reassured me when life turned bleak and I couldn't see anything good coming out of it. He'd tell me: *It's better this way.*

"Those are the very words I whispered when I signed the divorce papers, and at the time it seemed a stretch. Heath, it was because of that betrayal that I met you, and what we have, what we share, is by far better than anything I ever had with Eddie."

Chapter 28

Heath didn't have high hopes for this idea Julia and Lee had cooked up, but, having nothing better to offer, he went with it. All he could do was hope this fiasco didn't explode back at them.

Michael and Adam had been cool toward Heath ever since they'd learned he was unwilling to let Julia go. He'd left no doubt about his feelings for her. His sons had let it be known in subtle and not-so-subtle ways that they strongly disapproved. They had repeatedly warned Heath he was setting himself up for a world of hurt with his involvement with *that woman*. Heath assured them he knew what he was doing, and he had the distinct impression they viewed him as an old fool. He very well might be an old fool, but he was a happy one.

His doorbell rang and, squaring his shoulders, he opened it

to Michael and Adam. He'd invited his boys to watch the Seahawks play an away game. When he'd first mentioned it, they'd had a dozen excuses why they couldn't join him. For the last month they had begged off several of his invitations. He'd asked again, and his voice must have relayed more than his words, because both boys agreed to spend Sunday afternoon with him.

"Michael. Adam." He gave them each a bro hug, slapping their backs before leading them into the living room. He had beer out, plus a bowl of peanuts and a few other snacks.

"So, Dad, what do you think the Hawks' chances are against the 49ers?"

"Good, if the offensive line can protect Russell Wilson," he said. They all sat down together, and the boys each reached for a beer. They shared a love of football, and until recently had watched most of the Seahawks games together. It was these special times with his sons that Heath treasured most. His sincere hope was that at the end of today, they would still want to spend time with him.

Ten minutes before the game started, as casually as he could manage, he said, "I've invited—"

"Not Julia?" Michael snapped.

"Dad, if she comes, then Michael and I will leave."

"If you'd let me finish," he said, stabbing them with a glare as he swallowed down his irritation.

"Okay, fine. Sorry." It was Adam who spoke.

"I've invited a couple to join us."

"Who?" Michael asked.

"Anyone we know?" Adam added, his tone full of suspicion.

The timing of his question was perfect. No sooner had the

words left his mouth when the doorbell chimed. Heath stood to answer and welcomed Lee and Eddie into the condo. He turned around to see the shocked look that came over his sons' faces as their mother and Eddie walked into the room.

"Mom? Edward?" Michael breathed out, as if he was convinced he was seeing things.

"Edward?" Adam didn't seem nearly as surprised to find his mother as he did Eddie.

Lee's hand was linked with Eddie's as she smiled, as if this sort of thing happened every day. "I hope you don't mind that your father invited us to join you."

"You don't like football," Michael reminded her. He looked amazed to see her wearing a Seahawks jersey.

"I enjoy time with family, and if that means watching a football game, then I'm all in."

Except no one was watching the plays on the field. All eyes seemed to be focused on the newly arrived couple.

Finally, it was Michael who spoke. He pointed his finger in a circular motion, taking in Heath and his mom and Eddie. "When did this happen?"

Lee sat next to Michael. "Not long ago. We decided it was time to act like adults. It's been years since we split, and we thought it was silly to hold on to this enmity."

"Wow," Adam whispered. "This is a surprise."

"You never said anything." Michael posed the comment to Heath.

"Yeah, Dad, you might have given us a heads-up about this."

"Maybe," he said, looking to appease them both. There were more surprises to come.

They all turned to the game. Heath wasn't sure anyone paid much attention to the action taking place on the field.

"Heath, is there popcorn?" Lee asked.

"Oops. I forgot that's your weakness. I've got the microwave kind. Will that do?"

"Sure thing."

Heath started toward the kitchen when Michael leaped to his feet. "I'll help." He said this as if it was necessary for two people to microwave popcorn.

As they reached the kitchen, Michael backed Heath against the marble countertop. "What's really happening here?" he demanded. "You're not all chummy with Edward and Mom for nothing."

He knew his son was too smart not to realize something else was afloat. Although he wouldn't openly admit it, he was relieved when Lee moved to join them. "Michael, you'll never guess who got me this Seahawks jersey," she said, tugging the front of it away from her body so he could get a better look at it.

"Santa Claus?" he muttered sarcastically.

"No, a new friend of mine."

"You seem to be making lots of new friends these days."

"New and old friends," Lee said, turning to smile at Heath. "Your father and I were married for a lot of years. Our split was amicable. He's moved on, and so have I; there's no reason for us to remain estranged. Don't you agree?"

Brushing his fingers through his hair, Michael looked decidedly uneasy. "I guess. I thought, you know, that Dad was content to stay out of your life, especially now that you're with Edward."

Lee nodded. "Yes, I suppose we would have both gone our separate ways if it wasn't for Julia coming into his life. That changed everything."

"And I suppose Julia is your newfound friend."

"You just won yourself a Kewpie doll, son. You're smarter than I give you credit for. He got that intelligence from you, Heath," she teased.

Adam joined them, so that the only one keeping track of the game was Eddie. The popcorn started to pop when the doorbell rang a second time. Heath checked his watch and knew it was Julia.

"I'll get that," he said. "Lee, would you mind dealing with the popcorn?"

"Of course."

Heath opened the door to Julia, who looked uncomfortable and wary. While this had been her and Lee's idea, he knew Julia shared his doubts. Heath reached for her hand and gave it a gentle reassuring squeeze. "How's it going?" she whispered.

"About what we expected. It'll be fine," he whispered, although he wasn't sure this was going to end the way they'd all hoped. And this was only the first step in the women's plans for reconciliation.

Putting on a bright smile, Julia headed toward Lee. "Oh good, popcorn."

Putting on a show of affection, Lee hugged Julia. "I understand you all know one another."

Michael glared at his mother and then at Julia. "We've met." His words were clipped and unwelcoming.

Lee's face fell with marked disappointment. "You should

know that over the last couple weeks, Julia and I have gotten to know one another. She's actually quite lovely."

"I don't believe it," Adam said, standing next to his brother. He crossed his arms. The two stood side by side and looked like bouncers guarding the outside of a popular nightclub, their expressions none too friendly.

"Then you'd be wrong," Lee said, glaring at their sons. It appeared to be a practiced look she reserved for when they'd misbehaved as children. "That's quite enough of this foolishness from both of you. Julia and I have set our differences aside, and I expect you to do the same."

"But . . ."

"There are no buts about it. Heath loves Julia, and I heartily approve of their relationship. She's a much better match for your father than I ever was. Furthermore, I refuse to allow you to be unkind or mistreat her. She deserves your respect the same as your father and I do."

"Hey, what about me?" Eddie asked.

"And, of course, Edward," she added. "Sorry, love, I didn't mean to exclude you."

Michael and Adam exchanged looks, as if all this was beyond belief.

"I know this is a lot to take in," Julia said. "Still, we do share something in common."

"It's definitely not affection for your daughters," Michael said under his breath, but loud enough to be sure he was heard.

Julia smiled, and Heath was grateful she didn't take offense. "No, that would be hard for now."

"Now or ever," Michael returned.

"Michael," Heath warned in a low whisper.

"What we share," Julia continued, "is that we both love and care deeply about your father. How crazy is it that we would find each other?"

Heath scooted behind her and wrapped his arms around her waist. He kissed the top of her head. "In case I haven't made it clear, I'm crazy about this woman," he told his sons. "And, given the chance, I know you will come to love her, too."

Julia looked from Michael to Adam. "Would you be willing to give me a chance?" she asked gently.

Michael looked to Lee. "You're sure about this, Mom?"

"Very sure."

Sucking in a deep breath, Michael shrugged. "I'm going to need to think it over. But no matter what I decide, I don't want anything to do with either of your daughters."

Adam agreed. "Ditto for me."

Eric was late, which was a small problem with their relationship. He'd agreed to meet her in the lobby. They'd planned to spend the afternoon biking in Cal Anderson Park in the Capitol Hill area. She didn't need to guess what had held him up. Eric had gotten absorbed in some computer issue with one of his accounts, and time had slipped away before he noticed. He was much better, though, and seemed to look forward to their outings. They'd been on several such adventures over the weeks. At first she was the one who made the suggestions. It was Eric who'd suggested the biking, once he learned she enjoyed riding these special trails around the city.

Rather than call, she decided to collect him herself, otherwise he might easily get absorbed in his work until it was too late. It wouldn't take much for her to fall for this guy. What a contrast from Justin, who didn't seem to find a job necessary. Eric was a workaholic in recovery. Since they'd started seeing each other, he'd been willing to let go of some of the control he held over a few aspects of his business. It was necessary if he planned to have a life outside of his condo. Only last week he hired an executive assistant and took on a CPA full-time to deal with payroll, taxes, and other issues he'd been handling himself, freeing up his time so they could be together more often.

With her bike helmet in hand, Carrie headed to his condo. She paused when she heard voices on the other side of his door. She didn't recognize whomever it was with Eric. What she did discern was that his visitor was upset. His voice was raised and agitated, and he seemed to be pacing the room, because the volume grew louder then faded.

She hesitated before knocking, unsure she should interrupt.

Eric answered the door and looked relieved when he saw her.

"Should I come back later?" she whispered.

"Is that Carrie?" Eric's visitor called out.

Eric turned to answer his friend, bringing Carrie into the room with him. "Carrie, meet my friend Michael."

"We've briefly met," she said, recognizing Michael from the time he signed in to visit Eric.

Michael smiled and nodded at her. "I've heard a lot about you, Carrie. Now that we've met officially, I understand why Eric willingly left this condo. Good work. I was beginning to think my friend had turned into a vampire."

Carrie smiled. "I didn't mean to interrupt your conversation."

"It's fine," Michael said, and seemed to recognize he was holding up their biking adventure.

Eric didn't seem eager to leave, though. "Michael was just telling me about the Seahawks game. It seems his mother and stepfather showed up at Heath's along with Julia."

"Aunt Julia was there?" Carrie was surprised. She hadn't gotten wind of this development, and suspected her cousins hadn't, either.

The grin on Michael's face disappeared. "Julia is your aunt?" He didn't wait for her to respond. "I don't believe this." He slapped his hands against his sides in frustration "There's no escaping this family. I suppose your aunt is the one who got you this cushy job as concierge—"

"Hold on a minute," Eric said, cutting off his friend. "Nobody got Carrie this job, she earned it, and as for it being cushy, I'd like to see you fill in for her for a day and then tell me how easy it is."

Michael's eyes widened, as if Eric's defense of her shocked him.

"And as for escaping this family," Eric continued, "you'd be a better man to accept that you're part of it."

Michael's returning laugh lacked humor. "I don't suppose you've met Carrie's evil cousins?"

"As a matter of fact, I have."

"My cousins aren't evil," Carrie inserted, eager to defend Hillary and Marie. She was about to say more, but Eric stopped her.

Instead, he continued talking to his friend. "You came here this afternoon because your mother asked you to give Julia a chance. You made it sound like it was the worst thing in the world.

"What's the matter with you, Michael? Is it so important to hang on to your resentment that you are unable to move forward? Your dad loves Julia. If you'd ever seen the two of them together, you'd recognize it yourself. You want my advice, then fine, I'll give it to you. Get your head out of your ass, my friend, and man up."

Carrie's mouth gaped open. She'd never heard Eric talk like this or say as much at one time.

Michael appeared equally stunned.

"Furthermore," Eric added, "if you make me choose between our friendship and my relationship with Carrie, you'll find yourself on the losing end."

Michael's stunned look quickly moved to shock. "You can't mean that. We've been friends since grade school. Do you mean to say—"

"Yes."

Michael placed both hands on top of his head, as if he had trouble believing what he was hearing.

"Michael—"

Michael stopped her from continuing by stretching out his arm. "I need to think this through. Eric, you're my best friend and a good judge of character. But this is a lot."

Eric slipped his arm around Carrie's waist. "You know what you need to do," he told Michael.

Michael nodded. "I guess I do."

He left almost immediately. As soon as the door closed, Carrie turned into Eric's arms and kissed him long and hard. Eric kissed her back, and holy cow! They'd shared several kisses by this time. Nothing, however, had been this deep, or probing, or telling. Eric genuinely cared for her. And she for him. Their relationship had just moved to a deeper level, and Carrie couldn't be more pleased.

Chapter 29

Julia feared the ambush tactic wouldn't work with Hillary and Marie. The situation with them and their father was more complex than the antagonism between Julia and Michael and Adam.

Because her daughters knew Julia all too well, she couldn't invite them over and serve tea. That would be a dead giveaway. Laura offered to do whatever she could to help work their plan. Although on board with the idea, Julia was convinced it would be best if she dealt with this part alone. Laura would play a later role. The best way to reach Julia's girls was with honesty and fairness. If everything went as she hoped, then they could all meet with Eddie and Laura later.

She decided to invite her daughters and Carrie to lunch at the Thai restaurant they favored. The girls were happy to agree. A time was set for early Saturday afternoon. Before she left The Heritage, Heath gave her a pep talk and hugged her, lending her his strength and positive thoughts, which she badly needed. Even having prepared how best to appeal to the three, Julia continued to have misgivings. This could all go badly. It could also be a turning point for the two families and work the miracle they needed between Eddie and his daughters.

Julia made sure she arrived first. The server, who recognized her from her many visits, automatically brought her a steaming pot of Jasmine tea while she awaited the others.

"Mom." Hillary and Marie arrived together, and Carrie was only a couple minutes behind.

"What a great idea," Hillary said, as she slid into the booth, making room for her sister and Carrie.

Julia had used the excuse of getting an update on the wedding plans, knowing how eager Hillary was to share the latest news.

No one needed a menu, as they were all familiar with it and had their favorite dishes. "How are all the wedding plans going?" Julia asked, as she served them each from the teapot.

Hillary beamed as she shared the latest update. "Everything is coming together nicely. Blake and I have got the photographer we wanted. Thanks, Mom, she's the best, and way under what we had budgeted."

"My pleasure," Julia said, smiling as she sipped her tea.

"The cake is ordered."

"What about the dinner menu for the reception?" Carrie asked.

"Done. Chicken and salmon are what we could afford, and, of course, there's a vegetarian option."

"What about the flowers?" Julia asked, carefully studying her daughter, wondering what decision she'd made after visiting Laura's cousin's shop.

"Blake and I decided to go with the shop Laura recommended," she said, looking at her sister and Carrie.

"Laura?" Carrie asked, "as in Uncle Eddie's wife? That Laura?"

Hillary nodded. "She's been sending me text messages. I get one nearly every afternoon."

"You, too?" Marie sounded surprised, which told Julia the two sisters hadn't shared the news with each other. This was a little surprising, knowing how close they were.

Hillary nodded. "Mom went with me to the flower shop, which is owned by some relative of Laura's. Her prices were fair, and her work is great. Mom left it up to Blake and me if we went with her or not. It was a tough decision, although Blake seemed to think to refuse the best florist would be silly, especially since she's one we can afford. I agreed with him."

"You actually went with Laura's recommendation?" Marie repeated, as if she found it hard to believe.

Hillary looked a little embarrassed, as if she expected criticism.

"That's wonderful," Julia said, praising her daughter. She didn't want Carrie or Marie to put a damper on what had been a difficult decision for her oldest daughter.

"Wait," Carrie said, looking from Hillary to Marie. She had this wide-eyed, shocked look. "Did I hear you say Laura has been texting you both? When did that start?"

"A couple weeks ago, I guess—why?" Marie replied, with a hint of defensiveness. She chanced a look at her sister. "I didn't know she'd also been sending you texts."

Hillary lifted the fork from the place setting and then set it back down. "When the first one came, and I saw it was from Laura, I was tempted to block her."

"Why didn't you?" Carrie asked.

Hillary looked as if she wasn't sure she knew. "I . . . probably should have. I had Blake read it. He thought it showed effort on Laura's part, and, seeing how bad things are between me and Dad, I let it go."

"Did you answer her?"

"No," Hillary admitted.

"I didn't, either," Marie added. "I assumed it was a one-off thing, you know?"

"That's what I thought," Hillary added. "Then the next day there was another text, and the day after that, until I actually found myself looking forward to getting her silly jokes and stuff. She never tried to be my mother. The only really personal thing she offered was the name of her cousin, the florist."

"It was the same with me," Marie said. "I assumed that first text was a fluke. I decided to ignore it, and then they started coming every day like clockwork."

"Have you answered her back?" Hillary asked, in what sounded like a challenge.

With a guilty look, Marie said, "Yes, once."

"What did you say?" Carrie seemed intrigued. Everyone knew how strongly Hillary and Marie had objected to anything having to do with their stepmother.

Marie lifted one shoulder in a halfhearted shrug. "She sent a joke and it was really funny. I laughed out loud. I sent a text back that said: Funny. It was only that one time."

Carrie looked to Julia. "What do you think, Aunt Julia?"

It was a logical question, knowing the antagonism between Laura and Julia. It appeared Carrie knew more than she was letting on, although Julia didn't know how.

"Why should I mind? I'm the one who encouraged Laura to reach out."

Her words dropped like a deadweight onto the middle of the table.

"*What?*" Hillary and Marie cried simultaneously.

Julia set her small teacup down and nodded, as if it was no big deal for her to be talking to the woman they all considered a world-class home wrecker. With her daughters staring at her with openmouthed disbelief, she began to explain.

"A couple weeks ago, Laura asked to meet me. It was shortly after that fiasco with your father," Julia explained, looking to Hillary. "I debated if I should go or not, and was inclined to refuse, until I realized I couldn't ask you to practice forgiveness if I didn't do it myself. Unsure what to think, I agreed."

Julia could see the girls were fascinated, and so she continued. "Laura was as nervous as I was. Yes, there's bad blood between us, and I'll admit it was difficult for her to ask for this meeting."

"That woman isn't short on chutzpah," Marie murmured, using a word her father often used.

Julia talked about the awkwardness of that first meeting and what had transpired since. She watched as this news had the same effect on her daughters as it'd had on her. "Laura offered to do anything she could to help mend Eddie's relations with you girls and promised to stay away from the wedding."

"Dad won't be there without her," Hillary said, with a hard shake of her head.

"Which I mentioned," Julia added. "I also asked why she had never reached out to either of you. Perhaps if she'd tried at some point it would have helped."

"What did she say?" Marie asked with open curiosity.

Julia was pleased by her daughter's interest. "Laura admitted she was afraid of being rejected."

"Well, yeah," Carrie said, with more than a hint of defiance. "She should be afraid."

Hillary frowned. "You were the one who suggested she start with those text messages, weren't you, Mom?"

Julia sighed before she answered. "I know you think I probably should have refused to help her. The thing is, Laura didn't have a clue where to begin. She has sons, not daughters, and was at a complete loss. I helped her compose the first few texts."

"Are you like bosom buddies now?" Hillary asked.

"Not exactly. We've met and talked a few times and made a few plans to bring everyone together."

The stunned looks on their faces were almost comical. It was a good thing the server arrived when he did. He wrote down their orders, which broke the hypnotized gaze the girls had aimed in Julia's direction.

"Did I hear you right?" Hillary asked. "Dad, Laura, and those wretched sons of hers were all at Heath's place at the same time?"

"In the same condo?" Marie asked.

"In the same room?" This came from Hillary.

"Yes."

"Was there blood?"

Julia laughed. "No. When Michael and Adam saw that Laura

and I had set aside our differences, they asked for time to think it through. Since then I heard from Michael—"

"You did?" Carrie exclaimed. "What did he say?"

Julia was confused. "You know about this?"

"I do . . . long story, continue, what did he say?"

"Both Heath's sons have agreed to give me a chance."

Marie huffed. "That was big of them, giving you a chance and all."

"Given the circumstances, it was," Julia said, refusing to discount Michael and Adam's willingness to look beyond past hurts and slights.

"The bottom line, Hillary," she said, directing her attention to her oldest daughter. "Your father can be an idiot. Laura knows that as well as I do and was desperate to do something . . . anything to help him make up for his mistakes with you."

"Dad can be an idiot," Marie agreed.

"Tell me about it," Hillary muttered.

Julia was pleased with how well the conversation seemed to be going. "That ridiculous idea of inviting his friends and the seating chart were his bumbling attempt to be helpful," she said. "Your dad didn't mean to insult anyone. I sincerely believe he was looking for a way to make everyone comfortable, given our circumstances."

"Okay, I can give him that, but when he excluded Heath, that was insulting to you and just plain wrong."

"You'll be pleased to know your father and Heath have come to terms. They aren't going golfing together or anything, but they're cordial."

"Dad owed Heath an apology."

Carrie narrowed her gaze and asked, "Let me see if I've got

this straight. Aunt Julia and Laura are talking. Would it be a stretch to say you're friendly?"

"Not at all," Julia told her.

"Which blows my mind."

"Yours?" Hillary said, and shook her head. "It blows all our minds."

"And," Carrie added forcefully, apparently unwilling to lose her train of thought. "Heath's sons have accepted Aunt Julia being with their dad."

"Also," Marie added, when it looked like Carrie had finished, "Dad and Heath aren't threatening to kill each other."

"It never got that far," Julia felt obliged to correct them.

"Wow, that's a lot to take in," Hillary mumbled.

"You're telling me," Marie added.

Their food arrived, and Julia's daughters and Carrie looked at the steaming dishes, as if amazed they were now being asked to eat after such stunning news.

Undeterred, Julia reached for her fork.

"Where do we go from here?" Marie asked.

After swallowing her first bite and savoring the taste of basil and curry, Julia said, "That's up to you."

Hillary looked like she was a million miles away. "Dad was crying?" she said, picking up on part of their earlier conversation. "I've never known Dad to cry, not even when his dad passed."

"That tells you how badly he feels about this mess, doesn't it?" Julia said, letting her daughter draw her own conclusion.

Hillary didn't respond. She reached for her fork, and her phone pinged, indicating she had a text message.

Marie's pinged at the same time.

Julia knew the text was likely from Laura.

Hillary reached for her phone and so did Marie. They read the message and their gazes immediately went to each other.

"What is it?" Carrie asked.

"It's from Laura," Marie explained.

"Mine, too," Hillary said.

"Another joke?" Carrie asked.

"No. She asked if Marie and I would come to dinner."

"Will you go?"

Julia continued enjoying her meal, when all three faces turned to look at her as if seeking out her advice.

"Mom? Should we?"

"Don't look at me," Julia said. "This is your decision."

"But . . ."

"But nothing."

"If anyone wants my opinion," Carrie said, "you should, and I'll go with you."

Chapter 30

Carrie wasn't sure what had led her to insist on accompanying her two cousins to dinner with Laura. As soon as she offered, she'd changed her mind, and then Hillary and Marie claimed they wouldn't go without her. She apparently was to tag along as moral support.

Hillary sent a return text to Laura, stating Carrie would be joining them. She must have phrased the reply in such a way that indicated it was a package deal. No sooner had she sent the text when the okay came through claiming Uncle Eddie insisted he wanted to be there, too, and instead of meeting at a restaurant they should come to the house. Following that message, the three had a long discussion and decided to agree, seeing that Laura was happy to include Carrie.

Early that same evening, the three rode together, with Hillary driving. Blake had also been invited, but unfortunately had other plans that couldn't be changed on such short notice.

Or so he said.

Carrie got the impression Blake wanted Hillary to make peace with her dad first before adding him to the mix. She could understand his reservation, given the history between father and daughter.

When they arrived at their father's house, Hillary parked at the curb in front of the upscale one-level home. Carrie knew neither Hillary nor Marie had set foot inside before tonight.

Hillary turned off the engine, and no one made a move to climb out of the car.

"You ready for this?" Marie asked no one and everyone.

"I don't know," Hillary admitted, sounding uncertain.

"Is Laura a bad cook?" Carrie asked, hoping to lighten the mood. "Is that why you're hesitating?"

"Oh, for the love of heaven, this isn't about food, Carrie," Hillary snapped.

Carrie giggled. "I know. Come on, I think I saw your dad pull back the drapes and peek outside." She hadn't seen any such thing; she feared her cousins would remain in the car all night if she didn't prompt them to move.

"You're right. We need to go inside." Marie was the first to open the car door.

"Never in a million years did I think I'd be doing this," Hillary muttered under her breath. She continued to sound apprehensive.

Carrie had the feeling her cousins badly wanted to repair the relationship with their father, but pride and a sense of betrayal had blocked them. They'd both come a long way since Hillary and Blake had announced their engagement.

As they approached the front door, it flew open before they had a chance to ring the doorbell. Uncle Eddie was in the entry, his eyes wide and smiling.

"Hi, Dad," Marie whispered, and her voice cracked with emotion.

Uncle Eddie held his arms open and Marie walked straight to him, slipping her own around his middle. Carrie's uncle embraced his daughter and then slowly closed his eyes, as if he'd been waiting and praying for this moment for the last six years.

He released Marie, who stepped away. Then he looked to Hillary, and with tears in his eyes, opened his arms to her.

Hillary paused, and while it might have been wrong of her, Carrie nudged her from behind, pushing her in the small of her back.

Taking a halting step, Hillary went to her dad and allowed him to hug her after Marie.

When her uncle and cousin parted, Carrie noticed Eddie had tears in his eyes. He wiped the moisture from his face, smearing the tears over his cheeks. With another sniffle, he offered them both a huge smile.

"I thought I'd never get the chance to hug my daughters again," he said, and his voice shook as he whispered the words.

"You didn't make it easy, Dad," Hillary reminded him.

"I know. I know. I'm sorry. I never—" He didn't finish, because Hillary cut him off.

"Please, don't say anything more."

Surprise widened his eyes. "Why not . . . I want to tell you how sorry I am."

"I got it—you have regrets, yet every time you open your mouth it seems you make everything worse, so let's go with you're sorry and leave it at that."

"Now, that's a wise daughter," Laura said as she entered the room. She came to stand at Eddie's side and offered a tenuous smile. "I'd like to welcome you all to our home."

"Thank you," Marie said.

"And, Hillary, congratulations on your engagement."

Her cousin stiffened and, after a tense moment, gave a slight jerk of her chin. "Thank you."

"When do I get to meet Blake?" Uncle Eddie demanded. "If he's going to marry my daughter, then I want to have a heart-to-heart chat with that young man."

Laura looped her arm around her husband's elbow. "Baby steps, Edward. Baby steps. Hillary will introduce him when she's ready and not before."

"Right," he said and nodded. "I need to remember baby steps . . . tiny baby steps, a little at a time."

"I'm Carrie," she said, since it didn't seem anyone wanted to introduce her.

"Welcome, Carrie. The three of you look enough alike to be sisters," Laura commented.

"We hear that a lot," she said, and they did. The family resemblance was strong.

"Come in, please," Laura said, as she ushered them into the living room. It was tastefully decorated, but nothing like what Aunt Julia would have done with the place. Laura wasn't nearly as talented as Julia in that area.

The fireplace mantel held family photos of Laura with her

sons, and there were individual photos of Hillary and Marie, and then a couple more with her uncle and his daughters.

Carrie wasn't the only one who noticed the framed photographs. As if he was reading their minds, Uncle Eddie said, "And, no, I didn't put those up today. They've been on that mantel every day since Laura and I moved into this house."

At the mention of Laura's name, both Hillary and Marie turned their attention back to the other woman. Carrie didn't know what they wanted, and they seemed to be waiting for her to speak.

Laura sat on the chair arm with her hand resting on Eddie's shoulder. "I realize all of us started off on the wrong foot, and I want to apologize for the things I said and did that drove a wedge between you and your father. He loves you both very much."

"Have you apologized to our mother for the things you said and the things you did to her?"

Laura's cheeks filled with color. "I have, and the classy woman that she is, Julia has forgiven me. It was a stressful time and I behaved badly. I'm hoping you'll find it in your hearts to forgive me as well. And if you're willing, I'd like a second chance."

No one spoke, and Carrie worried what would happen next. Finally, when Carrie was convinced all Julia and Laura's efforts were to come to naught, Marie spoke.

"I'm willing to try."

Uncle Eddie looked to Hillary. "And you?" he asked.

Carrie heard the yearning and the angst in his voice, as if he was afraid and hopeful at the same time.

Hillary nodded. "If my mother is willing to let go of the past, then I guess I can, too."

"Thank you," Laura whispered.

Carrie wasn't sure, although she thought she might have seen the other woman blink away tears.

"One thing I want to get straight, though," Hillary said, her voice stern. "I refuse to have anything to do with your two sons."

Uncle Eddie barked out a laugh.

"It isn't funny, Dad."

"Right. It wouldn't be if Michael and Adam hadn't said the same thing about you two."

Hillary wasn't amused. "You should know there's not a snowball's chance in hell that the four of us will ever be on good terms. No offense, Laura, but your sons are . . ." She couldn't seem to find the right word.

"Barbarians," Marie supplied.

"No offense taken," Laura said. "When it comes to protecting me, my boys turn into alpha males. Normally they are regular pussycats."

"You mean alley cats, don't you? Feral ones."

Laura was good-natured enough to laugh. "You could say that. No worries, girls, Michael and Adam are as eager to stay away from you as you are of them. Perhaps one day—"

"Don't count on it," Hillary said.

Seeing that this line of talk could lead down avenues full of potholes, Carrie asked, "Is there anything I can do to help with dinner?"

"Thank you, Carrie, I have everything ready to serve."

—

To her surprise, the meal went well, the conversation centered on Hillary, Marie, and the wedding. Just as dessert was about to be served, Uncle Eddie looked at Hillary.

"If you want to exclude me from your wedding, I understand. What's important is that you and Blake are happy. I love you and am so very proud to be your dad. My prayer is that now that we've broken the ice, so to speak, we can move forward. Laura has promised to help me keep my foot out of my mouth, and I'll try my hardest to be the best dad, father-in-law, and, hopefully one day, grandpa possible."

Carrie noticed Hillary struggling to swallow as her eyes filled with tears. "I'd like you to be at my and Blake's wedding more than anything, Dad."

Uncle Eddie looked toward Laura.

"And, Laura . . ." Hillary paused, and Carrie knew how hard this was for her. "You are welcome to attend, if you'd like."

Laura nodded, and once again Carrie could see the other woman was holding back tears. "Thank you," Laura whispered, flashing a smile to Eddie.

Carrie knew this was a groundbreaking moment. Sure, Uncle Eddie and Hillary and Marie had a long way to go. The road wasn't going to always be smooth. Still, she felt confident that her cousins were happy to have their father back in their lives and were willing to give Laura the benefit of the doubt.

Time would tell.

And so would the wedding.

Chapter 31

Today was the long-awaited day of Hillary and Blake's wedding. Julia had been an emotional mess all day. Now they were in the church, and Hillary was with her sister, Carrie, and the other bridesmaids getting dressed in a room off the side of the sanctuary.

The bridal shop had sent a woman to dress Hillary. With the assorted bridesmaids and everyone else, the room had grown crowded. Seeing they weren't needed, Julia and Amanda found a quiet corner in the hallway outside and sat down on a bench. Julia struggled to get her tears under control.

Amanda handed her another tissue, which Julia carefully placed beneath her eyes to stop the flow of tears from ruining her makeup. After sitting for an hour being worked on by the makeup artist, she was determined not to ruin the woman's hard work.

"If you're all weepy now, what are you going to be like during the ceremony?" Amanda asked, a smile teasing her lips.

"You wait," Julia warned, waving her finger at her sister. "See how you react when Carrie's the bride."

"Remember Mom at our weddings?" Amanda said, reminding Julia of their own mother's reaction on their individual wedding days. "You'd think she was attending a funeral."

"And we each promised we would never be like our mother," Julia said, laughing and weeping at the same time.

"Mirror, mirror, on the wall, we are our mother, after all," Amanda said in a singsong voice.

Julia broke into laughter. "Oh, so true."

Eddie arrived, looking uncomfortable in his tuxedo and starched white shirt. He normally dressed for the golf course, and this wasn't his usual attire. He nervously paced the area in front of Julia and Amanda.

"Is Hillary dressed yet?" he asked.

"Patience, Eddie." It would be a good half hour before everyone was seated.

"Why are you nervous?" Amanda teased.

Eddie stopped his pacing and rubbed his fingers through his carefully combed hair. "I don't know, I just am. It's hard to believe the newborn baby girl I held in my arms is about to become a wife."

"I know," Julia whispered, grabbing another tissue from the packet her sister held in her hand. She sniffled. "This is ridiculous. Today is a happy day."

To Julia, this day was much more than she had ever hoped it would be. Even now, she had a hard time trusting this fragile truce between the two families. How grateful she was to Laura for taking that first uncomfortable step and contacting her. That had initiated a new beginning for the two families.

Despite Julia's multiple efforts to reconcile her daughters and their father, it'd taken the last woman she ever suspected to accomplish what had seemed an impossible task.

Laura joined them and looked lovely in her rust-colored dress. At one time, Julia had barely been able to tolerate the idea of the other woman. She viewed Laura much differently these days. While they would never be close friends, thankfully the distrust and resentment were gone. In Julia's opinion, this was about as close to a modern-day miracle as she ever thought she'd see. Her one hope now was that sometime in the future, their children would find the same acceptance toward one another.

Word came that all were ready for the wedding to begin. Laura left and was seated in the row across the aisle from Heath.

Hillary appeared, and Julia gazed lovingly at her beautiful daughter and blinked back fresh tears.

"Mom," Hillary said, nearly laughing out loud. "Why are you crying?"

Unable to speak, she shook her head. The emotion was so much more than looking at the beautiful woman her daughter had become. It was that her family was together and there was nothing but love here. The resentments were gone, they were a family again, perhaps not in the traditional way, but family nevertheless, gathered around the daughter they had created together in love.

"Dad?" Hillary said, sighing. "You, too?"

Eddie wiped his eyes. Julia hadn't been married to him all those years without knowing his thoughts matched her own. The tears were those of gratitude that Hillary and Marie had accepted him and Laura and were willing to have a relationship with them both.

"You're so . . . lovely," Eddie whispered brokenly.

Hillary laughed off his words. "I should be considering what you paid for this dress."

"It was worth every penny."

Amanda left and was seated with Robert and assorted family and friends. The bridesmaids lined up behind Julia. Blake's grandmother was seated first, then Julia was escorted to the front of the church by Blake's youngest brother, followed by his mother and another of Blake's brothers. Blake's twin brother, Bradley, was beside Blake at the altar, serving as his best man.

The organ started Pachelbel's Canon, the traditional bridal entry music, and, following the bridesmaids and maid of honor, Hillary and her father slowly proceeded down the middle of the church.

Heath reached for Julia's hand and held it tightly in his own. She smiled up at him, feeling a joy she never fully expected.

As father and daughter approached Blake, Hillary turned to her father and, instead of the traditional kiss, she hugged Eddie and whispered, "I love you, Dad."

"I love you, baby girl. Always have. Always will."

As Hillary and Blake exchanged their vows, Julia reflected back through the years when she'd been the young bride standing next to Eddie. They had been in love as well, eager to start their lives together. She thought their love would last a lifetime. She glanced at him and noticed him looking at her.

The moment was precious, to see the man she had once loved with all her being and not feel the terrible sadness of loss. She'd never wanted the divorce, would have willingly worked toward reconciliation, but it wasn't meant to be. As her father had so often reminded her: *It's better this way.* And it was.

Tearing her gaze away from Eddie, she glanced up at Heath and saw that he was closely watching her before his eyes skirted to Eddie. In case he assumed she was longing to have Eddie back, she leaned close to him and wrapped her arm around his waist. He gazed down on her, his eyes full of questions.

"Love you," she mouthed.

His frown disappeared and he smiled. "Love you," he returned, and tucked his arm around her shoulders. Julia pressed her head against the side of his arm.

All was right in her world. She hadn't expected to find love again, and she knew Heath felt the same. Their meeting had been providential, coming when they least expected to find someone else.

The incredulity of learning their divorced spouses were married to each other had badly shaken them both. For a time they'd faltered, until they realized they couldn't allow their relationship to be ruled by the others.

Once the ceremony was over, Heath was to drive Julia to the reception. After he'd helped her into the passenger seat and joined her, he glanced her way.

"It was a beautiful wedding."

"It was," she agreed.

"I've been thinking . . . you know, I do that sometimes, and it seemed, you know, that the two of us get along well and, you know . . ."

"Heath? What in heaven's name." He was stumbling over his words, and he kept repeating "you know," when she didn't know. "What's wrong?"

He leaned his head back against the headrest and heaved a giant sigh. "I'm nervous."

"About what?"

"This," he said, as if that was self-explanatory.

"The wedding reception and dinner? It's all settled. The seating plan puts us together and—"

"Not that," he said, cutting her off and making a noncommittal hand gesture. *"This."*

"O-k-a-y," she said, dragging out the word. "Only I don't know what *this* is?"

He leaned forward enough to press his forehead to the steering wheel. "I'm bungling it and I apologize. I had everything I wanted to say planned, and now the moment is here, I can't get the words out and I'm tongue-tied."

"Take a deep breath and start at the beginning," she advised.

He did as she suggested. "I'm badly messing this up. Forgive me."

"There's nothing to forgive, Heath. Tell me what's troubling you."

He nodded, sucked in a breath, and started again. "I realize you have your life and I have mine and it's been good."

"Yes, it has."

"The thing is, I'm finding that every minute I'm away from you is too long. I want you with me every minute of every day."

"That would be nice, but not possible."

"It would be if we were married."

So that was *this*! What he'd been trying to say. She hadn't meant to be obtuse, nor had she wanted to make assumptions, either.

"I realize there's more involved than loving you," he continued. "There's the problem with our kids disliking each other. I choose to believe that will work itself out in time if we're patient. You'd need to sell your condo, and then there are the mingling of finances or not, whatever you want. Second marriages can be complicated, The thing is, Julia, I am willing to knock down any roadblock you put up to convince you we were meant to be together. I meant it when I said I don't want to live another day without you. I love you and want you by my side for the rest of my life."

He paused, drawing in a deep breath as he continued to look expectantly at her, awaiting her answer.

As unexpected as this proposal was, and as much as there was to consider, her heart was screaming at her to accept. Still, there was more to consider than love, as he'd mentioned.

"Julia, please. Tell me what you're feeling."

"Overwhelmed, at the moment," she whispered, her mind whirling at the speed of light. "Can I think about this?"

"Of course."

Later at the reception, following the dinner, when the music started to play and Eddie and Hillary danced the first dance, Heath brought Julia onto the polished wooden dance floor.

As he brought her into his arms, she looked up at him and immediately knew what her heart had been telling her all along. She loved him, and only God knew how many years they would have left. Ten? Twenty? Thirty? The number wasn't important. What meant the most was knowing she would spend those years with Heath.

Smiling up at him, their eyes met. "I have my answer," she whispered into his ear as he held her close.

He raised his head, looked at her, and expectantly arched his brows, awaiting her reply.

"I'm crazy in love with you, Heath Wilson. *Crazy* being the key word. But like you, I don't want to live another minute away from you."

"Is that a yes?"

"Most definitely."

And then, right there in the middle of a crowded dance floor, Heath's hands captured her face. He stopped dancing and kissed her in full view of everyone at the reception. The very man who frowned upon PDAs kissed her like there was no tomorrow. Bending her backward, he kissed the very life out of her.

When they broke apart, they were greeted by a round of applause.

Life couldn't get any better than this, Julia mused.

Epilogue

"Mom." Hillary burst into the condo, her face red and her voice raised.

Julia looked up from the recipe she was studying in the kitchen. She'd become familiar with the appliances even before she married Heath. Her husband was meeting with clients and she hoped to have dinner ready by the time he returned.

"My goodness, Hill, what's wrong?" she asked, setting aside the recipe book.

Her daughter crossed her arms and heaved a deep sigh. "It's Blake."

"Trouble in paradise already?" Her daughter had been married nine months, and as best Julia could see, Blake and Hillary were happy. They certainly seemed to be.

"No . . . not really. It's complicated."

"Then tell me what's gotten you this riled." She came around the kitchen island and joined her daughter in the living room. Julia and Heath married barely a month after Hillary and Blake's wedding. Her condo had sold within the first week it had gone on the market. Carrie had proved to be an excellent concierge. She sincerely doubted the association would find anyone better, and Carrie had been given a substantial raise in appreciation for her excellent service. In addition, Carrie was sporting an engagement ring. Eric had proposed on Valentine's Day and she had accepted. Wedding plans were in the making, and Amanda was beside herself, eager to see her daughter settled.

"Blake and Dad have been golfing together."

"That's what I understand." Eddie had proven to be an excellent father-in-law, taking Blake under his wing, especially on the golf course. The two played often.

"What I didn't know until today is it's a foursome with Michael and Adam!"

Julia did her best to squelch her smile. This wasn't news to her or Heath. It was part of a determined effort to bring their children together. "Is that so dreadful?" she asked her daughter.

"Mom, Blake and Michael are now the best of friends."

"What are you going to do about it?" she asked, joining her daughter on the sofa, eager to see how Hillary would handle this.

Hillary sat with her arms crossed, frowning. "I don't know."

"Is it really important to hang on to your dislike of Heath's sons?"

She didn't answer, so Julia tried another question. "You trust Blake's judgment, and if he likes Michael, then clearly there's some good in him."

She shrugged. "Maybe."

"You're being a bit judgmental, aren't you?"

"Mom, you don't understand."

"Then explain it to me."

"It isn't just that Blake and Michael are friends, now Blake wants to invite Michael and his girlfriend to our house for dinner. Can you even imagine how awkward that would be?"

"And? Are you going to do it?"

Once more, Hillary shrugged, as if she hadn't come to a conclusion yet. "I told him I needed to think about it."

"That's a good start. While you're thinking, you might consider something. If Michael has agreed to the four of you getting together, that tells me he's willing to let bygones be bygones. The ball is in your court now."

Hillary slowly nodded. "If we could all be friends it would make Thanksgiving and Christmas go a lot smoother."

Scheduling between the two families on the holidays had been problematic, to say the least. Sorting out times when their children could arrive to not conflict with one another had turned into a logistical challenge.

"Yes, it would," Julia agreed. She added another bit of reason to the situation. "What does Marie have to say about this?" The two remained close, and this was sure to have an impact on Marie as well.

Hillary bounced her head against the back of the sofa. "She's all in. I suppose you heard she ran into Adam at the mall. He's engaged and introduced Marie to his fiancée. She said it wasn't nearly as awkward as she thought it would be."

Julia had heard all about it. She wasn't entirely sure what had taken place, only that the two appeared to have squared matters away. The last holdout was Hillary.

"What's your decision?" Julia asked. "Will you invite Michael to your home?"

Hillary straightened. "That's what Blake wants."

She remained silent while Hillary sorted this out for herself.

"Michael and you are on good terms, right?" she asked Julia.

"Yes. He's been wonderful. You know, he's the one who insisted on helping me move into Heath's condo."

"Yeah, I heard," she muttered.

"He isn't the Neanderthal you assume, Hillary."

She released a long, slow sigh. "You're right. I know you're right; the thing is, it's going to be hard to think of him as Blake's friend."

"Give it time and he can be your friend, as well."

She reluctantly agreed.

"And it would make your mother and Heath happy," Julia added.

"And Dad and Laura." She smiled over at Julia. "Okay, I'll do it. I'm not sure I'll like it. Still, if Michael's willing to give it a try, it'd be ungracious for me to refuse."

"Good for you, Hill."

"I'll let you know how it goes."

"You do that."

A week later, Hillary connected with her mother again: this time by phone. "Mom," she said excitedly, "Michael and Claire were here for dinner last night."

"It sounds like it went well."

"It did. Michael and I sort of pretended that there was nothing negative between us. He was gracious and so was I."

"And that worked?"

"Yeah. I discovered Michael's got a great sense of humor, and the funny part is, he's a lot like Heath. I didn't realize it until last night."

"And you liked Claire?"

"I did. She's great. She told me about this little shop in University Village and we've made plans to meet up to shop next weekend."

"That's wonderful, sweetheart. I'm grateful everything turned out."

They spoke for a few minutes longer before ending the call.

When she finished, Heath set aside the book he was reading on World War II. "Was that Hillary?"

"It was."

"I heard from Michael earlier, and he said he and Claire had a good time with Hillary and Blake."

"So it seems."

Heath grinned. "It looks like everything has worked out for the best."

Julia agreed. "As my dad always said: *It's better this way.*"

How right he was.

ABOUT THE AUTHOR

Debbie Macomber, the author of *Cottage by the Sea*, *Any Dream Will Do*, *If Not for You*, and the Rose Harbor Inn series, is a leading voice in women's fiction. Thirteen of her novels have reached No. 1 on the *New York Times* bestseller list, and five of her beloved Christmas novels have been made into hit movies. Macomber's Cedar Cove books have also been made into an original television series. There are more than 200 million copies of her books in print worldwide.

She lives with her husband in Port Orchard, Washington. Their children are grown and she is a proud grandmother.

Read on for a sneak-peek at Debbie's new festive treat . . .

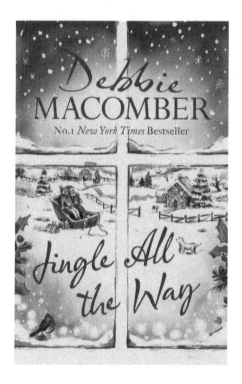

OUT NOW IN HARDBACK, EBOOK AND AUDIO

PAPERBACK COMING OCTOBER 2021

CHAPTER ONE

Everly Lancaster was ready to explode. Her assistant, Annette, the very one Jack Campbell, her business partner and CEO, had highly recommended she hire, who also happened to be his niece, had made yet another crucial mistake. One in a long list of costly errors. This time, however, this Gen Z, spoiled, irresponsible, entitled young woman had gone too far.

Annette Howington had mortified Everly in front of five hundred real estate brokers.

"It's really not that big a deal," Annette insisted, smiling as if to suggest this had all been a small misunderstanding. "You did fine without your speech."

The awards banquet held in the posh Ritz-Carlton Hotel, half a block off Chicago's Magnificent Mile, honored the top brokers for the online real estate company Easy Home. As Everly stepped onto the podium to deliver her carefully crafted speech, she discovered that her empty-headed assistant had downloaded the wrong talk and graphics. As a result, Everly had been forced to stumble through what she remembered of it. To her acute embarrassment, she'd sounded ill prepared, fumbling over words and names.

Everly was always at the top of her game. She did not stand up before a crowded banquet room and make a fool of herself.

"Not that big a deal?" Everly repeated, after the banquet. Annette had tried to escape without Everly noticing. No such luck. Everly had the assistant in her sights, and no way was she letting Annette sneak out.

"This is the last straw," Everly said, managing to keep her anger under control. "I've given you every opportunity. I'm afraid I'm going to have to let you go."

"You're firing me?" Annette asked in utter disbelief. "But I'm doing the best I can." For emphasis, she added a loud sniffle. "You've never liked me. From the day I started you've been demanding and critical." Her eyes filled with tears as if that would be enough to convince Everly to change her mind. She sniffled again for extra measure, her shoulders making dramatic shudders.

No way was Everly going to allow Annette to turn this on her. "Your best isn't good enough. You don't possess the skills I need in an assistant. The first thing Monday morning

I'll explain to your uncle that you will no longer be working with me or Easy Home." Everly couldn't think of a single position this ditzy girl could handle in the entire company. She'd even managed to mess up answering the phone on more than one occasion.

Annette's tears evaporated and a cocky expression came over her. "Uncle Jack won't let you fire me. I'm his favorite niece."

Everly gritted her teeth. "We'll see about that."

With a confident flair, Annette whirled around and stormed straight to her mother, who stood in the rear of the ballroom, waiting for her daughter. Everly watched as Annette burst into tears and pointed at Everly. A horrified look came over Louise Campbell as she started to weave her way around the tables toward Everly.

Bring it on, sister, Everly thought, more than prepared to face this tiger mom. Before that happened, however, Everly was waylaid by one of the brokers with a question. When they finished speaking, both Annette and her mother were nowhere to be seen.

Everly had a reputation to protect. She'd worked hard to make Easy Home the success that it was. What Annette said about Jack defending her was a worry, but nothing she couldn't handle.

The problem was Jack and his easygoing, everything-will-take-care-of-itself attitude. They'd met in college while getting their business degrees. Jack was the creative mastermind.

Everly possessed the business savvy and drive to take his idea of an online real estate company for Chicago and put it in motion. Six years ago they'd formed a partnership, and, working side by side, the concept had grown at a furious rate. With Everly at the helm, overseeing the everyday operations, Jack was content to rest on his laurels after handling the media-facing and investors. Basically, he left the running of the company to Everly. And she'd let him.

First thing Monday morning, Everly approached Jack in his office. "We need to talk about Annette."

Jack barely glanced up from his in-office putting green, where he stood, gauging the distance between the golf ball and the hole.

When he didn't respond, Everly said, "I've given her every opportunity, Jack. I'm letting her go."

Jack, ever willing to overlook his niece's complete lack of professionalism, sighed loudly. "I know. I know. And I appreciate the way you've taken her under your wing. This is my sister's girl and it means the world to Annette to have the chance to learn from you. You realize she idolizes you."

Then God help her if the young woman intentionally had it out for her, Everly mused. "Jack, take your eye off that golf ball and look at me. Favorite niece or not, I'm done."

Jack looked up and his eyes widened. "Annette was named after my mother."

"I don't care if she was named after the Statue of Liberty, I refuse to work with her a minute longer. The girl is incompetent."

His shoulders sagged. "Please reconsider."

That he would ask infuriated Everly. "No."

"No?" Jack looked both crestfallen and shocked.

After mentally reciting the alphabet, she tried again. "I know you love Annette and want to please your sister, but I'm the one left to deal with this pampered, entitled, inept girl."

Jack pretended not to hear and did a couple of practice golf swings. "I'll think on it," he said, as if this was his decision.

Which was so Jack. He had tunnel vision and refused to deal with unpleasantness, especially anything having to do with his family.

"Great. You want to keep Annette working here, then I have an idea," Everly said with an exaggeratedly cheerful note. "Make Annette your assistant."

"I can't do that," Jack insisted, leaning against his putter. "Maryann has worked with me from the beginning. Besides, Annette is family." To his credit, Jack looked uncomfortable. When he glanced up, a pleading expression came over him. Everly knew that look. He was trying to figure out a way to change Everly's mind. That wouldn't work. Not this time.

Jack smiled. "I know you're upset, and you have a right to be. It was a silly mistake, but Annette apologized . . ."

"Silly mistake? She apologized?" If he defended this nitwit one more time, Everly was going to walk out the door and leave the running of the company to him and see what he had to say then.

"You're not listening to me, Jack. I. Have. Reached. My. Limit."

Jack stared at her for a long moment. "I'm pleading with you, Everly. Give her one more chance, that's all I'm asking. With a fresh start I believe Annette will prove her worth. Don't make a hasty decision."

Hasty decision? Had Jack lost his ever-loving mind?

He must have noticed the stubborn expression she wore, because he added, "Remember, this is her first job out of college. We all make mistakes. You did. I did. We were fortunate that people believed in us. Is it so much to ask that we give my sister's daughter the same opportunity?"

"Admit it, Jack, anyone else would have been out the door weeks ago."

"Come on, Everly," Jack pleaded again.

Everly shook her head. "What you fail to realize is that Annette not only let me down, but she's failed you, and this entire organization. You aren't going to be able to turn this around. I'm not changing my mind."

Having had her say, Everly left his office.

———

Join us at

For competitions galore,
exclusive interviews with our lovely
Sphere authors, chat about
all the latest books
and much, much more.

Follow us on Twitter at
🐦 @littlebookcafe

Subscribe to our newsletter and
Like us at 🅵/thelittlebookcafe

Read. Love. Share.